ROBIN F(
THE POLO GRC

Robin Forsythe was born Robert Forsythe in 1879. His place of birth was Sialkot, in modern day Pakistan. His mother died when a younger brother was born two years later, and 'Robin' was brought up by an ayah until he was six, when he returned to the United Kingdom, and went to school in Glasgow and Northern Ireland. In his teens he had short stories and poetry published and went to London wanting to be a writer.

He married in 1909 and had a son the following year, later working as a clerk at Somerset House in London when he was arrested for theft and fraud in 1928. Sentenced to fifteen months, he began to write his first detective novel in prison.

On his release in 1929 Robin Forsythe published his debut, *Missing or Murdered*. It introduced Anthony 'Algernon' Vereker, an eccentric artist with an extraordinary flair for detective work. It was followed by four more detective novels in the Vereker series, ending with *The Spirit Murder Mystery* in 1936. All the novels are characterized by the sharp plotting and witty dialogue which epitomize the more effervescent side of golden age crime fiction.

Robin Forsythe died in 1937.

Also by Robin Forsythe

Missing or Murdered

The Pleasure Cruise Mystery

The Ginger Cat Mystery
(*aka* Murder at Marston Manor)

The Spirit Murder Mystery

ROBIN FORSYTHE

THE POLO GROUND MYSTERY

With an introduction
by Curtis Evans

DEAN STREET PRESS

Published by Dean Street Press 2016

Introduction copyright © 2016 Curtis Evans

Cover by DSP

First published in 1932 by The Bodley Head

ISBN 978 1 911095 12 5

www.deanstreetpress.co.uk

To

MY SON

JOHN

Robin Forsythe (1879-1937)
Crime in Fact and Fiction

Ingenious criminal schemes were the stock in trade of those
ever-so-bright men and women who devised the baffling puzzles
found in between-the-wars detective fiction. Yet although scores
of Golden Age mystery writers strove mightily to commit brilliant
crimes on paper, presumably few of them ever attempted to
commit them in fact. One author of classic crime fiction who
actually carried out a crafty real-life crime was Robin Forsythe.
Before commencing in 1929 his successful series of Algernon
Vereker detective novels, now reprinted in attractive new editions
by the enterprising Dean Street Press, Forsythe served in the
1920s as the mastermind behind England's Somerset House
stamp trafficking scandal.

Robin Forsythe was born Robert Forsythe—he later found it
prudent to slightly alter his Christian name—in Sialkot, Punjab
(then part of British India, today part of Pakistan) on 10 May
1879, the eldest son of distinguished British cavalryman John
"Jock" Forsythe and his wife Caroline. Born in 1838 to modestly
circumstanced parents in the Scottish village of Carmunnock,
outside Glasgow, John Forsythe in 1858 enlisted as a private in
the Ninth Queen's Royal Lancers and was sent to India, then in
the final throes of a bloody rebellion. Like the fictional Dr. John
H. Watson of Sherlock Holmes fame, Forsythe saw major martial
action in Afghanistan two decades later during the Second Anglo-
Afghan War (1878-1880), in his case at the December 1879 siege
of the Sherpur Cantonment, just outside Kabul, and the Battle of
Kandahar on 1 September 1880, for which service he received the
War Medal with two Clasps and the Bronze England and Ireland
until his retirement from the British army in 1893, four years after
having been made an Honorary Captain. The old solider was later
warmly commended, in a 1904 history of the Ninth Lancers, for
his "unbroken record of faithful, unfailing and devoted service."

His son Robin's departure from government service a quarter-century later would be rather less harmonious.

A year after John Forsythe's return to India from Afghanistan in 1880, his wife Caroline died in Ambala after having given birth to Robin's younger brother, Gilbert ("Gill"), and the two little boys were raised by an Indian ayah, or nanny. The family returned to England in 1885, when Robin was six years old, crossing over to Ireland five years later, when the Ninth Lancers were stationed at the Curragh Army Camp. On Captain Forsythe's retirement from the Lancers in 1893, he and his two sons settled in Scotland at his old home village, Carmunnock. Originally intended for the legal profession, Robin instead entered the civil service, although like E.R. Punshon, another clerk turned classic mystery writer recently reprinted by Dean Street Press, he dreamt of earning his bread through his pen by another, more imaginative, means: creative writing. As a young man Robin published poetry and short stories in newspapers and periodicals, yet not until after his release from prison in 1929 at the age of fifty would he finally realize his youthful hope of making his living as a fiction writer.

For the next several years Robin worked in Glasgow as an Inland Revenue Assistant of Excise. In 1909 he married Kate Margaret Havord, daughter of a guide roller in a Glasgow iron and steel mill, and by 1911 the couple resided, along with their one-year-old son John, in Godstone, Surrey, twenty miles from London, where Robin was employed as a Third Class Clerk in the Principal Probate Registry at Somerset House. Young John remained the Robin and Kate's only child when the couple separated a decade later. What problems led to the irretrievable breakdown of the marriage is not known, but Kate's daughter-in-law later characterized Kate as "very greedy" and speculated that her exactions upon her husband might have made "life difficult for Robin and given him a reason for his illegal acts."

Six years after his separation from Kate, Robin conceived and carried out, with the help of three additional Somerset

House clerks, a fraudulent enterprise resembling something out of the imaginative crime fiction of Arthur Conan Doyle, Golden Age thriller writer Edgar Wallace and post Golden Age lawyer-turned-author Michael Gilbert. Over a year-and-a-half period, the Somerset House conspirators removed high value judicature stamps from documents deposited with the Board of Inland Revenue, using acids to obliterate cancellation marks, and sold the stamps at half-cost to three solicitor's clerks, the latter of whom pocketed the difference in prices. Robin and his co-conspirators at Somerset House divided among themselves the proceeds from the illicit sales of the stamps, which totaled over 50,000 pounds (or roughly $75,000 US dollars) in modern value. Unhappily for the seven schemers, however, a government auditor became suspicious of nefarious activity at Somerset House, resulting in a 1927 undercover Scotland Yard investigation that, coupled with an intensive police laboratory examination of hundreds of suspect documents, fully exposed both the crime and its culprits.

Robin Forsythe and his co-conspirators were promptly arrested and at London's Old Bailey on 7 February 1928, the Common Serjeant--elderly Sir Henry Dickens, K.C., last surviving child of the great Victorian author Charles Dickens--passed sentence on the seven men, all of whom had plead guilty and thrown themselves on the mercy of the court. Sir Henry sentenced Robin to a term of fifteen months imprisonment, castigating him as a calculating rogue, according to the Glasgow Herald, the newspaper in which Robin had published his poetry as a young man, back when the world had seemed full of promise:

It is an astounding position to find in an office like that of Somerset House that the Canker of dishonesty had bitten deep....You are the prime mover of this, and obviously you started it. For a year and a half you have continued it, and you have undoubtedly raised an atmosphere and influenced other people in that office.

Likely one of the "astounding" aspects of this case in the eyes of eminent pillars of society like Dickens was that Robin Forsythe and his criminal cohort to a man had appeared to be, before the fraud was exposed, quite upright individuals. With one exception Robin's co-conspirators were a generation younger than their ringleader and had done their duty, as the saying goes, in the Great War. One man had been a decorated lance corporal in the late affray, while another had served as a gunner in the Royal Field Artillery and a third had piloted biplanes as a 2nd lieutenant in the Royal Flying Corps. The affair disturbingly demonstrated to all and sundry that, just like in Golden Age crime fiction, people who seemed above suspicion could fall surprisingly hard for the glittering lure of ill-gotten gain.

Crime fiction offered the imaginative Robin Forsythe not only a means of livelihood after he was released in from prison in 1929, unemployed and seemingly unemployable, but also, one might surmise, a source of emotional solace and escape. Dorothy L. Sayers once explained that from the character of her privileged aristocratic amateur detective, Lord Peter Wimsey, she had devised and derived, at difficult times in her life, considerable vicarious satisfaction:

> When I was dissatisfied with my single unfurnished room, I tool a luxurious flat for him in Piccadilly. When my cheap rug got a hole in it, I ordered an Aubusson carpet. When I had no money to pay my bus fare, I presented him with a Daimler double-six, upholstered in a style of sober magnificence, and when I felt dull I let him drive it.

Between 1929 and 1937 Robin published eight successful crime novels, five of which were part of the Algernon Vereker mystery series for which the author was best known: *Missing or Murdered* (1929), *The Polo Ground Mystery* (1932), *The Pleasure Cruise Mystery* (1933), *The Ginger Cat Mystery* (1935) and *The Spirit Murder Mystery* (1936). The three remaining novels—*The Hounds of Justice* (1930), *The Poison Duel* (1934, under the pseudonym Peter Dingwall) and *Murder on Paradise Island* (1937)—were non-series works.

Like the other Robin Forsythe detective novels detailing the criminal investigations of Algernon Vereker, gentleman artist and amateur sleuth, *Missing or Murdered* was issued in England by The Bodley Head, publisher in the Twenties of mysteries by Agatha Christie and Annie Haynes, the latter another able writer revived by Dean Street Press. Christie had left The Bodley Head in 1926 and Annie Haynes had passed away early in 1929, leaving the publisher in need of promising new authors. Additionally, the American company Appleton-Century published two of the Algernon Vereker novels, *The Pleasure Cruise Mystery* and *The Ginger Cat Mystery*, in the United States (the latter book under the title *Murder at Marston Manor*) as part of its short-lived but memorably titled Tired Business Man's Library of adventure, detective and mystery novels, which were designed "to afford relaxation and entertainment" to industrious American escape fiction addicts during their off hours. Forsythe's fiction also enjoyed some success in France, where his first three detective novels were published, under the titles *La Disparition de Lord Bygrave* (The Disappearance of Lord Bygrave), *La Passion de Sadie Maberley* (The Passion of Sadie Maberley) and *Coups de feu a l'aube* (Gunshots at Dawn).

The Robin Forsythe mystery fiction drew favorable comment for their vivacity and ingenuity from such luminaries as Dorothy L. Sayers, Charles Williams and J.B. Priestley, the latter acutely observing that "Mr. Forsythe belongs to the new school of detective story writers which might be called the brilliant flippant school." Sayers pronounced of Forsythe's *The Ginger Cat Mystery* that "[t]he story is lively and the plot interesting," while Charles Williams, author and editor of Oxford University Press, heaped praise upon *The Polo Ground Mystery* as "a good story of one bullet, two wounds, two shots, and one dead man and three pistols before the end....It is really a maze, and the characters are not merely automata."

This second act in the career of Robin Forsythe proved sadly short-lived, however, for in 1937 the author passed away from kidney disease, still estranged from his wife and son, at the age of 57. In his later years he resided--along with his Irish Setter Terry, the "dear pal" to whom he dedicated *The Ginger Cat Mystery*--at a cottage in the village of Hartest, near Bury St. Edmunds, Suffolk. In addition to writing, Robin enjoyed gardening and dabbling in art, having become an able chalk sketch artist and water colorist. He also toured on ocean liners (under the name "Robin Forsythe"), thereby gaining experience that would serve him well in his novel *The Pleasure Cruise Mystery*. This book Robin dedicated to "Beatrice," while *Missing or Murdered* was dedicated to "Elizabeth" and *The Spirit Murder Mystery* to "Jean." Did Robin find solace as well in human companionship during his later years? Currently we can only speculate, but classic British crime fans who peruse the mysteries of Robin Forsythe should derive pleasure from spending time in the clever company of Algernon Vereker as he hunts down fictional malefactors—thus proving that, while crime may not pay, it most definitely can entertain.

Curtis Evans

Chapter One

EXTRACT FROM "THE LONDON EVENING BULLETIN"

MYSTERY OF SHOT MILLIONAIRE.
SCOTLAND YARD MEN ARRIVE ON THE SCENE.
NUTHILL, August 14th.

Mr. Sutton Armadale, the millionaire sportsman, was
found lying shot dead on the private polo ground of his
palatial home, Vesey Manor, in Surrey, at an early hour
this morning. The body was discovered by his gamekeeper,
Stephen Collyer. Collyer, it appears, was awakened at five
o'clock in the morning by the sound of two shots and,
believing that poachers were at work in Hanging Covert,
near his cottage, immediately rose, hastily pulled on his
clothes, and went out to investigate. He was convinced
that the shots he had heard were due to the springing
of alarm guns which he had set in the covert. The sun
had just risen and, as he put it himself, "visibility was
good." He was about to enter Hanging Covert when he
happened to glance towards the manor. Between where he
stood and Vesey Manor, in the dell below, lay Mr. Sutton
Armadale's private polo ground, and as the keeper's eye
ranged over that level green expanse it encountered a
mysterious, dark object lying at its farther end. Using his
field-glasses, which he had thrust in his pocket prior to
setting out from his cottage, he at once distinguished it as
the recumbent body of a man. Giving up his intention of
trying to surprise intruders in the covert, Collyer hurried
down the hill and crossed the polo ground to ascertain who
the prostrate stranger might be. To his surprise and horror,
he discovered that it was the body of Mr. Sutton Armadale.
The dying financier, who was still breathing faintly, was

bleeding profusely from a wound in the right temple, and on examination the keeper found that his employer was also suffering from another terrible wound in the abdomen. In his left hand he was clutching an automatic pistol, a Colt of .45 calibre. Collyer rendered what assistance he could in the circumstances, but Mr. Armadale never recovered consciousness. Before expiring in his gamekeeper's arms he muttered the one word, "Murder." On this point Collyer is quite positive, and ridicules any suggestion that he may not have heard aright. Seeing that nothing further could be done, Collyer at once ran to Vesey Manor and roused the servants. They in turn conveyed the news to Mr. Basil Ralli, Mr. Armadale's nephew, who was staying with his uncle on a holiday visit from town. Mr. Ralli, after breaking the news as gently as he could to Mrs. Armadale, at once telephoned for the local doctor and the Nuthill police, who soon made their appearance on the scene. The small party of guests who were staying at Vesey Manor included Miss Edmée Cazas, who made quite a hit in the revue *What's Yours?* with her dancing and her song, "He kissed me in the Cinema but wouldn't see me home"; Captain Rickaby Fanshaugh, the well-known polo player, late of the 14th Lancers; Mr. Ralph Degerdon, son of Mr. Harold Degerdon, stockbroker of Drapers Gardens and Meadway Court, Godstone; Mr. Aubrey Winter, a cousin of Mrs. Armadale; and Mr. Stanley Houseley.

Displaying his characteristic energy and initiative, Captain Fanshaugh collected the male servants of the house, and with the aid of Collyer combed the neighbouring coverts in search of a possible assailant. Their efforts, however, proved abortive.

The tragedy presents several very perplexing features and is being thoroughly investigated by Detective-Inspector Heather of Scotland Yard, assisted by Detective-

Sergeant Lawrence Goss, who arrived during the day as the result of an urgent summons for assistance by the Chief Constable of Nuthill.

It appears that Mr. Sutton Armadale retired last night between twelve and one o'clock. He was in his usual good health and excellent spirits. During the afternoon he had played a brilliant game at No. 4 in a friendly polo match for the Pandits against a team of the 14th Lancers on the private ground at Vesey manor. Later he put in an appearance at the village flower show being held in one of the meadows adjoining the manor, at which Mrs. Armadale (she was, of course, the beautiful Miss Angela Daunay prior to her marriage two years ago) distributed the prizes. At cocktail time the guests indulged in a swimming party in the charming pool in the rock garden, and after dinner played bridge and billiards until midnight, when every one retired. Mr. Armadale, who was a martyr to insomnia of late, slept apart from his wife, but shortly before one o'clock he came into her bedroom and bade her good night. From that moment no one either saw or heard his host until he was found dying by his gamekeeper on the polo ground near the manor.

A very mysterious factor in the case is that, though Collyer is certain he heard two shots fired and his testimony is corroborated by Mr. Ralli, who happened to be lying awake at the time, only one spent cartridge case was found on the ground by the financier's body in spite of a most careful search by the police. In this respect it may be noted that an automatic pistol, unlike a revolver, ejects the spent cartridge and reloads itself as each shot is fired. Inquiries are being diligently pursued by detectives under Inspector Heather, who, it may be remembered, brought the mysterious Bygrave case to a successful conclusion some years ago. Sir William Macpherson, the famous pathologist, who is also an expert on gunshot wounds, has been summoned to Vesey Manor.

Mrs. Armadale, accompanied by Mr. Ralph Degerdon, was among the first of the inmates of the house to appear on the scene of the tragedy and render what little assistance she could to her dying husband. Though perceptibly suffering from shock, she is showing remarkable courage and fortitude in her bereavement and is doing her utmost to assist the police in their difficult investigations.

At midday to-day the police detained a man in the village of Nuthill, who had openly boasted of having committed the murder, but after searching inquiries he was discharged.

Such was the first account published in the early issues of the *Evening Bulletin* of the mysterious shooting of Sutton Armadale, the well-known London financier, racehorse owner, stockbreeder, and yachtsman, to whom the Press invariably referred as the "millionaire sportsman" whenever they had occasion to mention his name in their columns. Later editions added the further stimulating paragraph:

It was subsequently discovered that the secret safe in the library where Mrs. Armadale usually kept her jewels, especially her famous rope of pearls, valued at £20,000, had been rifled and that the rope of pearls was missing. The window of the library was open, and a mask, such as is sometimes worn by burglars, was found lying on the floor of the library between the safe and the window. From the evidence in hand it would appear that the financier surprised the burglar shortly after he had rifled the safe and gave chase. Mr Armadale, it is clear, eventually overtook him as he was making his way across the polo ground and was shot by the bandit when the latter found escape impossible.

The daily papers on the following morning gave lengthier accounts of the mysterious affair, but these were rather an ornate expansion of the descriptive reporter than a fuller record of the facts. The *Daily Report*, in which Sutton Armadale was financially interested, gave up nearly a column of its precious space to a sketch of his career. The following extracts are instructive, but the writer responsible for the sketch probably wrote with his tongue in his cheek. Again, this may be a magnanimous view of his activity; it is so difficult to know:

> No man who held such immense financial power and was such an outstanding figure in the sporting life of this country had such a meteoric rise to fame as Mr. Sutton Armadale. His rapid ascent from obscurity to the dazzling pinnacle of a phenomenal business success was solely due to his immense energy and his inherent ability for carrying through a deal.

There is something about the vagueness of that phrase "inherent ability for carrying through a deal" which is conducive to uneasy reflection. The reader is inclined to feel that the acquisition of immense wealth is not quite so simple a matter as all that, and instinctively decides that the use of the word "inherent" is a palpable trick to conceal the writer's unblushing ignorance of his subject. The biographer goes on to state with sustained confidence:

> He lived for work only, though his principal interest apart from his immense financial undertakings lay in the field of sport. He was a first-class shot, and used to practise at polo whenever he had a moment to spare from business. By his keenness he had made himself into a very fine exponent of this difficult and hazardous game.

He concludes this Press epicedium on a popular if rather reckless note:

> Mr. Sutton Armadale always believed in paying large salaries to every one in his employ and was as generous in private life as he was in public.

The statement is encouraging. Yet the news value of even a millionaire sportsman's death is a delicately relative affair to a modern daily paper, and Sutton Armadale's startling exit from the arena of his activities was crowded into insignificance by other and more alarming news which burst with reverberating effect over London on that bright August morning. The headline, "Amazing Share Slump in Well-known Companies," stretched like a signal of flags across the whole width of the *Daily Report*'s principal news page, and a sub-title screamed that "millions of invested money" were affected. (That the *Report* subsequently reduced this hint of countless millions to a definite figure and assured the public that they had from the first advised a wise abstention from anything in the nature of panic is irrelevant and deceived no one.) It was the first warning note to the world of what is now known as "The Great Braby Crash," a crash which resulted in a long term of penal servitude for that arresting personality, Raymond Braby, and left behind it a hideous trail of suicides by poison, coal-gas, disinfectants, fire-arms, and—cold water. Under this alarming headline, inset among the letter-press, was a portrait of Raymond Braby himself. To those who were fortunately not involved in the disaster there was something grimly ludicrous in this genial apparition of the cause of all the trouble smiling serenely from the midst of the havoc he had created. It led one to believe that on the morning of the disaster, when the glittering castle of Braby's hopes and dreams crumbled away and vanished before his vision as if beneath the dread wand of some evil magician, he must have savoured some morsel of cynical relish when he glanced at his copy of the *Daily Report*. For there, figuratively, the bugles sounding the last post over the grave of his own lurid career had effectually drowned the editorial requiem over the very corpse of his old enemy in the field of money-getting; in this hour of catastrophe he had positively hustled his dead, if successful, rival into a smaller space in one of the latter's own newspapers. For during their lives Braby and Armadale had been sworn business foes. And now? Well, "the tumult and the shouting dies, the captains and the kings depart!"

It must be humiliating even to millionaire sportsmen to learn in some moment of blinding illumination that the "paths of glory lead but to the grave." Whether such a moment of revelation had been granted to Sutton Armadale during the last days of his life no one will ever know; but, if it had, his more intimate friends could imagine him in that crisis of discovery quietly smiling, a pugnacious light in his blue eyes, his rather pronounced chin thrust out defiantly, and his hand wandering in search of his cigar-case. For Sutton Armadale was (if those intimate friends are to be believed) a sportsman in a sense quite different from that which is implied by the connection of the term with the possession of great wealth. To own a racing stud, to lead a winner into the paddock to the plaudits of successful backers, to be sufficiently wealthy to experience little excitement in betting, to be a member of the National Sporting Club, to possess a luxurious yacht, to tilt his hat at a rakish angle, to smoke cigars incessantly in public, to wear perennially an exquisite buttonhole—may be some of the outward and visible signs of sportsmanship. Sutton Armadale exhibited some of these stigmata, but he also possessed much of the inward and spiritual grace. He knew no fear; though he worshipped rank and title he was never obsequious to a superior or insolent to an inferior; he was never known to desert a friend in any possible circumstances; he always strove to be fair to an enemy. He always displayed a lively contempt for a sneak or a lick-spittle; he was genuinely sorry for a timorous man and loved a brave one. He gloried in a risk, however great the risk might be, often flouting chance with a suspicion of swagger, and in the midst of a cheery cynicism he had always shown, contradictorily enough, an unexpected regard for that adolescent type of romance which flavours, more or less, every revue and musical comedy and much of the popular literature of to-day. At fifty—he was killed on the eve of his birthday—he was one of the most distinguished-looking men in the City. Tall, broad-shouldered, active as a cat, his ruddy, cheerful countenance, his shrewd, sparkling blue eye, his ready tongue always alive with a quip or a caustic remark, made him a man whom anyone would be glad to call a friend. About all really big men in any walk of life there are unmistakable signs of greatness. The very movements of Sutton Armadale's body, its sense of strength and firmness in repose, his high cheek-bones, aquiline nose, square, pugnacious jaw, and unflinching eye all displayed that one quality which marks every genuinely successful man, namely, confidence, realized confidence in his own powers. This confidence in his own judgment never failed him, and he possessed the magic of being able to instil it in all those who were fortunate enough to be associated with him in business. But there was more than one Sutton Armadale. The business man of the city was an altogether different man from the Armadale of private or social life. Like most of those engaged in the incessant fight of making and retaining wealth, he treasured a different set of ethical values on the commercial side of his existence, and it seemed contradictory that a man, implacable in securing the last farthing of an advantage in some specific business deal, should a few hours later in his club draw a cheque for a thousand pounds in favour of some insistent charity in which he was not very greatly interested. But this duality is not uncommon in men, and the millionaire sportsman of social life could in business transactions be as ruthless and pitiless as a tiger. At a meeting of the directors of the many trusts or companies with which he was associated, where were gathered the shrewdest and hardest financial brains of London, he would trample down hostile opposition with a cold ferocity which made the boldest fear him. Few dared to challenge the plans of a man whose judgment had been invariably attended with success. Under the intoxicating spell of making money all those kindly, humane, and lovable facets of Sutton Armadale's magnetic social personality vanished and a demon appeared seized with an unquenchable lust for money and power. He had therefore incurred bitter hatreds and wakened in equally rapacious and determined men an ineradicable animosity—a never-sleeping desire for revenge. Yet opposition merely steeled his resolve and inspired him to livelier defiance, for fear was a sensation to which he was a stranger. As Captain Rickaby (known as "Fruity") Fanshaugh, one of his most intimate friends, relates, the only occasion on which Sutton Armadale was thoroughly scared was that of his proposal to the young and beautiful Angela Daunay, whom he married two years prior to his tragic death.

And now that colossus of business was no more! The spirit which had ridden unperturbed over many a nerve-racking financial crisis, which had flung itself with inflexible will and superb courage into every commercial struggle in which it had become involved, had slipped quietly out of the riven flesh without even a curse of defiance or a threat of reprisal. The indomitable leader in many a hard-fought battle had been despatched, almost ignominiously it seemed, by a predatory brother in a bolder, if less intellectual, field of acquisition.

The significance of the event was probably never more succinctly sketched than in a conversation between two clerks travelling comfortably in the Tube to their assured if arduous toil.

"Well, Harry boy, it appears that Mr. Sutton Armadale wasn't immortal after all! Bit of a sell, isn't it?"

"You're right, Bill. His sudden death calls up to me a picture of a dashing skater, arms outstretched, skimming the ice on twinkling steel. Then, all of a sudden, there's a round hole in the ice—rather a funny sort of hole, to be sure—and his nibs has vanished. Silence. Nothing more!"

"A few bubbles, perhaps, departing effervescence, so to speak. We'll be fair and grant him that. I'll see you at Mooney's at one o'clock."

And that was all!

In the City of London, however, the air was electrical. The shares of the various companies connected with Raymond Braby were cascading downwards to undreamed-of levels, and the awful tenseness that had permeated the financial atmosphere of the previous week had given way to the first thunderous crashes of the impending storm. Round Throgmorton Street the facts were beginning to filter out, and outside the Stock Exchange a hatless and jabbering crowd were excitedly discussing the momentous situation. When the news of the violent death of Sutton Armadale became more widely known, it was at once assumed that it had some sinister and immediate connection with the Braby debacle by all those speculators whose nerves had been frayed to an intolerable sensitiveness by the vagaries of the market in the Braby Group. For some hours financial circles, as the *Evening Bulletin* subsequently put it, "were staggered" by the announcement of the tragedy. Shares in the Armadale companies and trusts were recklessly thrown by the more timorous holders on the market and prices began to drop ominously. But not for long. Some Rupert of finance, quick to seize his opportunity and armed with surer information, flung himself gallantly into the fray and rallied the shaken squadrons to, as Pepys would have worded it, his "great content." It was beginning to gain credence before night closed on that eventful day that the sudden shooting of Sutton Armadale had no material connection with the synchronous Braby collapse, and all those investors who had pinned their faith to the millionaire sportsman were congratulating themselves, a trifle nervously, perhaps, on their own sound judgment of Armadale's financial stability and integrity. It was recorded, however, that one who had stood to lose all his possessions had the Armadale concerns tottered to ruin was ungrateful enough to remark:

"By God, I'm thankful, but damme if I ever liked the angle at which Sutton always wore his topper. A trifle, you may think, but psychologically pregnant. It always put the wind up me!"

The final editions of the evening papers announced the stupendous news that Mr. Raymond Braby had been arrested and that a warrant had been issued for the arrest of his partner and right-hand man, whose whereabouts at the moment were unknown. Dealings in the Braby shares were now being transacted at absurd prices. After the Exchange closed, 15s. shares were offered at half a crown in the street and nobody would buy, and through thousands of once bright little homes in Great Britain there stole the appalling conviction that all the hard renunciations of life, bitter oblations to the great God of Security, had been in vain. Those symbols of wealth which they had treasured as the visible rewards of the worship of that deity were so much waste paper. Ruin, to paraphrase Wilde, was drawing the curtains of their beds!

Meanwhile at Nuthill, a resident at the White Hart Hotel, but a stranger to the district, had been behaving in a very singular fashion. He had breakfasted on brandy and continued to drink brandy steadily until lunch. He lunched on brandy and became morosely drunk. John Salt, it appeared, bore some deep-seated and wholly irrational hatred to all financiers, whom he kept calling with increasing difficulty "silk-hatted sneak-thieves." He was foolish enough to remark when he heard of Sutton Armadale's death, which had occurred not a mile distant from the inn, that it "served the perisher damned well right too!" Later in the afternoon, in a grimly drunken mood, he loudly boasted to a crowded bar that he himself had "bumped the slab-jawed swindler off," and was promptly arrested. Growing sober under the cooling effects of police interrogation, he proved his complete innocence and was discharged. Of such incongruous stuff is the fabric of life woven!

Chapter Two

Anthony Vereker, known as Algernon, unabbreviated, to his intimate friends, sat in the comfortable studio of his flat in Fenton Street, W., with the morning papers strewn on a table in front of him. He was bending over the table, leaning on his left hand and glancing at the various reports of the shooting of Mr. Sutton Armadale. Taking a pair of scissors from a small drawer of a large cabinet in which he kept his assortment of canvases, watercolour papers, and tubes of paint, he cut out these reports, placed them side by side in the centre of the table, and hurled the remainder of the several journals in an untidy heap on the floor. Then he drew a chair to the table, lit a cigarette, and for about half an hour was absorbed in a close comparison of the text of the cuttings. Having mentally digested the principal features of the tragedy he thrust his hands deep into his trousers pockets and flung himself back in his chair. At this moment the door bell of his flat rang with a series of short, insistent peals which terminated in a sustained and irritating resonance.

"Hell's bells!" he exclaimed impatiently as he heard Albert, his man-servant, hurry to answer the summons.

"Mr. Ricardo would like to see you, sir."

"Show him in, Albert," said Vereker, and a smile erased the frown of impatience that had momentarily clouded his brow.

"Well, Ricky, I'm glad to see you, my boy. Come in and make yourself at home." Noticing the unusual gravity of his friend's demeanour, he asked, "What's the matter? In trouble again?"

Manuel Ricardo wearily flung his hat, gloves, and stick on to a settee before replying.

"I've come to stay," he said gloomily.

"You're welcome as ever, but I thought you'd just moved into new digs."

"I moved out again this morning."

"Cleared out bag and baggage, eh?" laughed Vereker.

"It's not quite as magnificent as all that. You see, the landlady is sitting tight on my trunks till—till—"

"I see clearly. Never mind, we'll remove her later. What was the cause of the trouble or who?"

"Who? Rachmaninoff!"

"A fellow-lodger?" asked Vereker, bewildered.

"No, the composer and his damnable prelude. Some musical student in the next house with his instrument of torture against my wall. Morning, noon, and far into the night—a whole week of the prelude and nothing but the prelude. Worked it up into a prelude to insanity. It was an incitement to murder as an interlude. I was getting dangerous!"

Ricardo's glance fell on the newspaper cuttings arranged on the studio table.

"Ah, the Armadale case! I thought it would put the kibosh on your painting. What about the Spring Show? Going to give it a miss?"

"No, I'm sending in three exhibits. That one on the easel's an oil. Finished it yesterday."

Ricardo walked lazily over to the painting and studied it for some seconds.

"Algernon, this is an outrage! I presume your modern art critic would call it architectural painting and say that you had enlarged your formal experience! Of all the gaseous nonsense ever mumbled by fatuous nincompoops... 'struth, I prefer Luke Fildes. What's it supposed to represent, anyway?"

"I've tried to visualize a scene from the Athenian Thesmophoria. The women, as you will remember, walked with phallic emblems in their hands and uttered obscenities. Those feasts symbolized the magic of fertility..."

"Good Lord above!" exclaimed Ricardo piously, and added quietly, "A pretty conceit, Algernon, but to-day, outside the Church the idea's moribund. If you could elaborate something similar about birth control it would be more modish. I'm glad you're returning to crime detection. The saving grace of murder is that it's non-controversial. After your picture I think I'd like a cocktail."

"It's no longer done, Ricky. Those who know prefer good sherry. There's a bottle of old golden on the buffet in the other room. Help yourself if there's any left. That's Albert's only fault; he has a palate."

"It's always expensive in a servant and ruinous in a guest," added Ricardo as he left the room. Returning with a bottle and glasses, he placed them on the table.

"Have you read what the papers have to say about this shooting mystery, Ricky?" asked Vereker, glancing up from the cuttings on the table to which he had suddenly returned.

"I devoured the *Daily Report*'s account. Their crime reporter's style's so good I never buy a thriller nowadays."

"Geordie Stewart, their editor, asked me this morning to go down to Nuthill on their behalf. He remembered my private work on the Bygrave case. Besides, I once met Sutton Armadale, who practically owned the *Report*. He bought one of my pictures some time ago. I had a standing invitation to Vesey Manor to see his little gallery of French painters. I've always been going to run down. He has a couple of Marchains and a Montezin I'd like very much to see."

"That's most convenient. I shall have the flat all to myself. I must get on with my new serial. About that baggage of mine, can you see your way clear—?"

"How much do you owe your landlady?"

"I've got to pay her three guineas in lieu of a week's notice."

"You're fairly up to date, then? Astounding, Ricky! And the guv'nor's cheque, isn't that due shortly?"

"What a pestilential memory you've got, Algernon! Yes, it is, but I've earmarked that amount for out of pocket—"

"Don't trouble to explain, Ricky. What's the lady's name this time?"

"Laura Hardinge. You know the Hardinges. I always think Laura's such a beautiful name."

"So did Petrarch, I believe. To return to the world, here's a tenner. Go and get your baggage and come back without divagation, as Thackeray would have put it. Your camping here while I'm down in the country'll suit me down to the ground. You'll be handy if I want you to ferret out any information up at this end. If I remember well, you were rather useful once before."

"Useful? Useful? My services were of paramount importance in the Bygrave case. Damned fine mess you'd have made of it without me! As you know, my forte is shadowing. I can follow your man into the most expensive pleasure resorts with the greatest of skill. Thanks for the tenner. I hope repayment by instalments won't inconvenience you. The only thing I liked about *Eric* was the little by little business."

Vereker was lost in thought for some moments.

"Look here, Ricky, if I leave another twenty quid in my bureau to be used for emergencies will you promise—?"

"Never, Algernon, never! You positively must not! For me every moment is an emergency. If you think your commission will run me into expenses, wire the cash with the commission. My whole life's a kind of post-dated cheque. In money matters you might truthfully say I've always been before my time."

"Very well, should the need arise I'll wire the money. What do you say to lunch?"

"I always say yes, emphatically! You see, I've been on a breakfast and dinner basis for weeks with a drink of water at midday. Water won't stay put."

"Then we will lunch at Jacques. You remember Jacques?"

"I never forget a good eating-house or remember a bad debt. I've been to Jacques occasionally since you introduced me to the place. In fact, I'm quite friendly with the *sommelier*. I used to take Edmée there for dinner."

"Edmée? Who the devil's Edmée?"

"Edmée Cazas. I was very much in love with Edmée."

"French, I suppose. Where did you pick her up?"

"My dear Algernon, you've assumed an expression as if you'd just encountered a bad smell. I don't pick up women; they always forestall me. I was introduced to Edmée by Aubrey Winter, if you'd like to know. Aubrey was also in love with her. A very high-spirited filly she is, and neither Aubrey nor I had the hands."

For a few seconds Vereker was silent, and then, bringing his right fist with a report into the open palm of his left hand, exclaimed dramatically:

"Now I've got her!"

"Well, I'm damned, Algernon! You sly dog! Still, you're welcome to her and have my sympathy."

"You misunderstand me, Ricky ; I mean that I've placed the lady."

"Sorry! I thought you'd misplaced your affections."

"No, with me that would be a tragedy; with you, it has simply become a bad habit."

"That's the natural evolution of tragedies, Algernon, but in what connection have you placed Edmée Cazas?"

"She was one of the guests staying down at Vesey Manor, Sutton Armadale's place in Surrey. Do you know anything about her?"

"Quite a lot! By profession she's a ballerina, by nature a Bacchante, behaves like a Begum, Belgian nationality, born in Britain, a bewitching brunette—in fact, she's everything beginning with a b except a bore or a Beguine!"

"Ricky, I see you're going to be helpful. Can you tell me how long she has known the Armadales?"

"She got to know them last year at Nice. The Armadales had taken a Villa there for the season. Aubrey Winter—he's Angela Armadale's cousin—was among the guests. Aubrey was painfully in love with Edmée—at the sonnet-writing stage, if you understand."

"I thought that stage was a sort of afterglow."

With a poet, yes, but Aubrey's merely a part of a motor-car, a Bentley spare, you might say. Well, Edmée was taken into the bosom of the family, chiefly Sutton's. The result was catastrophic. I don't know whether I should tell you the details. I got them from Aubrey."

"In confidence?"

"Not exactly. He poured out his tale of woe to every one patient enough to listen. Besides, to tell me anything in confidence would be as foolish as putting a burglar in command of the Bank Guard. You see it concerns Edmée, and I'm very fond of her."

"I thought Laura Hardinge was in the ascendant at the moment."

"I know, I know, but Edmée's not an ordinary woman, Algernon; she's a relapsing fever. She gets into your blood. You take an injection of common sense and you think you're cured. You even begin to look happy, and then without the slightest warning you're as bad as ever again. I may have a relapse at any moment."

"And Laura's an alternating fever, I suppose."

"No, no, she's too sweet for that. She's almost a convalescence."

"Well, never mind. I'm discretion itself, Ricky. You can trust me with the details; they'll go no further."

"Then let's begin at the beginning. It's just a little over two years ago since Sutton Armadale married Angela Daunay. She had been the loveliest debutante of her year, so every one said. It's a relative kind of compliment as a rule; the standard's so low. Still, every one would call Angela beautiful, I think, beautiful with a *noli-me-tangere* face. Flaxen hair, blue eyes, complexion of milk and roses. Not my colouring; I've always disliked Dresden Shepherdesses since I broke one of my mother's treasures as a small boy. There's one thing, however; Angela's a thoroughbred. 'Fruity' Fanshaugh says she has the most perfect pasterns he has ever seen. Everything about Angela is fine; it's an overpowering quality in some women. I'm rather afraid of her, to tell the truth. One glance from her turns me from a baboon into a courtier. About his first wife I don't know very much. A very estimable person, I believe, but not quite out of the top drawer. She was fourteen stone and always dressed as if she weighed seven. Had a bourgeois taste in jewellery and wore it like a publican's wife. I've seen her enter a room caparisoned like a durbar elephant. But she was an amiable, kind-hearted soul with a *Family Herald* streak in her mental make-up. I think her favourite author was Berta Ruck. Anyway, Sutton was very happy with her and was very cut up when she died. He knew her and understood her; he'd got the feel of her as one does of a favourite stick. Now, like many successful business men, Sutton had no insight where women were concerned. He met Angela Daunay, liked her streamline, knew she was a top-notcher as far as birth was concerned, and thought she'd put the right *cachet* on his wealth. Nobody thought Angela would look twice at him. But there's something about these financiers that's inexplicably, almost spookishly magnetic. I've a theory that it's the secret of their success. Angela, to everybody's surprise, accepted him. I was going to say jumped at him, but it would be wrong. She accepted him with about the same enthusiasm as royalty accepts a large donation to a charity. She was glad but impersonally glad. She had accepted him as if he were going to be a pleasant adjunct to her dignity and comfort—more of a rich fur coat than a husband. Sutton's second excursion, if rumour speaks the truth, was unfortunate. In less than six months they were cold soup to one another. Edmée says they ought to have taken a warning during their engagement when they found they couldn't dance well together. 'Their vital rhythms varied,' were her words, and I dare say lasting love's only a matter of good timing. In any case, there was a big disparity in their ages. Sutton was forty-eight and Angela twenty years younger."

"There's not much in that, Ricky; the woman usually makes up for it in intelligence. Intelligence is to experience what art is to craftsmanship."

"But Angela, like many aristocrats, isn't intelligent. With her the delightful capriciousness, the eagerness and glow of vulgar life have hardened into the glitter of good taste and perfect manners. She's a human crystal. She was brought up in the later feudal tradition of romantic love. In your own language, Vereker, she has been painted in the neo-classic style. At forty-eight, Sutton had outgrown his illusions, but he was stupid enough to give them lip service and always enacted a preposterous make-believe. His was one of those rather undeveloped minds that always think they ought to illuminate their sexual emotions with strings of fairy lamps. However, when the newly married couple discovered that they didn't live in the same street they were both very amiable about it. Sutton was too indifferent and Angela too polished to quarrel. Figuratively, Sutton sought the Garden of Eden, and Angela was all the time yearning for Paradise. Now, Edmée has always roamed the Garden of Eden. It's her natural habitat."

"A very modern Eve, I suppose."

"No, I wouldn't call Edmée modern. Ordinary women, like hymns, are either ancient or modern, but Eve is of all time. She's Isis, Aphrodite, Venus in a hundred guises and various coloured skins. Edmée is ninety per cent Eve and Sutton had achieved through experience seventy-five per cent Adam. They were bound to fuse. It didn't take Edmée a week to see that Sutton and Angela were a discrepancy, and that Sutton, to use her own phrase, was 'tout cousu d'or.' How distinctly I can visualize her mouth as she said 'tout cousu d'or' and the calculating gleam in her Belgian eyes! She translated for my benefit in Americanese—'he's lousy with money, Ricky.' Like all Eves, Edmée is passionately fond of money; not for its own sake, but as something to be quickly exchanged for the fruits of the earth. She came upon Sutton just as I might stumble on a fiver when I was hard up."

"Just as you might come on me for a tenner would be more accurate," interrupted Vereker, with malicious glee.

"You deserve the point, Algernon; I had dropped my guard. To continue the story, there followed the Sutton Stakes."

"What on earth was that?"

"Haven't you heard the yarn? Bless my soul, I thought it was in a cheap edition by now. I have much pleasure in telling you the scandalous story. It happened about a fortnight after Edmée had arrived in Nice. She had come to Nice because Aubrey Winter was there. As I have said, Aubrey was in love with her, he may be so now for all I know, but her affection for Aubrey was the affection she might have for a comfortable pair of house slippers. Aubrey's a delightful fool and, though Edmée hurts all her lovers indiscriminately, they are somehow never disillusioned. There's something of the snake and the bird in her relations with men. Well, to brighten things up the Armadales gave a little dinner and dance at their Villa, Les Aigles d'Or. What part Aubrey had in suggesting that dinner and dance, or whether Sutton was inspired to its realization by Edmée, it would be hard to say. Most likely Aubrey, because if a man's stupid Fate seems to take a grim delight in making him encompass his own ruin. In any case, the dinner was given, and when Sutton gives a dinner it is a dinner. The cost doesn't interfere with the dream, and Angela saw to it that the dream was delightful. Angela is all for English dinners, and one of the items on the menu was cygnets. I like that touch of cygnets; it's pure Angela. But the wines that flowed appealed to my imagination. They proved the *deus ex machina* in what followed. There were old golden sherry, Château Montbrun, Grand Musigny 1911, Clicquot 1919, Cockburn port 1904, and '70 brandy. Could anything be more reasonable? This selection of sound liquor produced a Bacchanalian atmosphere among the happy guests. Edmée, flushed with the fire of the grape, became Phryne incarnate; Aubrey's Boeotian wit began to caper whimsically, and even Sutton's merry mercantile eye took on a satyr's gleam. It was this vinous urge which promoted the Sutton Stakes. No one is certain to this day who suggested the rag, but it has generally been attributed to 'Fruity' Fanshaugh. He has never denied it. 'Fruity' is a cross between Kipling's Anglo-Indian and a Yogi. As a young officer in India he swallowed a lot of Yoga and got it inextricably mixed up with polo and pig-sticking. He's credited with the possession of a Bombay head."

"What's that? I don't understand," asked Vereker, with solemn interest.

"I'm not quite clear myself, but I believe it means that the owner has suffered at one time or another from a touch of the Indian sun—a bit 'gaga,' to put it vulgarly. In any case, towards the end of the dance 'Fruity' seemed to take charge of the company of guests, and there was a hurried consultation with much laughter among the males. In a few minutes it was seen that something unusual was afoot, and it was suddenly announced before the final dance that the Sutton Stakes was to be run. The gees were to be seven male members of the company who had pooled substantial stakes, and the riders were to be seven of the ladies present. The horses were to run on all-fours with their jockeys astride their backs, and the course was once round the ballroom. It was an astounding proposition, but, as I've said, a Dionysian spirit was abroad and the Greeks had a very natural taste in amusements. I can never remember just who the horses were, but I know there was an eminent K.C., a brigadier, a very famous playwright, an M.P.—I won't mention his name—and an R.A. among the field. Not a selling-plater ran. 'Fruity' Fanshaugh was weigher-in, starter, judge, winning-post, tote, Stewards of the Jockey Club, all rolled into one. It was a weight for youth handicap, and to Sutton, being the oldest horse, was allotted Edmée as his rider. She's a sylph, I may explain, a wisp of provocative feminine gossamer. One of the rules insisted that no rider should touch the ground with her feet. Infringement of this rule instantly disqualified. Edmée, trained for the ballet, found this acrobatic feat to her taste and had, moreover, the courage of her anatomy not to mention underwear. In any case, she rode a daring and graceful race. Sutton went well up to bridle and won, and from that moment lost his heart to his pretty jockey. Edmée at once took the reins and began to ride him for all he was worth in the everyday race of having a good time."

"And have you heard what Angela thought of this performance?" asked Vereker, with grave interest.

"Have I not? You could have iced the bubbly yards away from her. After the riders had mounted and Edmée had adjusted her rope of pearls—Ciro, of course—on Sutton as a bridle, Angela walked out of the room like a plate-glass Bellona. For a few seconds the air was susurrous, and then 'Fruity' shouted the word 'Go.' Angela went and sat out on the balcony in frozen meditation, gazing at the sweet moonlit shimmer of the Mediterranean while the race was in progress. Her old friend, Houseley—'Hell-for-leather' Houseley—accompanied her and gallantly held her hand in the courtliest manner. 'Masochistic vulgarity' was what Angela thought of the race, and remarked to Edmée afterwards that she was certain that 'Nebuchadnezzar at his worst could never have looked such a damned fool as Sutton did on all-fours.'"

"I've a soft spot for Angela already," remarked Vereker when Ricardo had finished his story. "Among the goddesses there's something devilishly attractive about Diana."

"I think I'll call you Endymion instead of Algernon in future," said Ricardo, with a loud laugh.

For some moments Vereker sat in thought, and then rose abruptly to his feet.

"Do you know, Ricky, when I hear of rags like the Sutton Stakes I long for an evening in company with Van Ostade's Dutch boors. I want to sit in an old picture and laugh over my mug of ale."

"Posing again, Algernon, in spite of yourself, and pure cussedness at that! Besides, it's completely out of fashion to hiccup the antithesis of beer and erudition or beer and art at the

British public—except at the Universities. Even the Sussex literary school is as dead as Van Ostade. The idea that poverty implies robust virtue won't wash in these democratic days. Give me the vivid amusements of the unorthodox rich. Money doesn't smell, but those that lack it frequently do!"

"Quite in your best vein, Ricky, but now for that lunch. My bag is packed and I start for Nuthill immediately after we've eaten. While I'm down there I want you to get in touch with Edmée Cazas."

"She's an expensive contagion," interrupted Ricardo gloomily.

"Never mind, I'll stand the racket. Connect up. Keep in touch with her and get from her her version of this shooting of Sutton Armadale. I'll bet she knows more than may ever be made public. With her hysterical desire to be interesting, you ought to have no difficulty in pumping her to a vacuum. I will run up and see you in a day or so, and I hope you'll have something important to communicate. And now for grub!"

Chapter Three

Half-way between Vesey Manor and the little, old-fashioned market town of Nuthill there stands a country inn called the "Silver Pear Tree." Somewhere in one of those interesting volumes published by the Surrey Archaeological Society on the history of that charming county there is a pleasing story about how this country inn acquired its fantastic name, but Vereker was too delighted with the name to trouble about its history. History, even when it falls back on legend for lack of fact, is inclined to be prosaic, and somehow Vereker was in a mood to accept the "Silver Pear Tree" as too good for investigation. He had been shown his room and ordered tea, which was to be served in what was called "Ye Olde Coffye Roome." He was obliged to smile on seeing this title freshly painted on the glass panel of the door of that apartment. For a few moments he was lost in amused reverie, and then quietly opened the door and entered. To his surprise, he found "ye coffye roome" occupied. In the most comfortable chair, by an open window, through which drifted the warm, flower-scented air of the August afternoon, lounged a bulky figure. On his entry, the figure moved, two powerful arms shot out and were stretched in lazy ecstasy; a pair of large grey eyes under heavy, bushy eyebrows slowly opened and were questioningly turned on him. With an agility amazing in so cumbrous a bulk, the figure sprang instantly to its feet.

"God bless my soul, Mr. Vereker!" came the exclamation.

"And my soul, too, Inspector Heather!" returned Vereker, with genuine pleasure.

"No need to ask you what brings you down here," remarked the inspector.

"Beauty, inspector, beauty! I sometimes come down into the country in search of it. Doesn't my old friend, Ralph—I mean Emerson, of course—say 'we ascribe beauty to that which is simple; which has no superfluous parts; which exactly answers its ends; which stands related to all things; which is—'"

"Good beer," interrupted the inspector hastily.

"Agreed. To quit fooling, I'm down here on this Armadale affair."

"Not a job for amateurs, Mr. Vereker."

"Why call in the Yard, then? I have here in my pocket-book a cutting from the *Daily Express*. It is wholesomely informative. Let me read it to you. 'Six murders have been committed during the first nine months of this year and the six murderers are still at large. Scotland Yard detectives were concerned in four of these cases.'"

"Sounds as if we committed them," interrupted the inspector testily.

"'Nine murders took place last year and are marked in the police records as "undiscovered,"'" continued Vereker relentlessly. "'Scotland Yard inquired into seven of those crimes. A plain fact must be stated—Scotland Yard, the most highly organized police department in the world, has lost the habit of catching murderers.'"

"Catching murderers is an art, not a habit, Mr. Vereker, with all due respect to the *Daily Express* correspondent."

"Perhaps you're right, inspector. But what are you going to do about it?"

"Catch 'em in future if we can. In the art of criminal investigation, just as in your job—if you can call it a job—of painting, there's a power of luck. Only you can burn your duds while ours are put on record for critical Press correspondents to chuckle over," replied the inspector, with a show of warmth.

"Neatly expressed, inspector, but only partially true. The critical Press correspondents generally manage to chuckle even over our successes. We have that disadvantage. But let's get to the Armadale case. You've been over the ground and got the general hang of things. I know only what I've gathered from the news—fragmentary, uncertain, inconclusive stuff—poor foundations to build on. Of course it was a murder and not suicide."

"Oh!" said the inspector, looking up with his slow, inquisitive glance. "How did you tumble to that?"

"Just a guess," replied Vereker lazily, "an idle guess. I don't think a man would commit suicide by shooting himself in the stomach. There were two bullet wounds: one in the head and one in the abdomen, I believe?"

"That's true, and the guess is quite a good one, but only a guess. If a man's determined to do himself in there's no saying how he'll do it if his mind is sufficiently worked up. A man has committed suicide by beating his head almost to a pulp with a hammer; another by driving a chisel several times into his skull. At first glance these actual cases looked like particularly brutal murders, and yet they were proved without any doubt to have been suicides."

"Amazing! What do you think about it yourself, Heather?"

"Like you, I've guessed it's murder. But it's too early in the day to say much more. For instance, suppose Mr. Armadale wished it to be thought that he had been murdered. There have been hidden reasons for such a trick on several previous occasions. It might be done to avoid trouble over insurance money; to incriminate some innocent person in a mad spirit of revenge."

"Quite so, but there's something fishy about those two wounds—one in the abdomen, the other in the right temple. It was in the right temple, wasn't it?"

"That's correct, and Mr. Armadale was gripping his Colt .45 automatic pistol in his left hand. What's the bright amateur deduction from that, Mr. Vereker?" asked the inspector, with his heavy, good-natured face breaking into a smile.

"I thought that would be the first, dull, official question, inspector. I guess it puzzled you immensely. I thrashed it out with myself this morning while I was hunting for my back collar-stud. As you've got a flying start of me, I must ask you a few questions. In the first place, was Mr. Sutton's left thumb on the trigger?"

"No, there was neither digit nor thumb within the trigger guard."

"Digit is luscious, inspector! You ought to be on the *Daily Report*. We'll leave digits out of the question. If Armadale had pulled the trigger of his automatic with his left thumb, it would have been as easy to shoot himself in the right temple with his left hand as with his right."

"That's sound enough, especially if he had turned his head for the purpose," agreed the inspector.

"I'm glad you follow me so easily, Heather. But the vital question is—what was Mr. Armadale doing with his right hand?"

"I wasn't there to see," replied the inspector dryly.

"You're dodging, Heather; it's not fair. Where was the dead man's right hand when you saw the body?"

"Lying limply at his side."

"It was covered with blood, I'll wager."

"That's true."

"Well, my bright amateur deduction is that when Mr. Armadale was shot in the abdomen the bullet entered on the right side. He promptly slipped his Colt into his left hand and thrust his right hand over the abdominal wound in his agony."

"Mr. Armadale was ambidextrous as far as I can gather, Mr. Vereker," replied the inspector quietly. "You're correct about the right side of the abdomen. We'll say he shot with his right hand. I think you've described what happened if he was murdered."

"You're still flirting with the idea of suicide, I see."

"I never draw hasty conclusions nowadays."

"What does Sir William Macpherson, 'the famous pathologist who is also an expert on gunshot wounds,' say?"

"He's non-committal so far."

"Has he extracted the bullets?"

"Well, the bullet which penetrated the right abdomen carried with it into the intestines a trousers button. This obstruction turned the bullet broadside on, and after making a shocking wound it was stopped by the top of the left hip bone, 'near the left iliac crest,' as Sir William put it. The bullet that entered the skull passed clean through and hasn't been found, but from the clean-cut entrance hole it was evidently fired from the same calibre weapon as the first."

"And what was the calibre of that weapon?" asked Vereker expectantly.

"The bullet was fired from a .45 automatic," replied the inspector, unable to restrain a shade of dramatic intensity.

"Well I'm damned!" muttered Vereker, as he thoughtfully stroked his chin with the fingers and thumb of his left hand. "That's a very singular discovery— almost a coincidence. I suppose you'll examine that bullet microscopically and be able to say whether it was fired from the Colt found in Mr. Armadale's left hand, won't you?"

"The bullet has been badly marked by its impact with the button, but if our luck's in we'll know very soon. It's always very difficult to answer such a question definitely. In the meantime, I'm working on the idea that it wasn't fired from Mr. Armadale's weapon. Colt .45 automatics are a very widely bought and used type of pistol. There are thousands of them in this country and tens of thousands in America. There may be automatics of other makes which take exactly similar ammunition."

"These technicalities put years on me, inspector, but I follow your argument. About those cartridge cases which are so neatly ejected by such a weapon, the *Evening Bulletin* states that only one cartridge case has been found, though two shots were fired."

"Perfectly true, but I'm going to have another very thorough search. We must find the other shell or shells: they may furnish very vital evidence."

"I thought as much. And what vital evidence has the first one furnished which you're discreetly hiding from me?" asked Vereker.

"I had a 'phone message this afternoon from our expert micro-photographer to say that that cartridge case was fired by the pistol found in Sutton Armadale's hand."

"They discovered that from the firing-pin impression on the cap?"

"Exactly. So it's clear that Armadale had one shot at his assailant."

"Clear? Clear? What do you mean, Heather? You're at your old game of throwing dust in my eyes. Pure jealousy, of course. If Armadale was shot twice by the burglar and himself took one shot at the burglar, that would make three shots. Collyer, the keeper, heard only two reports; Mr. Basil Ralli, who was much nearer the scene of murder, heard only two reports. Three shots into two reports won't go. Even Euclid would call it absurd."

"I always thought Euclid himself absurd, Mr. Vereker. What else can you make of it? I have an idea that there were three shots. People who hear reports in the night don't think of the number till they're asked about them afterwards. Have you ever waked up and suddenly become aware that a clock was striking?"

"Too often. I'd like to blow up the church behind my flat in Fenton Street. Its clock even strikes the quarters."

"Well, at night if you wake by chance you're almost sure to wonder what the time is, and if a clock is striking you promptly begin to count the chimes. But you consciously do that for a definite purpose. If, however, you hear a dog bark or a cock crow you don't bother about the number of barks or crows."

"I'd bother all right, inspector, but I wouldn't count them. I'd curse instead. Last time I counted clock chimes at night I made six. You can imagine my delight when I found it was only midnight. I'd missed the first six in my sleep."

"Just what I was coming to. Both Collyer and Ralli were probably wakened by the first report and only actually heard the last two. I'm pretty certain there were three shots and that two cartridge cases are still missing."

"That's possible, but I won't take it for granted. At what distance do you think the shots were fired, inspector?"

"It would be very difficult to say, but at a fairly close range, in my opinion. The difficulty is this. Modern smokeless powder doesn't blacken the skin, and if the shot is fired more than a foot away doesn't mark it at all. The wound in Mr. Armadale's forehead seems to have been inflicted at very close range. Again, no matter how close the pistol muzzle is held to clothing there won't be any signs of scorching with modern powder."

"I see I'm going to have an easier job than you this time, inspector," replied Vereker thoughtfully.

"How do you make that out?"

"I rely chiefly on psychology, while you base your investigations on facts. I find out why the crime was committed and thence by whom, while you always try to discover how the crime was committed and thence by whom. By the way, what clothes was Armadale wearing when they discovered his body?"

"Evening dress with dinner jacket, boiled shirt, and patent-leather shoes."

"That's interesting. Had he been to bed?"

"Oh, yes. He'd been to bed all right. The state of his bed-clothes and bed confirms that. His pyjamas were lying on the floor as if he'd flung them off in a great hurry when he dressed himself."

"This is all very strange, Heather. You say he had put on his patent-leather shoes?"

"Yes."

"And his socks?"

"Yes."

"He didn't trouble to put on his collar and tie, I suppose?"

"No. Instead of his collar and tie he had wound a large, black silk muffler round his neck and tucked the long ends into his waistcoat. He had also turned up the collar of his dinner jacket."

"Most peculiar, don't you think?" asked Vereker pointedly, as he flung the inspector a furtive glance.

"You didn't expect him to take the trouble to put on his collar and tie to chase a burglar, did you?" asked the inspector, staring up at the ceiling and quilling his moustache thoughtfully.

"What more reasonable, Heather? You can imagine the shock a burglar would get when he found the master of the house at four or five in the morning all dressed up to receive him—dinner jacket, black tie, collar, stiff shirt. What about his monocle?"

"Strange you should joke about a monocle, Mr. Vereker. Mr. Armadale always wore a monocle, and it was dangling from his neck by a silk cord when he was found lying on the polo ground."

"Random shot on my part, but quite an unexpected hit. Of course he'd want his monocle if he intended to use his automatic. It was possibly his aiming eye. He ought to have blazed at him instead of aiming. I dare say that confounded monocle was his undoing. The burglar got him first in the stomach and then settled him with a more deliberate shot through the head."

"That's how I figured it out," said the inspector.

"But you're keeping very quiet about one very important item, Heather. Doubtless you think I've forgotten all about it. Let me have a look at the burglar's mask that was found near the rifled safe. I know you've got it in your pocket."

Unable to suppress a laugh, Inspector Heather drew from his pocket the mask referred to and handed it to Vereker.

"I don't think it will tell you much," he remarked. Vereker drew the mask from the large paper envelope into which the inspector had carefully placed it. For a few seconds he examined it very minutely and then, slipping the elastic over his head, adjusted the mask to his own face.

"A mask has always intrigued me, Heather," he said. "Strange that a suppression of so small a portion of the face should effect so complete a disguise. It shows we recognize our friends not by the individual features but by a very intimate combination of all the features. The portrait painter knows that if you get that chord the slightest bit out of harmony the likeness suffers, and yet the human eye is so sensitive that it amazes me—"

"Bunkum! I know your little dissertations are a pure blind, Mr. Vereker," interrupted the inspector. "You've found something about that mask that interests you much more than the science of disguise. Am I right?"

"You're far too smart, Heather. As a matter of fact, I was just asking myself the question, 'Do burglars wear masks?' and the question reminded me of a newspaper article which I once read entitled, 'Have telephone girls It?'"

"Wearing masks isn't so common with burglars as it used to be. They're much more careful nowadays about wearing gloves," replied the inspector.

"I don't know what I'd do without you, Heather," said Vereker, as he replaced the mask in its envelope and handed it back to the detective. "You're a mine of information—an inexhaustible mine," he added ironically. "I'm always learning something new from you. Who'd have thought that burglars were careful to wear gloves?

Well, well! Why didn't you add that it was to obviate leaving finger-prints? I suppose you believe in imparting antiquated knowledge in small doses. I promise you I'll get my own back, so look out, my old friend!"

At this moment a maid knocked at the coffee-room door and entered with a tea-tray.

"You'll join me, Heather?" asked Vereker.

"Thanks, Mr. Vereker. There's nothing I like better than a cup of tea after waking up from an afternoon nap."

"Blows away the effects of lunch beer, Heather. Afterwards you might conduct me up to the polo ground, and we'll thoroughly examine the scene of the murder, for I'm now convinced that it was a murder. I dare say there's a lot you've missed that I shall be able to discover. I really must help you to regain some of your lost prestige. I know how they'll write it up for the *Daily Report*: 'Smart piece of detective work by Inspector Heather, who distinguished himself some years ago, etc.,' and not a word about your old pal, Anthony Vereker."

"Never mind, Mr. Vereker. You must put on the injured air of an unrecognized genius and feel terribly superior. Genius is its own reward when you've got no virtue to boast of!"

The inspector indulged in a hearty laugh at his own joke.

"Nice cos lettuce that, Heather. I can recommend it. There's one thing that's troubling me a lot. I suppose you're quite unable to say how many shots were fired from Mr. Armadale's pistol by the number of cartridges left in the magazine? Leave out of the discussion for the time being the evidence of the reports that were heard."

"That's always impossible unless you know the number of cartridges that were in the magazine before any were fired. Take this automatic, for example"—here the inspector produced a Colt .45 from his pocket—"the magazine can take any number of cartridges up to seven. They're simply loaded into the magazine against a spring clip, and the magazine is inserted in the stock of the pistol. The cartridges are released into the barrel, the first one by hand, the remainder automatically as each shot is fired. It's an ingenious bit of machinery, and quite different in action from the ordinary revolver."

"Thanks, inspector, but I know a lot about automatic pistols. The point I wish to make is that you've no idea how many cartridges were originally in the magazine?"

"There were six live cartridges in the magazine of Mr. Armadale's pistol when I took charge of it. It's reasonable to surmise that there were originally seven and that only one shot was fired by him."

"I don't like the assurance of that 'fired by him,'" remarked Vereker, pouring himself out another cup of tea.

For some moments the inspector was silent over the mastication of a generous mouthful of home-made cake.

"You have an idea that some one may have shot him with his own pistol and then thrust it in his hand?" he asked at length.

"It seems a likely supposition; it would account for only two reports. When a man commits suicide with a revolver or pistol he usually relaxes his grasp of the weapon, and it is nearly always found at some little distance from the body."

"There is that alternative, and yet a missing cartridge case to explain away. But, Lord bless us, Mr. Vereker, we could go building variations on the theme till doomsday. In the meantime—"

"We'll go up and have a look at that polo ground," interrupted Vereker, rising. "There's one point that I had nearly forgotten. What's this yarn about Mr. Armadale as he was dying murmuring the word 'Murder' to Collyer? What do you make of it?"

"We've only got Collyer's word for it. It's so easy to be wrong on such a point," replied the inspector gravely.

"Only too easy, inspector. It may have been the word 'Mother.' It's a strange thing that proud, self-reliant man in the last great crisis of death will sometimes unconsciously call for help to her who gave him birth and who was his comfort through so great a part of his growing years. In the mystery of existence, womanhood seems to be imbued with terrible significance!"

"It's nearly opening time," interrupted the inspector, noisily clearing his throat. "I think we'd better be going."

"Knowing ourselves very thoroughly, inspector, I quite agree. I see you're as sentimental as ever!"

Chapter Four

On leaving the "Silver Pear Tree" the inspector turned eastward along the road which runs between Nuthill and Burstow and thence onwards to the north-east right away to Canterbury. To the north of this highway swell the rolling masses of the Surrey Hills, and roughly parallel with it wandered the old Pilgrim's Way. Those comfortable hills were now bathed in the hot August sunshine, and the atmosphere about them trembled mistily—a golden transfiguration. The two men had barely walked a hundred yards along this thoroughfare, both lost in their own thoughts, when the inspector halted at a gate leading into a field on their left.

"We'll take a short-cut across the fields from here, Mr. Vereker," he said. "It chops off a big bend in the road, and Armadale's polo ground lies on this side of the manor."

"How far from the house does the polo ground lie?" asked Vereker suddenly.

"About two hundred yards. The gardens and lawns surrounding the manor are enclosed by a ten-foot wall except on a short frontage near the main gates, where there are posts and chains and a low quickset hedge, over which a beautiful view of the front drive and its flanking lawns and borders can be seen. These grounds are roughly rectangular. The western wall, that is the wall nearest us at the moment, is pierced by a folding iron gateway into a courtyard. This courtyard contains the stables for the polo ponies and hunters, and also a garage for Mr. and Mrs. Armadale's cars. From this courtyard wide wooden gates again open out on the field which Mr. Armadale has had converted into a first-class private polo ground."

"An inspiring picture, Heather. It fires my imagination and is an arraignment of the disgusting crime of poverty," interrupted Vereker.

"Armadale was immensely wealthy," commented the inspector simply.

"And immensely intellectual, if we are to believe my friend Emerson. 'Property is an intellectual production,' he says. 'The game requires coolness, right reasoning, promptness, and patience in the players. Man was born to be rich.' Sutton must have been a plucky and tenacious man as well."

"I'm glad to hear that man was born to be rich," sighed the inspector, and added, "I don't know so much about that gentleman's pluck."

"You must admit it. He gets up before five o'clock in the morning to surprise a burglar who wished to acquire some intellectual production quickly by a bold display of coolness and promptness. Without troubling to ring for assistance or rouse the house, he chases him out of the building, follows him through the stable-yard into the polo ground, some two hundred yards of dogged pursuit, and tackles him single-handed with an automatic pistol and a monocle. Then that limitation we call Fate intervened. In a grossly immoral mood Fate sided with the burglar, and twenty-five years of financial acquisition was shot like a rabbit in a ride. On second thoughts, perhaps, Fate has a stern criterion in moral values. God knows!"

Inspector Heather's face broke into a smile.

"To put it in a few words, that burglar business has got you guessing, Mr. Vereker."

"Mightily, inspector. I don't feel quite happy about that burglar, and the more I think on the subject the more mysterious does his mask seem. Can you tell me why burglars wear masks?"

"To avoid identification should we subsequently clap our hands on a suspect."

"To avoid identification? Ah, there's the rub! And yet at the very moment when his mask ought to have been fulfilling its purpose, he recklessly flings it off. Can you explain that action?"

"I've thought about it a good deal. It may have been a bit of a hindrance when he was cracking the safe; or, when he was disturbed and found that it might be necessary to use his gun, he reckoned he'd be able to shoot better without it."

"You've taken good care so far to hide from me all particulars about the cracking of the safe, inspector. Did the burglar use the latest gadgets to do the job—the oxy-acetylene blow-pipe, for instance?"

"That's just what he didn't do. The safe had simply been unlocked with a key."

"The mystery deepens. I suppose it was a modern safe?"

"Yes, but not a very massive affair. A similar safe can be found in any club or hotel in England."

"Where was the key kept, and who had charge of it?"

"There were two keys. Mr. Armadale always carried one on his key chain. He was wearing the chain when he was shot. The other, Mrs. Armadale always kept in a jewel-case in her bedroom. When it was discovered that the safe had been rifled and her £20,000 pearl necklace stolen, she rushed into her room to see if the key was in its usual place. To her surprise, it was there."

"Amazing! Now how did the burglar manage to get a duplicate of one of those keys? It seems to have been a carefully planned affair by a skilled man who took his time, did things with aforethought, and of course left no finger-prints."

"There were no finger-prints on the bolt handle of the safe. The few prints we discovered on the inside walls of the double doors will doubtless prove to be those of the master and mistress of the house. We can't hope for much from finger-prints, and there were no footprints. The man knew his job."

"Was there no electrical burglar alarm on the door of the safe?"

"Yes, but it was out of order."

"You should have said it 'wasn't functioning,' inspector. Is the safe a concealed structure?"

"A bookcase which opens and swings out like a door on hinges hides it very neatly, but as I've said, the man knew his job. He had probably been at work for months finding out all about this safe and its contents. Even if he had spent a year on preliminary scouting the result was worth while. Burglary is highly paid work if you know how to get rid of the swag."

"Your skilled burglar rarely carries fire-arms; you must admit that much, Heather."

"The old hands seldom did, Mr. Vereker, but what with the example of the American crook and the suggestive education of Yankee films, our chaps are taking to the dirty habit more and more. For all we know, an American crook has followed that necklace across the Atlantic; it was bought at Tiffany's in New York."

For some moments Vereker was silent as they crossed a meadow crimsoned with sorrel and powdered with the warm gold of buttercups over which the air hovered in quivering heat. He was walking with head bent in thought. Every now and then he would look up, and his searching eye would drink in the still beauty of the landscape with its drowsy elms drooping in bluish-grey festoons. Above their soft masses shone the distant hills crowned away to the east by a water-tower, now looking in the transforming glow bold, feudal, chivalric.

"How did this burglar enter the house, Heather?" he asked suddenly, as if his thoughts had been utterly detached from his roaming and appreciative vision.

"A folding glass door, or French window, if you like, of the library opens on to a long balcony supported by stone pillars. The library is on the first floor, some twenty feet from the ground and quite an easy climb for an active man. Underneath this balcony is a veranda, which looks out on to a magnificent rock garden. The French window was found ajar when the burglary was discovered, and certain scratches on the stone balustrade of the balcony and down one of the supporting pillars showed that the thief had escaped that way. If this window had accidentally been left open, he may have got in that way by shinning up a pillar and climbing over the balustrade. All the doors and windows on the ground floor were found firmly fastened and hadn't been tampered with."

"You're talking poppycock, Heather. You don't mean to tell me that Armadale clambered over the balustrade and slithered down a pillar after his man?"

"It looks mighty like it, anyhow," replied the inspector. "How is the French window of the library fastened?"

"With an ordinary handle catch and a lock and key. One-half of the window is made fast, of course, with a bolt into the transom and a bolt into the floor. This half was closed and bolted; the other half was ajar."

"The thing's as simple as pie, Heather. One of the servants was in collusion with the burglar and kindly left the window open for him. This servant coached the crook as to the concealed safe, got an impression of the safe key for him, and disconnected the burglar alarm on the safe door, so that you've just got to choose him out of the staff and clap the bracelets on him as an accessory. Arrest the trusted butler for choice!"

"I've got my eyes on the staff, Mr. Vereker. There's a lot in your suggestion," said the inspector gravely.

"I'm going to concentrate on the guests, Heather. There's a Raffles among 'em. Life's daily creeping up to fiction, or vice versa. Bothered if I know. The tragedy of this problem is that nobody will ever know exactly what wakened Armadale in the early hours to go down to the library."

"His bedroom is right above the library," interrupted the inspector. "The noise below probably woke him up."

"Then that's the first logical thing I've heard about this astounding affair, Heather."

"The second is that we've arrived at the polo ground," added the inspector.

At these words, Vereker's lackadaisical manner was at once sloughed, and for some moments he stood silent, his eye taking in every detail of the scene. From the polo ground with its boarded edging it crossed to the gates opening from the stable-yard, thence to the upper windows of Vesey Manor, peering over the enclosing walls of the grounds and kitchen garden and now aflame with the westering sun. He noted that a good view of the polo ground could be obtained from the upper windows of the second and third stories. Thence his glance swept northward to where Hanging Covert frowned over the valley. It was an ideal covert, he could see, for driven pheasants. With their homing habits they would make for Wild Duck Wood to the south-east, flying across the narrow intervening valley, and supply the rocketers beloved of every good shot. Due east of Hanging Covert his eye picked up a puff of bluish smoke issuing from a red chimney-pot burning like a tiny flame against the dark green of the surrounding foliage.

"That's Collyer's cottage nestling on the slope of the hill, I suppose, Heather?"

"That's it, Mr. Vereker. Collyer was making for, and had nearly reached the fringe of, Hanging Covert when he spotted Armadale's body lying near the goal flags at the end of the ground."

"It would take him a good twenty-five minutes to reach the covert after leaving his cottage even at a steady jog-trot. He probably walked, and that would give the murderer half an hour to make himself scarce before Collyer came into a position from which he could view the polo ground. He could have been spotted from the manor windows, but evidently no one was roused or took the trouble to look out. It would probably be more than an hour before Captain Fanshaugh suggested combing the surrounding grounds and woods, so that the man had plenty of time to clear without being seen. In any case, he was careful enough, it seems, to pick up his ejected cartridge cases—a nice point, Heather, don't you think? I should say a man who had committed a murder would be desperately eager to quit the scene of the crime without stopping to hunt for cartridge cases."

"It suggests he was a crook who knew the danger of leaving any clue behind. If we could get hold of one of his empty shells we might be able to trace the weapon, and if we traced the weapon we should probably be able to lay hands on our man."

"You're deadly efficient fellows, Heather," commented Vereker, and hastened his pace towards the northern goal flags of the polo ground. Some twenty paces from those goal flags he noticed a cross marked in whitewash on the close-shorn turf. "Is this the spot where Collyer found the body?"

"Yes. Mr. Armadale was lying on his back with his feet towards the house and his head towards the west."

"With his feet towards the house," repeated Vereker slowly, and was lost in a brown study. After a few moments he added, "That looks as if he had fallen forwards after being shot, and subsequently turned on his back."

"How do you make that out, Mr. Vereker?" asked the inspector quickly.

"If he had fallen backwards, the man who shot him must have been between him and the house. As we are presuming he was chasing the burglar from the house, that would be ridiculous."

"Fairly sound, Mr. Vereker. You've made a big advance since the Bygrave case."

"There's another thing I've learned since then, inspector."

"What's that?"

"The sun rises in the east and sets in the west. Perhaps the burglar manoeuvred Armadale so that the sun would be in his eyes. But tell me, which direction do you think the murderer took after he'd done his dirty work?"

"I've been figuring that out. I should say he hugged the stable and kitchen-garden wall until he reached the main road. This would cut out any risk of his being seen from the house. And now I'm going to give you a valuable bit of information. Very early that morning, Mr. Ralli, as he lay awake, heard a car start up on the main road, and Mrs. Burton, the gardener's wife, heard that car pass the lodge at the front gates at great speed. Unfortunately neither is certain at what time that car passed, but it's significant and probably fits in rather neatly."

The inspector had hardly finished speaking when Vereker suddenly knelt down on the ground and began to examine a small hole in the turf which the whitewash line marking the spot had made clearly visible.

"What have you got there?" asked the inspector curiously.

"I thought at first it was a bullet hole, Heather, but it's not. It's too large for that. There is also the run of a circular impression round it. What do you make of it?"

"I told Sergeant Goss to mark the place with a cross, and I dare say he shoved in a sharpened stake as a temporary indicator."

"Possibly," returned Vereker thoughtfully, "and possibly not. In any case, I suggest we make another thorough search of the ground round here for those two cartridge cases—if there are two."

"That's why I came up here," replied the inspector, and getting down on hands and knees commenced the irksome task.

"A nice snap you'd make for the picture page of the *Daily Report*, Heather," remarked Vereker, laughing. "Detective Inspector caught grazing in an unguarded moment. Pity there's not a clump of thistles in the foreground!"

The inspector was too intent on his search to reply to this facetiousness, and for the next half-hour neither man spoke as he diligently covered every inch of the ground round the cross marking the spot where Sutton Armadale fell. Vereker was the first to break the silence.

"Here's a thing and a very pretty thing," he suddenly exclaimed as he rose to his feet and approached the inspector.

The latter jumped up quickly and glanced anxiously at the small brass object which Vereker held out on the palm of his hand.

"By God, that's a rare bit of luck!" he exclaimed. "A .45 automatic cartridge case. We must recommend you for promotion for this, Mr. Vereker. I wonder how we missed it on the first search."

"I can explain, Heather. I found it down the hole which you think Sergeant Goss made with a sharpened stake. Your friend Goss oughtn't to be trusted with sharpened stakes. He's dangerous enough with a baton. I've made another find, Heather. There's another hole made by Goss's sharpened stake some twenty or thirty yards off. There's nothing in it, I'm sorry to say."

The inspector took the empty shell from Vereker and, after examining it carefully, wrapped it in cotton-wool to prevent further scratching or abrasion and placed it in a match-box. Thrusting the box into his pocket with a shade of jubilation, he exclaimed:

"That ought to settle once and for all whether there was more than one pistol used in this shooting."

At this juncture the attention of both men was arrested by the emergence from the stable-yard gate of Sergeant Goss himself. The sergeant was carrying under his arm a brown paper parcel, and on seeing his chief he hurried his pace almost to a run. He was unmistakably excited, which was a most unusual emotional state for Sergeant Lawrence Goss.

"Well, sergeant, got our man wrapped up in that parcel?" asked the inspector.

"Tidy bit of him, I think, sir," replied the sergeant^ as he untied the parcel and displayed to view a well-worn but recently cleaned suit of clothes.

"What the devil!" exclaimed the inspector with a puzzled frown as he glanced at the garments. "Where on earth did you find this packet?"

"Burton, the head gardener, found the parcel tucked away under some bushes near the swimming-pool, not fifty yards from the house," replied the sergeant. "He thought it was a bit rum and might have something to do with our case so he 'anded the lot over to me."

"Any tailor's or cleaners' marks on them?" asked the inspector.

"Not a hiota, sir," replied Goss, gravely aspirate.

"May I have a look at them, inspector?" asked Vereker eagerly.

"Certainly, Mr. Vereker; though I can't for the life of me see what they've got to do with our case at the moment."

Taking the suit, which consisted of trousers, waistcoat, and jacket, from the sergeant, Vereker examined them very carefully, turning over the garments one by one.

"This waistcoat interests me particularly," he exclaimed at length, as he held the garment close to his face and sniffed at it suspiciously. Then handing the suit back to the sergeant, he added, "Reach-me-downs, recently cleaned. They still smell of benzine or petrol. You have a little line of inquiry there, inspector. I hope you'll be generous enough to let me know what you discover. I can't waste my time hunting up old do' shops and cleaners."

"I'll play fair, Mr. Vereker," replied the inspector, and glancing at his watch remarked, "I think I'll get back to Nuthill police station. Any other news, sergeant?"

"There was a 'phone message from headquarters for you, sir. I took it. Sir William Macpherson reports that he is almost certain that the bullet extracted from Mr. Harmadale was not fired from the Colt pistol found in the dead gentleman's 'and."

"Good. So you see, Mr. Vereker, we can safely take it that Armadale was murdered and didn't commit suicide. The cartridge case you found just now ought to confirm, and then for the weapon itself! By the way, Goss, did you mark the spot here on the polo ground with a sharpened stake?"

"No, sir. I marked it temporary with my 'andkerchief and a pair of 'andcuffs," replied the sergeant.

At this information Vereker was obliged to laugh.

"I think we can say right away that those holes were made before the murder was committed, Heather. Otherwise the cartridge case wouldn't have found such a neat little hiding-place."

"I'm not so sure about that," remarked the inspector, "but it's a nice point. I'll make a sleuth of you yet, Mr. Vereker. Now I think I'll get back to Nuthill."

"I feel I ought to nose round for a bit, Heather," said Vereker, as the inspector and sergeant turned to go. "I've a notion that there ought to be another shell somewhere. I'm working on your statement that you think there were three shots fired. Don't stop too long at the 'Silver Pear Tree.' You've got a big day's work in front of you to-morrow."

Chapter Five

On Inspector Heather's departure, Vereker glanced at his watch, and finding he had still two hours of daylight before him decided to explore what he called the "physical geography" of the case. Leaving the north end of the polo ground, he skirted the western wall of the manor grounds and came into the meadows forming the valley between the house and the gently swelling wooded hills to the north. In front of him, across those meadows, Hanging Covert loomed hazily through the golden sun-dust, and to the right frowned Beech Wood, in which he could now clearly discern the western gable of Collyer's cottage. At the eastern end of this valley and closing it lay the dark mass of Wild Duck Wood. After a careful survey of this scenery, he wandered towards Wild Duck Wood, with the intention of making a circuit of the meadows which lay like an emerald arena in this natural amphitheatre.

As he walked leisurely through the lush grass, his hands thrust into his jacket pockets, his mind was turning over in a series of permutations the matter of those two reports heard by Collyer, the keeper, and Basil Ralli. If Armadale's assailant had fired two shots and the murdered man had fired one, the conflicting evidence of the reports heard was mysterious. The only satisfactory deduction that he could make at the moment was that only two shots had been fired, and that both had been fired from Armadale's own pistol. The second empty cartridge case which he had found and which Heather had taken for examination would clear up this puzzle. Sir William Macpherson's report upon the bullet which he had extracted ran contrary to this supposition, but even Sir William had been guarded in his statement, and it was notoriously difficult to be certain on such a point. The number of live cartridges left in Armadale's pistol also conflicted with his theory, unless there had been one in the barrel in addition to the usual seven in the magazine. He also had a recollection that some of these magazine clips in automatic pistols were fairly elastic. If his theory were correct, the question at once rose—how did the burglar obtain possession of Mr. Armadale's pistol? It was obvious that he might have wrested it from him in a struggle, but Vereker was instinctively chary of accepting the obvious in criminal investigation. If the shell which Heather had taken with him for examination proved to have been fired from a weapon other than that found loosely gripped in the dead man's hand—and such a question might be finally answered by micro-photography—his assumption at once fell to pieces. The supposition that the burglar had obtained possession of Sutton Armadale's pistol prior to his robbery opened up an engaging problem for solution. It simply bristled with possibilities and blew a cloud of suspicion over the staff of servants and the guests in the house. It was going to be a thoroughly intriguing and intricate piece of work, and at the very thought Vereker's eyes shone with excitement.

In his preoccupation, he had sauntered at an easy pace along the north wall enclosing the main grounds of the house. His head was bent, his eyes scanning the grass through which he brushed and noting the gradual accumulation of buttercup pollen in the creases of his shoes. Suddenly he looked up, to discover a few paces in front of him the back view of a man dressed in a light tweed suit and grey felt hat. His head was thrust forward and downward, so that only the back half of the curved rim of his hat was visible, and on his shoulders could be seen the rosy finger-tips of two slim feminine hands. There followed the sound of an ecstatic kiss, the tweed suit drew itself erect, raised a hat with easy, theatrical grace, and next moment the recipient of the kiss turned and fled across the meadow towards Wild Duck Wood. Vereker stood rooted to the ground in embarrassment, but his eye did not fail to notice the beauty and symmetry of that fast-receding figure. Never had he seen a woman run with such delightful freedom. Most men, he thought, would be willing to play Hippomenes to such an engaging Atalanta. Then her lover, who had stood entranced watching her, seemed suddenly to become aware of an intruding presence, for he turned sharply round and confronted Vereker. The latter, in spite of an effort at detachment and the assumption of a clumsy air of not having witnessed the recent delicate expression of human passion, looked painfully gauche. He expected to see a similar manifestation of discomposure on the stranger's face, but to his surprise that singularly handsome countenance, after an almost imperceptible frown, made a strong but not quite successful effort to avoid a broad grin.

"A sense of humour!" thought Vereker, and was about to pass unconcernedly on his way when the stranger accosted him with the question:

"I suppose you know you're trespassing, sir?"

"Oh, yes," replied Vereker, in whom the word trespass always raised a sudden and furious combativeness, "but it's a confirmed vice of mine. I'm always willing to pay for any damage I may do, and don't mind being prosecuted in the least. Unless I'm greatly annoying other people, I take it as a right to wander across my own country—shall I be lyrical and say, 'England, my England, England my own!'?"

"Monopolize it by all means," said the stranger reflectively and without any show of annoyance. "Personally I raise no objections to your claims; but, as a murder was committed on the adjacent polo ground yesterday morning, the police are rather anxious that no unauthorized persons should be allowed about the place."

"I understand," replied Vereker, considerably mollified. "I came up here in company with my friend, Detective-Inspector Heather of Scotland Yard, as a sort of unofficial helper. I'm also a representative of the *Daily Report.*"

"Then there's nothing more to be said," interrupted the stranger quickly, and after a steady scrutiny of Vereker's face, asked, "Is your name Algernon Vereker, by any chance?"

"Anthony, to be correct, but I've always been known to my friends as Algernon—unabbreviated."

"I thought I couldn't be mistaken. For two or three terms I was your contemporary at Magdalen."

"I can't say I remember you," replied Vereker.

"Ah, well, being forgotten is one of the major advantages of mediocrity. I remember you chiefly through a series of wickedly malicious caricatures. They long outlived your going down. You do draw, don't you?"

"I'm afraid I do. It has been a bally curse from a worldly point of view. The sarcasm of art is never forgotten, and you can't give it the lie," replied Vereker, with a laugh. "Still, I'm annoyed at not remembering—"

"My name's Ralli, Basil Ralli. I'm a nephew of the Sutton Armadale who—Of course you've heard?"

"Oh, yes, that's why I'm here. I'm awfully sorry."

"Please don't condole with me. Polite hypocrisy in another makes me more uncomfortable than it does in myself. My uncle was never very fond of me, and towards him my feelings were no stronger. Some realist has said that a large legacy assuages grief. I had damned little grief to assuage, and my uncle, to my surprise, left me all his fortune and this rather jolly estate to assuage it with. I feel like a child who has suddenly been given the moon."

"Then let me congratulate you heartily," said Vereker.

"Thanks," replied Ralli solemnly; "the sentiment fits better with my feelings and the facts. I see you're naturally not a humbug. But are you staying anywhere in the neighbourhood?"

"I've taken a room at the 'Silver Pear Tree.'"

"Oh. I hear it's a comfortable enough inn, but old inns frighten me. Parasitism even on the comic *ad infinitum* basis scares me stiff."

"You don't say the place is buggy?" asked Vereker, with sudden alarm.

"I know nothing about it and wouldn't like to venture an opinion, but while you're engaged on this investigation stunt, won't you accept our hospitality and stay at the manor? My Aunt Angela will be delighted to welcome any friend of mine, and we're certainly not buggy!"

"It's very good of you, Ralli. I shall probably be glad to accept your invitation. In the meantime, I hope you'll leave it open. I can't decide on the spur of the moment."

"Certainly, Vereker, certainly. Don't hesitate to come and explore the place if you think it'll help in your detective business. The sooner you get to the bottom of this appalling mess the better Angela and I shall be pleased."

"You're sure Mrs. Armadale won't mind?"

"Absolutely certain. She's anxious to help all she can."

"Splendid! Incidentally I'm rather eager to see your late uncle's collection of modern French paintings."

"You're welcome. They're in a gallery by themselves. Angela calls it the 'Museum of Psychopathy,' rather aptly, I think. Why not come up and lunch with me to-morrow? I shall be alone. Angela has gone to Sutton Pragnell for a day or two. She's terribly upset."

"Thanks, I'll turn up. In the meantime, I'll continue further to trespass on your grounds."

"Go anywhere you like. If Collyer catches you in any of the coverts he'll take you by the scruff of the neck and fling you out. While you're struggling with him, try and explain that you have my permission. Au revoir. We lunch at one."

With these words, Mr. Basil Ralli turned, and opening a wooden door in the north wall passed through and closed the door behind him. Vereker heard him fasten the door by pushing two bolts into their sockets, and then wandered leisurely on his way towards Wild Duck Wood. The contretemps had been so unexpected and his embarrassment at seeing a pretty woman frankly hugged and kissed so acute that for some minutes he could not dismiss the subject from his mind. His embarrassment had risen from the fact that he had felt his presence at the moment something of a boorish intrusion. He figuratively kicked himself for his clumsiness, a clumsiness of inadvertence, and inadvertence was frequently equivalent to faulty manners. Ralli's smile had saved the situation. He recalled that smile. How pleasantly it had lit up the olive-skinned face, with a flash of perfect teeth and the sparkle of dark humorous eyes. The face was not English; the whole cast of countenance was Mediterranean. Ralli's mother was Sutton Armadale's sister, but Basil Ralli must have taken after his father. And, brief as had been their meeting, Vereker had learned the startling news that Sutton Armadale had left his nephew his fortune and estate. This was significant news in itself. He remembered Ricardo's story of the marital incompatibility of Sutton Armadale and Angela, and wondered whether this had been a stroke of posthumous vindictiveness on the financier's part.

Absorbed in his speculations, he had wandered into the fringe of Wild Duck Wood and was suddenly brought to his senses by the sound of a woman's voice raised in vehement protest.

"I don't want to see you again, Frank, and I'm not going to. If you persecute me any longer as you've been doing lately, I'll put the matter in the hands of the police. Understand that once and for all! I don't want to be unkind, but I'll stand no nonsense!"

"You're welcome to your fancy man, but you'll be sorry and so will he. Mark my words, Trixie, you'll be sorry for this. So-long."

The speakers could not be seen by Vereker, but he knew from the directional sound of their voices that they were screened from his sight by a dense tangle of blackthorn undergrowth. Much to his annoyance, Fate seemed determined to thrust on him the role of eavesdropper. Turning impatiently on his heel, he retraced his steps into the open, and hastening his pace, as if eager to get away from the place, was about to cross the meadow in the direction of Hanging Covert when a woman suddenly stepped out of the wood a few paces in front of him. On seeing him she promptly halted and uttered an exclamation of pained surprise. At once Vereker was aware that she was Basil Ralli's beautiful companion of half an hour ago. Immediately recovering her self-possession, she approached him.

"I'm sorry, sir, but I must warn you that you're trespassing. My father has strict orders to keep all strangers off the grounds at present."

"Thanks for the warning, but it's all right. I've Mr. Ralli's permission to explore the place. My name's Vereker. Please tell your father; it will save any further trouble till he gets definite orders from Mr. Ralli. Am I speaking to Miss Collyer?"

It was a guess on Vereker's part. The girl spoke with a cultured enunciation not usually associated with a gamekeeper's daughter, but modern education, he remembered, was swiftly blurring the lingual demarcations of social status, and he had risked the shot.

At once the air of inquisitive suspicion that had qualified her glance vanished, and she smiled.

"I'm Miss Collyer, and I beg your pardon, Mr. Vereker. I didn't know you knew Mr. Ralli. I thought you were just another of the crowd of strangers who've been over-running the place since Mr. Armadale was shot, yesterday."

At this moment a burly figure in breeches and gaiters with a shot-gun under his arm stepped leisurely out of the wood and approached. He came forward with the slow, heavy tread of the countryman, his head turning now to the right and now to the left as his eyes swept across the meadows and piercingly scanned the edges of the surrounding coverts. They were the eyes of a man trained in a natural school of observation. A beautiful cocker bitch followed him close at heel. When a few paces off, he suddenly halted, pressed the lever opening the breech of his gun, extracted the cartridges, and slipped them into his pocket. Then his eyes wandered over Vereker from head to foot.

"Anything the matter, Trixie?" he asked slowly.

"No, dad. This gentleman is a Mr. Vereker. Mr. Ralli has given him permission to look over the place. I was just going to send him about his business, thinking he was a stranger, when he explained matters."

"Good evening, sir," said the keeper, addressing Vereker. "We got to be a bit particular since this shootin' business. Police are very strict about strangers pokin' round." Turning to his daughter, he asked, "Worn't you in the wood a little time back?"

"Yes, dad," replied his daughter, her cheeks suddenly flushing.

"I thought I heard young Frank Peach's voice," commented the keeper casually. "Perhaps you was chatting to him?"

"Yes. I happened to meet him by chance as I was on my way home."

"You was going a tidy bit out of your way to get home, Trixie," remarked her father dryly. "Mebbe you had an appointment?"

"No, dad; I had no appointment. You know very well I don't want to see him."

"So you say. Then when you see young Peach again, tell him I've strict orders not to let him trespass on these grounds. He knows it well enough, but won't take no telling from me. Perhaps he'll listen readier to you nor me."

"I've already told him," said Trixie quietly.

"Then he's asking for a boiling of trouble. If you will go home now and get the supper ready, I'll be back in an hour's time. Mr. Ralli was looking for you; did you see him?"

"Yes, I've just left him. It's a quarter to seven now. I'll expect you back about eight," replied the girl, glancing at her wrist-watch, and without further words turned on her heel and hurried away.

"Is there anything I can do for you, sir?" asked the keeper, turning to Vereker. "Anything you want to know particular mebbe I can tell you."

"Thanks, Collyer. As I'm working on this shooting mystery you may be helpful," replied Vereker, as he glanced furtively at the keeper's face. It was a hard, weather-beaten face, with a thick, grizzled beard which completely hid the mould of his chin and jaw. The barely visible lips seemed thin and firm. Underneath the capacious peak of his old tweed cap bushy eyebrows shaded a pair of dark, shrewd eyes. There was a distrustful glint in those eyes which declared that Stephen Collyer would be hard to deceive and slow to accept human nature as wholly good.

"Inspector Heather seems to think there were more than two shots fired, Collyer. What's your private opinion?" asked Vereker.

"I told him, sir, I was pretty sure there weren't no more, but of course I might be wrong. There's no saying for certain in these things. These tecs always know better, far as I can see, and them newspapers talk a lot of nonsense. *Daily Report* said I thought poachers had sprung alarm guns. I know the sound of alarm guns better nor that, and I can generally tell the report of a poacher's gun when the barrels have been sawed off short. I had a suspicion it were neither. There was a something about those two shots as was different from a shot-gun. That's what made me take particular notice, so up I gets to see what was the matter."

"You made your way to Hanging Covert, I believe?"

"Yes, because you can get a good view from there of a tidy bit of the estate. I weren't bothering about poachers at all."

"How long did you take to get there?"

"It would be a good half-hour after I heard the shots. I went at a smartish pace."

"After you spotted the body lying on the polo ground you went straight there?"

"Not exactly. I went across to Wild Duck Wood and then along by the north wall of the manor gardens. You see, sir, I wanted to come on the polo ground sudden-like."

"I see, a sort of flanking approach to surprise the intruder."

"I suppose that was it. More of a habit nor anything else."

"You saw no one else about at that hour?"

"Nobody as could be connected with the murder."

"Then you saw some one you knew?"

"Oh, yes. I come across young Frank Peach, who was startin' early for Nuthill. He was going down into Sussex to see about a job on Sir Conway Rigden's estate."

"Did you speak to him?"

"I passed the time o' morning with him, and we chatted a little while quite pleasant. You see, sir, Peach used to be underkeeper to me, but him and Mr. Armadale couldn't get on with one another, and so the guv'nor sacked him about a week or so ago."

"What was the trouble? I believe Mr. Armadale was an easy man to get on with," asked Vereker in as casual a tone as he could assume.

For some moments, Collyer was silent as if weighing his words.

"I couldn't say for certain, sir," he replied at length. "Mr. Armadale were easy enough to get on with if you humoured him, but you never knew when you had him and when you hadn't. He was very touchy about some things. Take his shootin', for example. He couldn't shoot for nuts, sir, and nothing worried him more. He wanted to be a good gun, and he tried mortal hard. But men is like dogs, there's some as you can never break in to the gun. He hadn't the hands nor the temper'ment. Far too excited he got, and he always handled a gun as if it were an umbrella as didn't belong to him. Him and young Frank had words when we were driving pheasants last year. Frank was loading for Mr. Armadale, and the guv'nor was missing most of his birds as usual. Suddenly he turns round and says to Frank, 'In the name of God, what's wrong with my shooting, Peach?' Instead of smoothing him down or holding his own tongue as he oughter done, young Frank tells him blunt, 'Your footwork's uncommon bad this morning, sir.' 'Footwork be damned,' says Mr. Armadale. 'I'm shootin' at pheasants, not kicking goals with 'em.' 'You couldn't be worse at that, sir,' says Frank, and there weren't no excuse for him being impertinent like that. Young Peach is mortal touchy, and he took it to heart. He was dyin' to see the guv'nor killing his birds proper, and honestly it was gallin' to see the mess he was making of it. Even those he hit weren't no use to anybody but a plumber afterwards. A little later Frank was talking to one of the beaters, and he says, 'It's Zeppelins tied to a mast the boss oughter try his hand at and not tall birds coming fast downwind.' Mr. Armadale overheard the words, and that, I think, was the beginning of the trouble. You see, sir, Mr. Armadale was not what we call a real sportsman. Terribly touchy about his shootin', he was. You had to handle him gentle as an egg."

Amused as Vereker was by this narration, he was secretly convinced that it was an evasion. Something more than this, he felt sure, had led to Peach's dismissal.

"Can you take me to the spot near Hanging Covert from which you first saw Mr. Armadale's body, Collyer?" asked Vereker, to change the subject.

"Certainly, sir," replied the keeper, glancing shrewdly at his questioner as he led the way across the meadows, followed close at heel by the cocker bitch.

As they were about to climb a portion of post and rail fencing, along which ran strands of barbed wire, the keeper suddenly stopped to observe a footprint in the soft earth of the ditch.

"Not there yesterday morning," he muttered aloud.

"More trespassers?" asked Vereker, interested in the keeper's observation. Here, he thought, was one of Nature's detectives at work.

"Only a courtin' couple," replied Collyer, with a smile. "There's the mark of a lady's heel as well. Courtin' couples ain't exactly troublesome, but some will bring a dog with them. You see that dog's hair stickin' to the barbed wire? Sheep-dog type, from the look of it, and I'd like to bet it's young Norman Sparrow's mongrel. I'll have to tell him if he wants to kiss and spoon in these meadows he'll have to do it without the help of his cur."

Having crossed the fence into the next meadow, the two men walked along without further conversation until Vereker asked suddenly:

"Is Frank Peach courting your daughter, Collyer?"

The blunt question took the stolid keeper by surprise but with unexpected rapidity he covered it and smiled slowly.

"You be smartish good at guessin', sir," he replied. "Young Frank has been dead sweet on Trixie for some time, but she don't know her mind about him. She says she likes him but don't love him serious. He's a moody lad and sulks very bad. Trixie can't stand no sulkin', and about a month ago she told him straight she didn't care that way for him. The young fellow won't take it she means what she says. He's obstinate as a donkey."

"She's pretty enough to warrant a little obstinacy, if I may say so," said Vereker tactfully.

"She's comely," continued the keeper casually. "You see, sir, she's had a decent schoolin'. Mr. Armadale saw to that and sent

her to a finishing school at Eastbourne, so as she could have
a better chance nor I could possibly give her. He took a great
interest in Trixie, having no children of his own. That schoolin'
was the trouble, and has put big notions in her head. She wants
to be like the gentry. If you ask me, she thinks young Peach ain't
quite up to her standard of varnish, and perhaps he ain't when you
come to think of it."

"I see," said Vereker quietly, and was lost in his own thoughts.

As they climbed the slope to Hanging Covert, the keeper's eye
was again arrested by some impression on the chalky ascent.

"See them claw marks, sir?" he asked.

"Now you've pointed them out, Collyer, I do. They look like a
dog's."

"Much too long for a dog's, sir. Those are a badger's claws. I've
got a trap set for him, but he's a cunnin' old devil. I'll have him yet
or my name's not Steve Collyer!"

A few minutes later they reached the fringe of Hanging Covert,
where Collyer halted.

"Here's where I stood when I first saw Mr. Armadale's body
on the polo ground," he remarked, and produced a pair of field-
glasses from his pocket. "If you'll look through them, sir," he
added, "you'll get a good view.

Vereker took the binoculars and, adjusting them to his vision,
scanned the shorn turf of the polo ground until he distinguished
the white cross which marked the spot where Sutton Armadale's
body had been found. Handing the glasses back to Collyer, he
asked:

"Do you think it was murder, Collyer?"

"Certain, sir! Murder was the only word Mr. Armadale could
say when I got to his side before he died, and he said it quite
distinct. The inspector tried to mix me up about that word, but I
could give my oath on it. What's more, I'm sure Mr. Armadale was
expecting something of the sort. He has been acting very queer
lately."

"What makes you think that?" asked Vereker, with suppressed eagerness.

"One thing in particular, sir, but it don't do for me to talk. What I say might be brought up in evidence in court, and I don't fancy bein' bullied by coppers and lawyers till I don't know whether I'm on my head or my heels. Mum's the word with Steve Collyer."

"I've nothing to do with the police, Collyer. I'm only making a private investigation for Mr. Ralli, to safeguard his interests in this business," said Vereker, feeling that the moment warranted a certain elaboration of the truth.

"In the first place, sir, Mr. Armadale was always practising with a Colt pistol. He became a first-class shot with one too. Strange, because he could never handle a shot-gun. I've been out with him many times, and at twenty paces he could smash a small tea saucer nearly every time. I often thought he was expecting to use his Colt in real earnest some day. That was the notion he gave me, though of course I may be mistaken. He didn't do it for sport, because—well, pistol shootin' ain't a sport; it's only a silly kind of game unless you mean business. Puzzles me how he missed his man when the time came. Lost his head, I suppose, like he always did with birds. You'd only to see him flurried when a woodcock had been flushed to understand. He was a dangerous gun then."

"Did anyone on the estate bear him a grudge?" asked Vereker.

"No, sir, not a soul. On the whole, he was very well liked. He was a generous man. Chucked his money about a bit too flash for a real gentleman. Still, there ain't too many generous men in these parts nowadays. Frank Peach didn't exactly love him after he got the sack, but, bless my soul, Peach wouldn't commit murder for that. I've my suspicions Mr. Armadale had bigger enemies among his own class."

"I dare say. Where there's a dog-fight for money there's always some kind of trouble," commented Vereker lazily.

"It's not always money that causes the mischief, sir; it's just as often a bit of skirt," hinted the keeper.

"I hear that Mr. Armadale and his wife didn't quite hit it off together," commented Vereker in the hope of eliciting extraneous information.

"It would be hard to say, Mr. Vereker. If you're to believe the servants in the manor they was always mighty polite to one another—a bit too polite for man and wife. I never had much to do with the good lady myself, but from what I gather she was very fond of Mr. Armadale for about six months after their weddin', and then she took a sudden turn against him and froze up. Lately she got a bit reckless."

"She began to quarrel with him?" asked Vereker.

"Oh, no, sir; they never quarrelled in front of their servants. But Madam was always hanging about with a Mr. Stanley Houseley and didn't seem to care whether Mr. Armadale saw her or not."

"Did her husband seem to mind?" asked Vereker.

"He didn't show it. On the other hand, you could never say what was at the back of his mind. He was a deep 'un was Mr. Armadale. Only last Wednesday, after Mrs. Armadale had given out the prizes for the flower show, the guests came back to the manor and were having a dip in the swimming-pool. The guv'nor didn't care for swimming parties, so he walked up to my cottage, and we took a stroll round the shoot. He was asking what the prospects was for partridges. I told him they was none so rosy because the weather was perishing bad just after the young birds was hatched. He was only pretending to be listening, and I could see there was something on his mind. As luck would have it, we went towards the manor through Wild Duck Wood, and Mr. Armadale had just stepped out of the wood when he suddenly turned and rushed back again. I thought perhaps he'd forgotten to give me some order, and I was hurrying towards him when he waved me back with his hand and said, 'It's all right, Collyer, I don't want you.' Of course I wondered what had made him dodge back into the wood and, being nosy, I skirmished round a bit. Then I saw the cause of it. Strolling along the edge of the covert, thinking they was out of sight of every one, came Mrs. Armadale and Mr. Houseley with their arms round one another for all the world like an innocent courtin' couple. Thinks I, that's put the cheese in the trap, and as I was looking at them they came to a standstill, and the young gent starts kissing Madam as if she were under the mistletoe. Just then the guv'nor stepped out of the wood looking all puffed up and went straight towards them. I thought there was going to be blows, but I was mistaken. After a bit of a jawbation they all walked back to the house together as if nothing had happened. Still, Mr. Houseley left for Nuthill Station shortly afterwards in Mrs. Armadale's car. He didn't stop for dinner as was expected, so I heard from the butler. Of course, sir, it's none of my business, and perhaps I oughtn't to have mentioned it. I don't say it has anything to do with Mr. Armadale bein' shot by a burglar, but it looks mighty bad, in my opinion. There's more than we see on top of the water in this business, sir."

Vereker made no comment on the information he had received, but he was not slow to appreciate its possible importance. Caution, however, was one of the predominant characteristics of his mental make-up. Factors, he argued, which might point to subsequent proceedings in the Divorce Court might not, among civilized beings with a none too romantic outlook, be strong enough emotionally to lead to murder. Collyer's story had, however, awakened his interest in Mr. Stanley Houseley, whom he now remembered Ricardo had called "Hell-for- leather" Houseley; but his interest was tinged with a recollection of society drama as presented by modern playwrights balancing delicately values somehow relieved of their basic sordidness by an intensity of stress on a peculiarly English culture. Things somehow didn't happen quite in that way; on its emotional side life was cruder and more brutally natural. For the moment, Vereker's mind was preoccupied with an altogether different line of speculation. He took leave of Collyer, and made his way in a ruminant mood across the meadows until he reached the main road running between Burstow and Nuthill. It was growing dusk when he reached the "Silver Pear Tree" and wandered into the tap-room. Here a few of the neighbouring rustics were smoking placidly over their pints of ale, and among them loomed the bulk of Detective-Inspector Heather, who seemed to be thoroughly enjoying their companionship.

"I thought as much, Heather," said Vereker, with a well-feigned air of deprecation.

The inspector chuckled comfortably. "This is about the nicest time of the day in the country, Mr. Vereker. Peace perfect peace, and pint after pint. I once read a poem that ran:

'I cannot eat but little meat,
My stomach is not good,'

and it wound up:

'Back and side go bare, go bare,
Both foot and hand go cold,
But belly, God send thee good ale enough
Whether it be new or old.'"

"Marvellous, Heather! It was written by a Bishop of Bath and Wells. In fact, it's about the best thing a bishop ever wrote. He must have been spiritually sound. Oddly enough, his name was Still!"

"Just the man for a Liquor Commission," agreed the inspector, and asked, "Make any discoveries after I left you, Mr. Vereker?"

Vereker, taking a seat beside the officer, carefully related what he had learned from the gamekeeper, Collyer. The inspector listened intently to the story, and on its conclusion made his usual non-committal remark.

"Altogether a rum business, a rum business!"

"I knew from the first that the burglary was a fake," said Vereker solemnly. "It's a crime of passion, Heather."

"What makes you think the burglary was a fake?" asked the inspector quickly.

"It's clear on the face of it. If Armadale had been awakened by the sound of unusual movements in the library beneath his bedroom he'd have pulled on his dressing-gown, shoved his feet into slippers, and gone down to investigate. Now, instead of behaving like an ordinary man, he took the trouble to dress, except for collar and tie. He even went the length of pulling on socks, shoes, and a monocle before leaving his room. Ask yourself, Would any reasonable man behave like that in similar circumstances?"

"You can't chase a man in slippers, Mr. Vereker," suggested the inspector, "and I've never heard that a dressing-gown was the thing to sprint in."

"Your arguments are sound enough in their way, Heather, but a man getting up at night to investigate doesn't count on chasing a problematic burglar across country. It seems to me that Armadale knew that he would be obliged to leave the house and prepared for the contingency. Again, why didn't Armadale rouse the servants or some of the males among his guests to help him hunt the robber. By pushing a bell at his side he could have summoned his personal man-servant at once to his room."

"I see your line of thought, Mr. Vereker. You're secretly convinced that the burglary was merely a cunning cloak for the murder. Now that you've discovered that Mrs. Armadale and Mr. Houseley are a bit gone on one another you're letting your imagination run away with your common sense. I suppose you'll try and find out whether Mr. Houseley returned or not in the early hours of the morning and by what trick he got Mr. Armadale to chase him on to the polo ground where he could murder him comfortably without any hindrance. Am I right?"

"I hadn't advanced quite as rapidly as that," replied Vereker, smiling, "but you'll agree that such a line of inquiry suggests itself."

"Too much in the air for me," said the inspector stolidly, and asked, "What do you think has happened to Mrs. Armadale's necklace?"

"I leave that to you, partner. I dare say you've got your men in London on the look-out. They'll possibly be able to guess what fences are likely to deal with such a valuable haul. The police seem to be on quite cordial terms with fences in general, so that the job oughtn't to present insuperable difficulties."

"It's not so easy as all that, Mr. Vereker. The modern fence is such a respectable business gent that it's very hard to spot him. He takes big risks, and he has to be doubly cunning. Of course we're on the trail of that necklace, but I'll admit right away we may never set eyes on it again."

"I dare say I shall be able to track it down for you," remarked Vereker blandly, as he regaled himself from his heavy mug, and lighting a cigarette added, "I suppose you've considered the possibility that Mr. Armadale might not have been shot on the polo ground at all."

"Not for a moment," replied the inspector emphatically. "If he had, he'd have been dead as mutton when Collyer arrived on the scene."

"Steady, Heather, steady! You're surely not going to swallow Collyer's yarn as unadulterated truth? Collyer's not as easy as all that. He's as cunning as a fox and has all his wits about him. I can assure you, from certain observations of his this evening, that he's a man of very acute perception. Nothing escapes his eye, and he can draw inferences from what he sees better than any detective in Scotland Yard that I know, barring present company, of course."

"Yes, Mr. Vereker, every good gamekeeper has woodcraft at his finger-ends, but I think I know my man. I'm not in love with your suggestion that Mr. Armadale was shot elsewhere and his body carried out to the polo ground. It's possible but not probable. Take simple explanations first, the complicated ones will come without being asked."

"You throw cold water on all my glowing fancies, inspector. By the way, Mr. Ralli has asked me to put up at Vesey Manor while I'm on this business. I'm in doubt whether I should or not."

"Don't. You'd be putting yourself under an obligation to Mr. Ralli. You may yet be the direct cause of his being hanged," returned the inspector, "and it would be a shabby way of acknowledging his hospitality." Vereker glanced quickly at the inspector to see if he were joking, but the officer's face was gravity incarnate.

"Perhaps you're right," he remarked. "I hadn't pictured Mr. Ralli swinging for this job. Thanks for the tip."

"It might be a trick to keep in touch with your investigations," continued the inspector quietly, "and when the pursuit became too hot you might be the second victim of a—of a burglary!"

"Look here, Heather, it's not fair to put the wind up me like that. I'm too young to die. If I get thoroughly scared, I'll vamose and leave you to make a ghastly mess of the whole show. Take this final notice." The inspector finished his beer and, knocking out his pipe against the leg of the table, rose smartly to his feet.

"I feel strong enough to walk into Nuthill now," he said. After carefully quilling his moustache, he leant over to Vereker in a confidential manner. "I don't think it would be cricket if I hid certain information from you that may be vital to your side of this job, and yet I don't particularly want to send you down the wrong street."

"Spit it out, Heather. I had a feeling in my bones that you were concealing something weighty."

"You remember I mentioned that a motor-car was heard starting up on the main road by Mr. Ralli in the early hours of Thursday morning? It was also heard passing the lodge by Mrs. Burton, who says it was going at a great speed."

"I remember, inspector, but I don't attach importance to everything you say," replied Vereker.

"You will to this, I'll bet. That car, we're pretty certain, was a Rover Meteor, and we're also fairly sure that it belonged to Mr. Stanley Houseley."

"Aha, Heather, I thought my imagination would run away with your common sense! Perhaps you'll pay more attention to young gentlemen who openly make love to their hostesses and have earned the dashing sobriquet of 'Hell-for-leather.' There are always nasty possibilities to such a pastime. When I see you again I hope you'll be able to shed some light on that suit of clothes that Burton, the gardener, found near the bathing pavilion."

"I'll play the game as fairly as I can," replied the inspector, "and now I must go. I hope to see you again before you've completely solved this mystery. So-long."

On Heather's departure Vereker dined and then retired to his room. Here he made himself comfortable in a capacious Minty chair, and lighting his pipe reviewed at leisure all the incidents of the tragedy at Vesey Manor that had so far come to his knowledge. Theorizing at this stage of his investigation was, he felt, somewhat futile; a further accretion of facts was necessary. But his mind began to play with the evidence in hand much as the solver of a jig-saw puzzle plays with the exasperatingly incongruous pieces with which he wishes to construct his picture. The mystery of the number of shots fired and the two bullet wounds in the dead financier's body particularly intrigued him, and he pondered on them far into the night. Before retiring he extracted a well-worn notebook from his pocket and jotted down in pencil the following notes:

"Two pistols, A and B. Two bullet wounds. One bullet extracted by Sir William Macpherson is said by him to have been fired by a pistol other than Armadale's, B. One cartridge shell found has definitely been proved to have been fired by Armadale's pistol, A. This would suggest that three shots were fired: two by the murderer and one by Armadale. A second shell found by me has still to be examined. If this cartridge was fired by pistol B, there is still one shell fired by B missing, unless Armadale was killed by one shot from B and a second from A. It the latter supposition is correct, all the shells are in hand, only two shots were fired, and one bullet is still missing. If, on the other hand, the shell found by me is proved to have been fired from A, and if Armadale received two bullet wounds from pistol B, four shots must have been fired altogether, and three bullets and two shells are still missing. Though this supposition is at variance with evidence of reports heard by Collyer and Ralli, it declares that the murderer picked up both his empty shells."

At this juncture Vereker's pipe went out. He thrust his notebook into his pocket and, exclaiming, "Damned if it doesn't remind me of a problem in permutations and combinations," began to undress.

Chapter Six

"A landscape painter has a delightful day. He gets up at 3 a.m. before sunrise. He goes and sits down under a tree and waits and watches. At first there is little to be seen. Nature hides behind a white veil through which some vague masses are faintly visible. Everything is sweetly scented and trembles under the wakening breeze of dawn."

These words of Corot's from a letter which is an incomparable idyll had impelled Anthony Vereker on innumerable occasions to rise before daybreak and wander abroad with easel and painting gear to capture even remotely some of the sharp, scintillant spirit of the morning and imprison it on canvas. Nowhere, he thought, was the crystalline sweetness of early light the blithe tremor of yawning animation, the pungent yellows and greens of clean, supple foliage, the luminous purplish gloom of shadows so entrancing as in the heart of a wood at sunrise.

After getting into bed on the previous night, he had lain awake for hours pondering on the intricacies of the Armadale case until he had fallen into an uneasy drowsiness in which his head seemed to throb to the rhythm of "One bullet, two wounds, two shots, two shells, and only one dead man." Then sleep and a pleasant dream in which he was in New York on a holiday, visiting again the Metropolitan Museum of Art where he had, a year or so before, first seen a study of trees by Narcisse Diaz. The picture had made a very deep impression on him, and on waking it was the first thing he remembered. At once he was all aglow with enthusiasm, and though it was only five o'clock he rose. In another hour the sun would be up. It was only four o'clock by solar time. He must make some notes for a picture. On the fringe of Wild Duck Wood he had seen some magnificent oaks and beeches the evening before, and they had then suggested a composition, but the urge had been stifled by other and more insistent business. Now the desire had returned with renewed vigour and, as he hurriedly dressed, Vereker could already visualize those trees caught in the first rays of the morning sun. He could even see them through the eyes of Diaz. Picking up his easel and an old army pack which contained his painting gear, he went downstairs. Early as it was, the landlady of the "Silver Pear Tree" was up and bustling round. Would Mr. Vereker like a cup of tea? Yes, Mr. Vereker was very fond of an early cup of tea. Then he should certainly have one. He should also have a biscuit, because a biscuit kept an early cup of tea from "gnorin' the stummick." Up to this moment Vereker had been ignorant of this vicious propensity of early cups of tea, but if they gnawed the stomach perhaps a biscuit was a sovereign antidote. He had faith in mother-wit. After tea and biscuit he set out, saying he would be back at eight o'clock for breakfast. He left with the assurance that a nice gammon rasher and a couple of duck eggs would await his return. On reaching Wild Duck Wood the light pearly mist which had swathed the landscape was already beginning to vanish under the dynamic warmth and light of the risen sun. Making his way into the centre of the wood he came to a space where the brushwood and undergrowth were thin and a grouping of oaks all splashed and blotched with cool sunlight offered an arresting subject. There he settled down to work, making rapid studies of the play of light through foliage and of boles latticed with the shadows of branches and leaves. He was absorbed in his work and heedless of the swift passage of time when the crackle of a twig snapping under human tread attracted his attention. It was possibly Collyer making his way through the covert. On the previous evening he had said something about having bushed the meadows against poachers after partridges with drag nets. Rising from his painting stool, he stretched himself. IIe was stiff, and his eyes were tired from close application. Lighting a cigarette, he left his easel and wandered idly in the direction from which the sound had come. All at once he heard the intermittent rustling of some one making his way rapidly through the wood, and glancing quickly round caught a glimpse of a brown Harris-tweed Norfolk jacket and cap through a gap in the scattered mountain-ash and guelder undergrowth. Next moment the wearer had vanished, but in that brief space the set of his head and shoulders had photographed itself on his retentive visual memory. The man was certainly not Collyer and could hardly be one of the woodmen on the estate. The cut of the jacket and cap bespoke some one with sartorial taste and the money to indulge it. Vereker was nothing if not highly inquisitive, and at once hurried to the spot where the man had been when he had caught sight of him. Here he found that the bracken had all been trampled underfoot as if the unknown had been wandering about in ever-widening circles. It was suggestive, and as he stood surveying the ground his eye was suddenly caught by a tiny puff of blue smoke rising from a patch of sunlit bracken. In a couple of strides he was on the spot and, bending down, picked up the still burning end of a cigarette. It was a Russian cigarette, one of Bogdanov's of Petrograd, his well-known Zephyr brand. The stranger had evidently a cultivated and expensive taste in tobacco.

"Might be priceless, simply priceless!" exclaimed Vereker, as he extinguished the butt and carefully placed it in his wallet. He knew the particular brand, and he knew the tobacconists in the city of London who imported them. This was at present an insignificant trifle, but how often had he discovered the overwhelming possibilities of such. After a further fruitless investigation he returned to his easel, and there, to his astonishment, stood a figure bending over and critically scrutinizing his work. It was Basil Ralli, and so absorbed was he that he was unaware of Vereker's approach until the latter was almost upon him. Then he turned with a start and an anxious glance, which almost at once changed to pleased recognition.

"Good morning, Vereker," he exclaimed. "I hope you don't mind my having a squint at your work. I love preliminary sketches; they have a liveliness which you seldom find in the finished picture."

With these words he stood back from the easel and surveyed the canvas appreciatively. He was hatless and clad in light flannels with a silk sports shirt open at the neck, and as he posed reflectively, his hands thrust in his pockets, his brow slightly furrowed, Vereker was obliged to admit to himself that he had seldom seen such a handsome specimen of fresh and vigorous youth. In reply to Ralli's greeting, Vereker mumbled something conventionally depreciatory, but without heeding him Ralli continued:

"I always think painting's such a jolly sort of religion, such an admirable blend of the intellectual and the sensual. Like all other religions it promises a perfection to which you never bally well attain, but with the majority of its adherents it has sunk to a superstition fostered by a tribe of fraudulent high priests." The words were spoken almost in soliloquy, and then, turning to Vereker, he swiftly changed the subject by remarking, "I didn't expect to see you about so early. Do you always practise your rites at dawn?"

"No; a landscape painter may be summoned at any moment by some inner muezzin to prayer. I felt in the mood this morning when I woke. Now, I feel more like bacon and eggs."

"A natural reaction, though I always prefer fish after a communion service. I don't know why. Come and breakfast with me up at the manor."

"Sorry, but I ordered breakfast at the 'Silver Pear Tree' at eight," replied Vereker, hesitating.

"It's nearly nine now, so that settles it. You can't go back to stale bacon and eggs, and I've got a lot to talk about on the subject of my uncle's death. The assumption that he was murdered puts me in a bally awkward position, and I'm jolly glad you've arrived on the scene. I'm a friendless sort of oaf, and there are a lot of private family complications which I'd hate to be made public, as much for Angela's sake as my own. We don't want the Armadale skeletons yanked out of their cupboards to perform a dance of death for the British public. You inspire confidence, Vereker, and I'd like you to handle matters on my behalf. Can you do so without it mucking up your connection with that awful rag, the *Daily Report*? I mean, of course, on a business footing."

"I won't accept the business footing," replied Vereker. "Detective work's only a hobby with me. My connection with the *Daily Report*'s merely a species of passport and means nothing."

"Good! Then I can take it you'll accept the job?"

"On a mutual basis the offer is reasonable," replied Vereker cautiously. "You tell me all you know and I'll help you all I can."

"Right-o! You can have free access to the house; come and go when you like; the servants are at your beck and call, and you can ask me anything you wish. I won't accept your help for nothing, but I won't offend your sense of material independence. You must leave that to my tact—I've got lots of it."

"It's not altogether a question of independence," said Vereker thoughtfully. "After all, independence is generally a swagger assumed by people of small social intelligence. I want complete freedom of judgment."

"I see," replied Ralli, with a smile. "You wouldn't like me to pay you for bringing me to the gallows. Damn it, your talk about bacon and eggs has made me ravenous. Pick up your gear and let's make for home."

Before gathering his equipment together, Vereker made an ostentatious search in his pockets, which produced the result desired.

"You're hunting for a fag?" asked Ralli, and promptly producing his case offered it to Vereker.

"Thanks; I've got mine somewhere, but I can't just place them," replied Vereker, as he took one of the proffered cigarettes.

"I don't know whether you like Russians, but they're supposed to be pretty good. They're Bogdanov's of Petrograd."

"So I see," returned Vereker reflectively, as he struck a match. "They're very nice. My own tastes run to something cheap and deleterious. Even depravity, I sometimes think, is more or less a matter of habit. Don't you find these rather strong before breakfast?"

"I never smoke before breakfast," said Ralli, as he returned the case to his pocket.

"Then you've never plumbed the delights of the vice to its depths," remarked Vereker, but his thoughts were centred on the butt of the cigarette which he was carrying in his wallet. Customers of Bogdanov seemed to be strangely numerous in the district.

For some minutes they walked along in silence.

"Do you always get out and about before breakfast, Ralli?" resumed Vereker, as if forcing conversation.

"If there's any sunshine I generally manage to, but this morning I made an appointment for a short tramp before breakfast with Trixie—Miss Collyer—she's my fiancée."

Though the information came as a surprise to Vereker, he hoped his demeanour completely hid it. He refrained from any comment in order to let Ralli continue, a course to which he seemed not at all averse.

"I think at this point I ought to take you into my confidence about Trixie. We've been secretly engaged for a month, but now it doesn't matter a rap who knows."

"You hid the fact from your uncle, I suppose?" asked Vereker.

"You bet. He found out somehow that I was in love with her and raised Cain. He wanted me to marry some one of good birth, whatever that may mean. The *roturier* always talks of good birth, and the skivvy's child worships the baroness very much as people who chatter about good manners invariably lack them. Civilization teems with such paradoxes. Breeding's all right, I dare say, with pigs and horses and dogs, but as a specimen of *homo sapiens* I've always wanted to follow my own inclinations—I won't call it choice in these days of philosophical confusion. I'm a natural romantic in spite of our rational age. I argued with my Uncle Sutton, but he was a hopelessly confused thinker on everything except finance. In fact, I might say he could never rise above a syllogistic inference. It was useless. Prior to our discussion, I was to benefit comfortably under his will—the bulk of the estate was to go at that date to Angela. If I'd been rational I'd have comforted myself with the assurance that after all love is a purely temporary contraption on Nature's part and that an assured income for life isn't. Nature offered me Trixie, reason offered me an end to all money troubles. But Nature's a hypnotist, and I'm under her spell. I wouldn't promise to surrender Trixie, so my uncle cut me out of his will. Fantastically enough, I was delighted because we had both acted strictly according to a faded and fragrant romance. In this instance

I agreed that *vox populi* was *vox dei*. It sounds reckless, but love is never sciurine; it simply won't hoard up nuts for winter grub."

"*Amare et sapere vix deo conceditur*," quoted Vereker, and asked, "Your uncle knew at last that you were engaged to Miss Collyer?"

"No bally fear. After our little rumpus I refused to discuss the matter with him any further, and until recently I never came near Vesey Manor if I could help it. His attitude caused a temporary estrangement between Trixie and me. In a spirit of almost morbid self-sacrifice she refused to let me lose my inheritance on her account and tried hard to break away from me. Self-sacrifice is too often a wallowing in pain as a virtue. At length, with feminine practicality, she pointed out that we might ostensibly part until my uncle weakened. It was a saving gesture that re-established my confidence in her sanity. I didn't like the idea, but love can transfigure even dishonesty. Neither did I like the delay. I forgive procrastination for being the thief of time, but to put love to a lingering death is an unpardonable crime. It's more humane to kill it swiftly by marriage!"

"What caused your uncle to relent?" interrupted Vereker pointedly.

"He never relented on that score. He was utterly deceived. Finding out that Trixie and I never met, he thought I'd repented and sent for me just a month ago. He tried to bring up the subject again, but I was dead off and refused to discuss the matter. He had kept up a childishly simple system of espionage on us, and convinced that although beaten I was defiant, he said: 'I see you've acquired common sense, Basil, but you've got the indomitable pride of the Armadales and won't admit defeat. I admire you for it, my boy!' The pride of the Armadales forsooth! You see, Vereker, the infantile sort of self-adulation and the truly pitiable homage of the pleb to lineage that his words implied. They almost conjured up to me our hatchments, a coat of arms, a column in Debrett, and I could hear myself murmuring piously, '*Noblesse oblige*, my dear uncle.' Can you wonder at his objection to Trixie? He was an aristocrat, not by birth, but by auto-suggestion. It's a widespread form of delusion.

"Then, to my surprise, he told me he had left the whole of his fortune and this place to me. He couldn't have surprised me more if he'd turned up at a hunt meet in November in a pullover and a ski-ing cap. I didn't tell him at once that the relations between Trixie and me hadn't changed. I was momentarily flabbergasted and felt that I'd just collared something like two millions of money by false pretences. All I could ask was, 'What are you going to do about Angela? ' 'I've cut her off with an annuity of five hundred a year,' was his reply. I protested, but he told me to mind my own business. There our interview ended. For a week I was terribly depressed. I was the battleground on which the romantic spirit put up a staggering fight against two millions sterling. Cupid fought Croesus over my body for possession of my soul! And then my uncle was murdered, and I discovered that silence for once had been golden!"

Ralli concluded his narration with a sigh of intense relief. He seemed to have mentally reacted that bitter struggle of his spirit as he talked, and the following quiet suggested to Vereker the image of a canoe that has shot through the thundering welter of a barrier reef into a sunlit and glassy lagoon. Ralli resumed in a matter-of-fact tone:

"The whole damned business looks too jolly opportune, Vereker. I almost feel guilty of my uncle's murder. People professedly believe in chance or a deity, but they always bank on human intervention. I shall suffer agonies till this shocking affair is cleared up."

"I suppose your aunt feels hurt at being cut off with the time-honoured bob?" asked Vereker casually.

"No. Angela's made of a finer texture. She doesn't care two hoots—I might say one hoot—about that side of this tragedy. I'm very fond of my aunt $ she also is a natural romantic. Besides,

I've told her I shall go fifty-fifty with her over the income from the residue. She actually cried when I made this surrender, and Angela's tears are jewels. They were neither tears of joy nor of grief, but of religious ecstasy. She was overwhelmed by the victory of our common belief in the romantic tradition. She'd been damnably afraid that I was going to apostatize at the last moment. Our slogan is, 'Mammon for Monkeys!'"

With these words the two men entered the magnificent hall of Vesey Manor.

"And now for breakfast, Vereker. Let's be monkeys shamelessly! A month ago it would have been boiled eggs, probably Polish, with toast and marmalade and a cup of tea. This morning I fancy a bunch of my own Muscat of Alexandria, a portion of cold grouse, and a glass of still Moselle. No man can grow a big heart on Polish eggs and tea. From the moment you discover the dependence of soul on stomach, you can progress spiritually with leaps and bounds!" said Ralli, with boyish jocularity.

"I heartily agree," laughed Vereker in reply; "it's a basic part of my philosophy. Nobody can be a good Christian on crystallized ginger. Cheap claret will turn any man into a misogynist, and fish and eremitism are synonymous. Oysters—but perhaps I'd better not say anything about oysters."

"Frederick, when you've disposed of Mr. Vereker's kit, kindly show him to his room—the one next to mine," said Ralli to a footman, and turning to Vereker added, "While you're in this neighbourhood, Vereker, that room will be reserved for you. Count it your headquarters. I'll join you at breakfast in about ten minutes. There's a lot more I've got to tell that maybe helpful, and we can start jaw-wagging after our grub."

Chapter Seven

During breakfast both men were unusually silent. Ralli seemed intent on the enjoyment of his food. Vereker was deep in thought, weighing with critical appreciation the general tenor of the story Ralli had told him. On the face of it it seemed sincere and true, but the difficulty of detecting falsehood, he knew from experience, was far greater than is generally admitted. There are men who are bad liars for the simple reason that they are bad actors. They lie unconvincingly because they have no histrionic genius. Instead of living their parts they are merely dissimulating. Vereker would not have gone so far as to say that all fine actors could, if they chose, be accomplished liars. Here moral principles might be too strong to allow a full expression of their talent for playing a part. But a man without moral principle, gifted with histrionic genius, was a danger to society. Perhaps Ralli possessed this combination. He had a quick, supple mind, with a faculty for glib generalization, an easy and assured manner, and a supreme confidence in himself. His claim to be a natural romantic savoured of pose. At Oxford that sort of posture, assumed with all the gravity of youth, might be forgiven as a pardonably silly phase, but to carry it into social life or the world of affairs was detestable. As Ricky had once vulgarly put it, "Any man who does so should have his nose rubbed in it." On the other hand, Ralli might be perfectly sincere and flinging a challenge to what he considered the cynical nastiness of his contemporaries. It was impossible as yet to decide, and Vereker impressed upon himself that he must move cautiously.

After breakfast Ralli suggested that they should sit out on the solarium and, having made themselves comfortable in wicker chairs and lit their pipes, he commenced to talk.

"As people may suspect Angela of having something to do with her husband's death—" he opened.

"Why should they?" asked Vereker abruptly.

For some moments Ralli seemed discomposed, but, recovering himself, resumed:

"That's just what I want to explain, Vereker. While the police are poking their snouts into this mystery, her relations with her husband are sure to be questioned. To all her friends and relatives they were pretty well known. I'm going to tell you something which is not generally known and which neither she nor I would like to be yapped abroad. I must leave it in your hands as to whether it will be necessary to make it public."

"I will be tact itself," assured Vereker.

"When Sutton married Angela two years ago his first wife, Sarah, had been dead about six months. It's not necessary to go deeply into the history of my Aunt Sarah. She was a homely Yorkshire woman without any pretensions of her own. Sutton thrust those upon her as his fortune swelled and his own social pretensions grew. He was, as I've said, an aristocrat by auto-suggestion and, though he was fond enough of Sarah, he began to think she was not quite cast for the role of a society leader. It was an illuminating comment on his outlook when he suddenly ceased to call her Sarah and insisted on either Maureen or Renee. 'Sarah' smelled of the scullery. My aunt loathed Reeny, as she pronounced it, and fought a retreating battle over Maureen and all that Maureen implied. Finally she surrendered and tried to live up to it. It was a tragicomedy that used to make me laugh and weep alternately. She was dreadfully unhappy, but she did her best. She even tried to learn to ride, though she feared horses more than she dreaded cows. Bovine horns had always seemed to her less capricious than equine hoofs. But the advent of a butler was the climax of her troubles. Dunkerley always scared her stiff because he came to Vesey Manor from Lord Bravington's. To her he was a terrible embodiment of the hierarchy of caste. I shall never forget when he told her, 'You mustn't put your whisky in a tantalus, madam; it's only done among the poorer middle classes. The tantalus is now honly seen on suburban sideboards.' At this time, too, my Aunt Sarah's physical charms began to wane. She grew stout and, in spite of all sorts of mortification, persisted in growing stout. Sutton was mature enough to dislike the Rubenesque, and developed a secret promiscuity which ended in the seduction of his wife's maid. She was a very beautiful and rather ingenuous young woman. It was a stunning blow to Sarah. Though infidelity was abhorrent to her, the prospect of a scandal was infinitely more so. Sutton allayed her fears on the latter score to such an extent that she almost forgave him his unfaithfulness to her. Mrs. Grundy was more exacting than Venus. She was genuinely sorry for her maid; it's a commentary on her thundering good nature. The family went abroad for a year; the maid disappeared, and gave birth to a daughter, which was secretly farmed out, and after a wangle adopted by Collyer, the keeper's wife. She was christened Beatrix, is now called Trixie, and is my fiancée."

Ralli paused to allow the significance of this *denouement* to sink in.

"What became of her mother?" asked Vereker quietly.

"She subsequently married a seaman and now lives, I believe, in West Hartlepool."

"Of course your Aunt Angela knew of this before her marriage to your uncle?" asked Vereker.

"No, she didn't. She found it all out about six months after her marriage. I don't think she had ever really loved Sutton. He had appealed rather to her imagination than to her heart. His wealth dazzled her, and he always had a tremendously forceful way with women. The discovery simply destroyed any affection she had for him, and she never really lived with him as a wife again. This, in fine, was the Armadale skeleton, and rather a difficult one to box in a cupboard. It got a strangle-hold on my first aunt and worried her into her grave. She lived the last years of her life in perpetual fear that it would thrust a conspicuous finger through the keyhole. She developed diabetes, and after some years of ill-health died."

"Can you tell me if Trixie's mother told her sailor husband of her pre-marital trouble?" asked Vereker.

"No, she didn't. This I only found out quite recently. After the birth of her child, Sutton allowed her an income which was paid quarterly through her solicitors. Whether she told the sailor before her marriage of this quarterly payment, I can't say. But it's strange that only a month ago he turned up at the solicitors' office, and in a circuitous way wanted to know all about the blinking history of his wife's income. They fobbed him off with some yarn that it was by instruction of my late Aunt Sarah's executors that she was paid this money for her faithful services to my aunt during her stay with her. He was apparently not quite satisfied with this explanation and came down and put up at the 'Silver Pear Tree' for some days. During that time he sought and obtained an interview with my uncle. Needless to say, he learned nothing from him, but while he was here Sutton went about with some of the hesitancy of a man carrying an infernal machine in his pocket. Then Sinbad vanished, and we haven't seen or heard of him since."

"Do you know his address?" asked Vereker.

"No, but I can get it from my solicitors whenever you want it. His name is unforgettable to me because of its singularity—Jonathan Portwine."

"Do you know the nature of his interview with your uncle? Do you think he was trying to blackmail him?"

"I couldn't say. The possibility occurred to me, but until my uncle's death I never gave it further thought. Now it seems likelier than it did then."

Vereker glanced up quickly at Ralli's face. Through his own mind had suddenly flashed the idea that his interlocutor might be tactfully leading him on to a false trail. But from Ralli's face he could learn nothing; his gaze was wandering idly over the sunlit grounds in front of the house, and he was puffing at his pipe with quiet enjoyment. For a few minutes the conversation languished, and then Vereker broke the silence with the question:

"Can you tell me the names of the guests who passed Wednesday night in the house?"

"Let me see now. There was Ralph Degerdon, son of Harold Degerdon, the stockbroker; he has suffered very badly through the Braby financial crash. There was Captain 'Fruity' Fanshaugh, who lives on the outskirts of Nuthill. He was a very intimate friend of my uncle, who followed his advice on everything to do with his polo ponies, his hunters, and his shooting. Fanshaugh is none too well off and probably got something for his services to my uncle, but on this point I wouldn't be positive. There was Miss Edmée Cazas. You've possibly heard of her. An entertaining young lady of questionable antecedents, if I'm not mistaken. I've never liked her myself, but my uncle seemed to be hypnotized by her rather sinister beauty and scandalous wit. I may be biased, but I've always felt that she worships at the shrine of Venus Apostrophia. There was Aubrey Winter, ostensibly very much in love with Edmée, whom she enjoyed torturing in a spirit of pure sadism. Aubrey is rather a nice, simple fellow who, if he wasn't fairly rich, might shine as a sports master at a second-rate school for the sons of English gentlemen. He's a cousin of Angela's. To these add my uncle, my aunt, and myself, and you have every one except servants who stayed at Vesey Manor on Wednesday night."

"Wasn't Mr. Stanley Houseley one of the guests? I think the *Evening Bulletin* mentioned him in its list."

"You're referring to 'Hell-for-leather,'" exclaimed Ralli, with a laugh. "No, he didn't stay the night. He had to get back to town early and didn't even wait for dinner. I don't remember what excuse he put up, but Stanley's excuses are always as patent as his shoes. *Laudator temporis acti*, especially of Victorian and Edwardian times, he's an exact replica of his father. Beachcomber's Mr. Thake is perhaps rather a wild caricature of him, but there's a distinct likeness. He has been Angela's faithful cavalier for years. His favourite author is Whyte-Melville, and his favourite show a Gilbert and Sullivan opera. You observe the paternal echo. Though he's an ardent motorist, one of his pet pastimes is to inveigh against the use of a motor-car as a covert hack. He hitched on to this topic at tea on Wednesday, and Miss Cazas remarked that she objected to a Baby Austin being used as a *cabinet particulier*. It interfered so with the legitimate traffic."

"Have you seen or heard from him since?" asked Vereker.

"No, but he writes to Angela once a week. Houseley would make love with a calendar in his hand."

"About those shots you heard, Ralli? Are you certain there were only two?"

"I'm damned if I am. I was wide awake, and I think I heard only two."

"What time was it?"

"It must have been about an hour before sunrise; the dawn had just broken. There's a curious point about those shots which I've remembered since. I didn't recall it when being questioned by the inspector. There was a comparatively long lapse of time between the two reports."

"That's very strange," commented Vereker, deep in thought. "How long was the interval between them?"

"Five or six minutes, I should say."

On hearing this, Vereker rose from his chair and paced nervously up and down the solarium. Ralli's recently imparted information had set fire to an exciting train of thought.

"That's damned intriguing!" he exclaimed at length. "May I have a look at the library and the bedrooms?"

"Come along," replied Ralli, with sympathetic enthusiasm. "I'll show you round the whole place."

After examining the dining, drawing, and other rooms on the ground floor, they entered a small room which Sutton Armadale had always called the gun-room. Here in a case against the wall were several shot-guns of twelve, sixteen, and twenty bores; polo sticks stood in odd corners or hung in a rack; a bookcase with none but books on sport lined one of the sides of the room, and near the window was a desk of very beautiful wood, its top thrown open and the desk littered with papers and copies of the *Field*, *Sketch*, and *Punch*. In an angle formed by this piece of furniture stood two shooting-sticks, and on a small table close by was a tray with a decanter of whisky, soda, glasses, a box of cigars, and two silver boxes of cigarettes. It was a thoroughly comfortable, untidy, man's room. Crossing to the small table, Vereker opened the silver cigarette boxes. One contained Virginian and the other Bogdanov's Russian cigarettes.

"Your uncle was fond of Russian cigarettes," he remarked to Ralli, who was watching his movements with concentrated interest.

"Well, I can't say he was. He rarely smoked, and then only a cigar, usually after a meal. He always kept a stock of these Russian cigarettes, chiefly, I think, because they're expensive and uncommon. He felt that they lent him a sort of individuality. It was a curious little weakness which in the matter of cigarettes he borrowed from 'Hell-for-leather' Houseley. He was always stealing other people's idiosyncrasies and caricaturing them to fit his own flamboyant personality."

"I know the type," smiled Vereker. "There are people who are unconsciously individual and those who are consciously so. Your uncle was doubtless one of the latter, but was either too lazy or too afraid to choose his own pigments."

With these words he crossed over to the roll-top desk, picked up one of the shooting-sticks, and examined its steel extremity.

"That was another fad of my uncle's," remarked Ralli. "He carried a shooting-stick on every possible occasion, and once absent-mindedly took one to morning service at the village church. To him shooting-sticks stood as the insignia of the Order of Antiquated English Gentlemen!"

"I've often thought of trying one as a sketching- stool," remarked Vereker casually.

"Then take one by all means and see how it works," replied Ralli.

Vereker tucked the stick under his arm, and from the gun-room Ralli led the way up to the second floor. Here were the billiard-room, music-room, library, Angela Armadale's suite of rooms, and guest-rooms. From the billiard-room a door led on to the solarium or sun terrace running the whole width of the southern face of the house; through the library another door opened on to a balcony on the northern face. This balcony overlooked the extensive and beautifully-laid-out rock garden with its swimming-pool and pavilion, and from it an extensive view of the Surrey Hills could be obtained.

On entering the library, Vereker at once cast a searching glance round the shelves and asked:

"Where's the safe, Ralli?"

Crossing over to a bookcase by the fireplace, Ralli pressed a hidden button and a section of the bookcase swung slowly out on hinges, revealing a safe with double doors let into the masonry of the wall.

"Shall I open it, Vereker?" he asked. "I've my uncle's bunch of keys in my pocket."

"No, thanks, not at present," replied Vereker. "I don't think it would tell me anything new," and stepping over to the door opening on to the balcony he carefully examined its lock, bolts, and catch.

"Who sees to the locking of the doors and fastening of windows at night?" he asked.

"Old Dunkerley usually. Dunkerley's what a medical man loves to call 'podagrous.' His affliction is due to his trustworthiness and an intimate knowledge of the best port. When he is particularly podagrous, he deputes Frederick, the first footman, or even George, the second, to see to the locking up. On the night of my uncle's murder this door was found open. Frederick says he locked and bolted it before going to bed."

After a brief survey of the balcony outside with its stone balustrade and a glance at the supporting pillars springing from the veranda below, Vereker asked to be shown the bedrooms. A few yards down the corridor from the library, Ralli flung open a door leading into Mrs. Armadale's suite. Vereker entered with a strange sense of suppressed excitement, which he would have found difficult to explain. In spite of his general practicality a thread of philosophical mysticism ran through the texture of his mind. He could never dismiss from any general speculation the profound riddle of human personality. Here was ostensibly an expression of Angela Armadale's predilections, an unwitting revelation of the myriad diverse desires, convictions, caprices, which formulated her taste, liberated by the magic touch of great wealth. The scheme of decoration was in coral and green, and through an open door he caught a glimpse of a coral and green bathroom. There was something cold and virginal in the atmosphere, a suggestion of an intellectual rather than a physical pleasure in existence. He glanced at the bed with its exquisite spread of Chinese embroidery, and thought that even its voluptuous comfort must have been disturbed of late by the fretful tossing of an uneasy human spirit. And that uneasiness must have been due to her unhappy marital relations with Sutton Armadale, to an error in her vital adjustment with the profound emotion of love. As Vereker stood lost in reverie, a smile crossed his face, for he had suddenly remembered some words of Bertrand Russell's which ran, "Speaking broadly, the actions of all living things are such as tend to biological survival," and he muttered to himself, "beds and biological survival."

"You're admiring my aunt's wonderful taste?" suddenly asked Ralli.

"I'm very much impressed by it," replied Vereker thoughtfully.

"Then I'm sorry to disillusion you," continued Ralli, with a note of mischievous satisfaction; "it's entirely the work of Sam Ramsbottom, the architect, and his assistants."

The remark brought Vereker to earth, and his attention was at once arrested by the folding glass doors opening on to the balcony. They were almost exactly similar to those of the library farther eastward along the corridor. Noticing another door in the bedroom, he asked:

"I suppose that leads into your uncle's room?"

"He hadn't slept in that room for the last eighteen months. I needn't explain why. He had moved into a room exactly above the library and on the next floor, but 'not a step nearer heaven,' as Angela spitefully remarked."

"And Miss Cazas, where did she sleep?" asked Vereker.

"In the next suite on this corridor. It was practically always reserved for her, and you can understand the influence she exercised over my uncle when I tell you that it was furnished and decorated throughout according to her specific instructions," replied Ralli, as he led Vereker to the rooms in question.

The colour scheme chosen by Miss Cazas was pale bluish-grey and silver, and every touch in the room revealed a nervous sensitiveness to beauty of line. Here and there an ardent spot or splash of flame in cushion or coverlet suggested the coquettish disclosure of a passion curbed by the delicacy of a refined taste. Vereker was surprised. He had looked for some evidence of natural vulgarity, of a riotous and clamorous personality. No trace of such met his appraising eye. But as he stood surveying the room he was struck by the prevalence of a delightful but very insistent perfume. He knew that scent, warm, languorous, and insinuating. It was not now generally used, but its name for the moment escaped him. He was racking his memory in an effort to recall it when he noticed a book lying on a small table by the high Italian bed. He picked it up and glanced at its title. It was Sherard Vines's *Movements in Modern English Poetry and Prose*.

"Miss Cazas seems to have a more literary turn of mind than I was crediting her with," he remarked to Ralli, as he indicated the volume.

"Good Lord above! What tempted her to take that book from the library? It was one of my contributions. Edmée would take as much interest in it as she would in *The Voyage of the Beagle*. When she asked me to recommend her something to read the other day, I said I didn't know her taste, but that one of the most amusing books we had was Dekker's *The Honest Whore*. She promptly went off to search for it."

"By the way, Ralli, how did she take the tragedy of your uncle's death? I suppose it meant a lot to her."

"She was a bit hysterical at first, but soon regained her composure. She returned to town about three o'clock. She ate a fat lunch and excused her shameless hunger by remarking that she'd only had a cup of tea and some lipstick for breakfast. She's what a kindly reviewer of fiction would call an unsympathetic character. But let's get out of this. I can't stand her scent."

"I've been trying to remember that particular scent ever since I entered the room," remarked Vereker.

"Can't say what it is," replied Ralli, as he turned towards the door, "but it reminds me of a civet cat. Matter of association, I suppose."

On entering the corridor once more, Ralli turned to the right where a staircase led to the floor above.

"You'd better have a look at my uncle's room, Vereker. There, your hawk's eye may be able to pick up some scrap of information that may be useful."

Sutton Armadale's room was one of almost monastic simplicity. There was little in it that was suggestive of comfort. Vereker had looked for Sardanapalian luxury; he found by contrast the asceticism of an Antisthenes. He wondered whether this had been part of his pose or a true expression of his inner self. A set of "Quorn Hunt" aquatints by Henry Aiken were an illuminating disclosure of his pitiably obsequious worship of a cult.

A writing-table stood by the window, and beside it a plain chest of drawers in light oak. On the table was a telephone standard, a telephone directory, a blotting- pad, a stationery box, a desk fountain-pen, and a surveyor's round leather measuring-tape. Two doors facing one another led into a dressing-room and a bathroom respectively. Vereker walked over to the writing-table

and surveyed the various articles on it critically. He picked up
the measuring-tape, looked carefully at it, and replaced it slowly
on the table. His face had suddenly grown thoughtful. Then he
casually put his hand on the handle of the right-hand top drawer
and pulled the drawer open. It contained an empty cardboard box
such as is supplied with a Colt automatic pistol when bought, two
cleaning rods, two cleaning brushes, and two boxes of .45 calibre
pistol cartridges. Picking up the boxes of cartridges and almost
oblivious of Ralli, who now stood beside him, he examined them.
One was still intact, and from the other fourteen cartridges had
been taken. Returning the cartridges to the drawer, he took out
the cardboard box and turned it over casually as he inspected it.
All at once something arrested his eye. Two words were scribbled
hurriedly in pencil on the bottom of the box. They were written in
an execrably bad hand, but after some trouble Vereker deciphered
them as "Gastinne Renette." Turning to Ralli, he asked:

"Is that your uncle's handwriting?"

"Yes, that's his fist. What are the words?"

"Gastinne Renette—obviously French or Belgian."

"They're Greek to me," commented Ralli, "but they sound like
a name."

"I think you're right. I wonder who he is. Can you remember if
your uncle possessed two .45 automatic pistols, Ralli?"

"I didn't know he possessed even one. I've heard 'Fruity'
Fanshaugh say my uncle was a rattling good shot with a pistol,
though he always added that he handled a shot-gun as if it was a
fly-swatter and made a day's shooting as nerve-racking as trench
warfare when the enemy was strafeing. His record was two beaters
a season."

"Strange that he should have two cleaning rods and two
brushes for one pistol," remarked Vereker, and returning the
cardboard box to the drawer closed it.

Then he carefully examined the blotting-pad. The paper was
immaculate except for a few ink impressions on the centre and

a sentence written in pencil on the corner. The sentence written in pencil read, "It has a strange quick jar upon the ear. D.J. C4. S.41.", and the ink impression, when reversed in a mirror, showed where an envelope had been blotted. The address ran, "Mr. J. Portwine, Learoyd Street, W. Hartlepool." Taking a note of these, Vereker remarked:

"They may possibly fit into a scheme of things. Won't do to leave a stone unturned. We needn't trouble your solicitors for Portwine's address in any case, Ralli. I suppose you know what these drawers contain?"

"Indeed I don't. Haven't had time to go through them yet, but I believe they contain all my uncle's private papers. If you'd like to go through them with me, I shall be glad."

"When will it be convenient? It'll possibly take us some time."

"I'm ready now. We might be able to run through them before lunch. What do you think?"

To this proposal Vereker at once agreed, and Ralli, producing a bunch of keys, unlocked all the drawers on both sides of the writing-table. For two hours both men worked busily together, carefully scanning the contents of neatly tied and methodically arranged bundles of correspondence. On completion of the task, Vereker was constrained to admit that they had apparently drawn blank. Besides these letters and copies of letters, the drawers contained nothing but two small volumes by the late Walter Winans. They were *The Modern Pistol and How to Shoot It* and *Automatic Pistol Shooting*.

"I'd like to run through these two books when I find time. May I take them with me, Ralli?"

"By all means. I'm sorry you've dug out nothing worth having."

"On the contrary, I think I've made one or two rather startling discoveries. I'm just beginning to get thoroughly excited."

"Good Lord, I'm glad to hear it! You look about as excited as an Egyptian statue. You didn't shout the good news to me."

"As a huntsman would say, I'm not a 'babbler.' I never speak when I'm not sure of the scent."

Glancing at his watch, Ralli now proposed that they should adjourn for lunch. Before descending to the dining-room, however, Vereker insisted on looking into the bedrooms that Ralph Degerdon, Aubrey Winter, and Captain Fanshaugh had slept in on Wednesday night. Of these apartments he made a very careful survey, noting their order in the corridor and their disposition in relation to Sutton Armadale's rooms, to the staircase, and to the rooms below. He also examined every object that might still bear some trace left by the last occupant. During this search, Ralli watched him with quiet but unflagging interest, alert to notice what those inquisitive and observant eyes might seize on with suddenly awakened curiosity.

"You say that Aubrey Winter's very much in love with Miss Cazas?" asked Vereker, looking through the room which Winter had occupied.

"He's in love with her all right, but Aubrey's attitude to Edmée always reminds me of the attachment of an affectionate poodle to its mistress. He's a quiet, matter-of-fact youth without any fire. Slow but sure combustion!"

"Would he be capable of jealousy?"

"Not of violent jealousy, in my opinion."

"He was quite friendly with your uncle?"

"A great admirer of him. The ability to make money always struck Aubrey as something supernatural. You can't blame him; everybody thinks so more or less."

"Did he know that your uncle was infatuated with Miss Cazas?"

"He had some sort of inkling, I suppose, and I dare say he questioned Edmée about it. But you know the subtlety of a woman of her type. She'd mesmerize poor Aubrey into the belief that her relations with my uncle were as innocent as a child's. If he doubted her, she'd at once assume an outraged air and threaten instant dismissal from favour. Aubrey would promptly crawl and promise never to be a bad boy again. She'd then give him a peck of a kiss as a sort of figurative hanky with which to blow his nose and wipe away his tears."

"Poor Winter, I'm sorry for him. I've been through that hoop. *Improbe amor, quid non mortalia pectora cogis!*" said Vereker.

*"After that mouthful—lunch!" exclaimed Ralli, and led the way downstairs.

Chapter Eight

After lunch, Ralli suggested a siesta on the veranda under the balcony on the north side of the house. There, Vereker turned the conversation on the happenings of the eve and morning of the murder.

"Can you remember, Ralli, at what time Dunkerley woke you and broke the news on Thursday morning?" he asked.

"It was dawn when I heard the two shots fired, that's roughly five o'clock, summer time. Then I fell asleep and was roused by Dunkerley shaking me like a terrier shaking a rat. The sun had just risen, so that it must have been about six. The old boy was in such a state that he had some trouble in blurting out, 'Wake up, sir, your uncle has been murdered!' I was half asleep, and I took his words as 'your uncle's being murdered.' In my dazed state I thought it was some one playing a brutal sort of practical joke. The shock I got wasn't conducive to my bothering about the time. I simply leaped into my dressing-gown and rushed downstairs to break the terrible news to Angela."

"That reminds me, you forgot to show me your own room, Ralli," interrupted Vereker.

"Damn it all, so I did! It's next to my uncle's, the farthest bedroom along that corridor from the staircase. Have a look round any time you like."

"I'm not suspecting you at present," smiled Vereker amiably.

"I'm not so sure about that," replied Ralli, glancing up with a quick, nervous lift of his eyes. "You needn't, anyhow. But reckoning that it took Collyer about three-quarters of an hour after he heard the shots to make his way to Hanging Covert and thence to the polo ground and another quarter to reach the house—which is cutting it a shade fine—it would be as near six o'clock as damn it—perhaps a little more."

"Was your aunt asleep when you entered her room?"

"Sound as a drum. I didn't know how to break the news to her. But Angela guessed at once by my face that something was seriously wrong. When I told her, I thought she'd faint. She didn't. She pulled herself together, jumped out of bed, and straightway began to dress. I rushed upstairs and burst into Fanshaugh's room. To my surprise he was half dressed, and promptly asked, 'What's all the bother? I was just getting up to see.' I told him, and then roused Winter and Degerdon."

"Was Winter asleep?" asked Vereker.

"No, he was sitting up in bed, and on my telling him what had happened, he jumped up with the words, 'Good God! Have you told Edmée yet?' Without troubling to answer him, I hopped into Degerdon's room. He was fast asleep, and it seemed to me that I took the deuce of a time to wake him. After I'd shaken the liver out of him, he simply rolled over with a muttered, 'I shan't get up yet. Call me in another hour.' Finally I managed to bring home to him the seriousness of the situation, and he began very collectedly to get up."

"Was he at all upset?" asked Vereker.

"Not the least bit at first. Degerdon seems at times to be slow in the uptake, but he gradually realized what a horrible tragedy had occurred and appeared to be overwhelmed. This was my impression, but you must remember I wasn't in a condition myself to be very observant. By the time I had pulled on my clothes, Fanshaugh had already left the house. Degerdon had dressed, met Angela, and was accompanying her out, taking her arm. He shouted to me to ring up a doctor and the police and follow as quickly as possible."

"I wonder why he should suggest police before he was certain it was murder," remarked Vereker.

"Damn it, but that never struck me," said Ralli, with a shade of surprise. "In any case, I think I told him it was murder, and I suppose he took it for granted. One doesn't think beneath the surface at such a moment."

"Perhaps not. Who was the last to arrive on the scene?"

"Edmée and Aubrey together. Aubrey, phlegmatic in temperament, was rather chalky about the face but otherwise perfectly calm. Edmée, nervous and highly strung, was, as I've said, quite hysterical at first, but recovered later in the morning."

"Fanshaugh seems to have kept his head," commented Vereker.

"It's what one would expect from a soldier. Frankly, I was mighty glad Fanshaugh hadn't gone back to Nuthill on the previous night, as had been his intention. He was simply splendid!"

"Was it very late when you turned in the night before?"

"Not exceptionally. Excusing myself, I went to bed at eleven. To tell the truth, I was feeling bored with the company. They weren't in a particularly cheerful or bright mood. I had just got a copy of Richard Oke's *Frolic Wind* and had made up my mind to have a go at it in bed. Reading in bed's a habit of mine. I started with the expectation of falling comfortably asleep over it, but for the life of me I couldn't lay it down. About half-past twelve I heard Fanshaugh and Degerdon coming along the corridor. They were in a chirpy mood and talking at the top of their voices. I may add that they both appreciate a drop of really fine whisky. Then, at one o'clock I heard Aubrey Winter enter his room rather quietly, and a quarter of an hour later the closing of my uncle's door told me that he had followed suit."

"And then you fell asleep?"

"No, I read on till about two o'clock, when I switched off my light and settled down. I fell into a doze, but was wakened by the sound of movements from the floor below. It sounded as if either Angela or Edmée was up and treading rather lightly about her room. I didn't pay much attention to this, for Angela is a restless sort of soul at times. If she can't sleep she'll often get up and rake around for an aspirin tablet or fish out the manuscript of a novel she's writing. No one has ever seen that manuscript, but she admits that she has been at work on it for seven years. She says her genius is volcanic and has alternate periods of eruption and quiescence, but chiefly quiescence. Then I fell off again, but was wakened by the sound of a window being opened. The night was tropical, so that this incident didn't fire my curiosity. Shortly after, I heard a car start up and make off eastward along the Nuthill road. Once more I slipped away to the land of Nod. The dawn light woke me up, as it nearly always does, and it was then I heard the shots. To tell the truth, I wasn't quite sure at the moment that they were shots. I persuaded myself that I'd heard a car backfire on the road and dozed off again. My next sensation was seismic in its violence, and its origin, as I've related, was dear old Dunkerley."

Ralli had hardly finished speaking when the sounds of footsteps on the gravel announced the approach of some one, and next moment two figures suddenly appeared at the western end of the veranda. At once Ralli greeted them and introduced them to Vereker as Ralph Degerdon and Captain Fanshaugh.

"Frederick told us you were on the back veranda, so we said we'd stroll round and wake you up," said Fanshaugh, as both men seated themselves.

"Any further news?" asked Degerdon.

"None whatever," replied Ralli. "What do you know?"

"Rather startling development in the village of Nuthill," said Fanshaugh. "A man called John Salt drowned himself last night in the village pond. He ought to have chosen the sea with that name. He's the walla the police arrested the other day as a suspect in connection with Sutton's shooting. At the time of his arrest he was tight as an owl and was boasting about having done the job. It came out later that he'd lost all his dough in the Braby crash and was merely drowning his woes. Now he has gone one better."

"Poor devil, I'm sorry for him," remarked Degerdon, with feeling. "He's not the only one. The crash has brought Degerdon and Co. down with it. We've got to pack up and quit. I don't know what the old boy will do. I shall look out for a job abroad."

For some moments there was a sympathetic silence, and then Ralli asked:

"Is there any truth in the yarn that my uncle was the indirect cause of this smash? I know he and Raymond Braby were bitter enemies in business, or the 'world of finance,' as it's politely called."

"It was mainly through Sutton that the whole swindle was brought to light. The Public Prosecutor simply had to take action. I know Braby came to your uncle, and on bended knees begged him to try and save him. But Sutton was out for scalps and drove him from the office with twinkling feet and a hammy knife. I doubt whether he could have given him a hand in any case. It was bound to come out in the end, and it was jolly cute on his part to refuse to filthy his own hands," replied Degerdon.

"Look here, Degerdon. I'm not a business man," said Ralli, with a kindly note in his voice, "and I've an idea that business morality is not of a seraphic order. It hurts me to think my uncle was the cause of your misfortune, even indirectly. If there's anything I can do to give you a lift out of the ditch, call on me."

"Very good of you, Ralli, but you've got troubles enough of your own just now without being worried by mine. In business, as in sport, you've just got to be prepared to take a fall. Though we've come a nasty purler, I'm not going to blame your uncle for it. I don't even bear Raymond Braby much of a grudge, if it comes to that. It's no use, and we ought to have kept our eyes wider open. The only thing to do is to keep a stiff upper lip."

"That's the spirit, Ralph," agreed Fanshaugh. "It's all in a day's hunting. You've got a check; the only thing to do is to cast and get on the line again."

During this conversation, Vereker was making full use of an excellent opportunity to observe the outward bearing and characteristics of the newcomers and trying to cull from them some indication in each case of the true man that moved behind the exterior. Rickaby Fanshaugh conformed unexpectedly in appearance to his preconception of him. Of medium height, lean and wiry, with a sharp, bronzed face, a light moustache and light hair which barely showed incipient greyness, he suggested a cavalry officer who had seen much service abroad. From that bronzed face shone a pair of eyes of almost startling brightness of a very pale blue-grey. There was something about those eyes which intrigued Vereker. Their colour gave an impression of flatness and declared a man whose views, if not wide, were sharp and irrevocably definite. Unflinching courage was there, and the whole set of his face bespoke resolution and a certain virile challenge which bordered on contemptuousness. In spite of a perpetual guard over his feelings, Vereker instinctively liked him. He was a soldier—a soldier by choice—and to Vereker there were few types of men who were preferable.

Ralph Degerdon, on the other hand, seemed to him to be of a different fibre. The face was frank and jovial, with a softness and roundness which gave it an expression of exaggerated boyishness. His eye was dark brown and deep, with peculiarly long lashes; the mouth firm but somewhat full and sensitive. At the moment there hung about him an air of weariness bordering on exhaustion, and at intervals there shone in his eye a gleam of sudden desperation. In spite of his attitude of philosophical acceptance of misfortune, it was clear that the financial ruin which had overtaken his family had had its effect on him. He gave the impression of a man recovering from a shattering crisis.

"I came up here, Basil, to-day to see you about a rather pressing business," said Fanshaugh, breaking the silence which had followed his last words. "I don't suppose you feel a bit like discussing business, but the world has got to go round, you know. Have you decided what you're going to do about the ponies and hunters?"

"I haven't given them a thought. What's the business?"

"If you're going to get rid of them, Dixon of Lingfield would like to buy Nutcracker. Cub-hunting's ahead, and now's the time to sell. He's a top-sawyer, and Dixon's generous when he wants a thing badly. I shall shed tears when he goes, but business is business, and he'll go to a damn good man to hounds. A good man deserves a good horse even more than he does a good wife. Then there's Proserpine. She's a ewe-necked, sickle-hocked, pig-eyed, flat-sided mistress of hell, and I'd cheerfully give her away with a truss of hay to that 'thruster,' Morton, only I know he wouldn't take the trouble to come and fetch her. Sutton bought her off his own bat, and she started her gay career by kicking Foxglove, one of the best hounds in the pack!"

"Dear old 'Fruity,' don't worry yourself. I'm not going to get rid of them. Just carry on as you've done for my uncle. Give Proserpine to your worst enemy. I leave everything in your hands. Later on I may become an ardent disciple of old Jorrocks. Fox-hunting's as good a qualification for heaven as any other faith."

"You don't know how damned glad I am to hear you say so. It's the first bit of common sense I've heard on religion for years. To refer to an unpleasant topic, I saw Inspector Heather with a small army of assistants, about an hour ago, near the 'Silver Pear Tree.' I suppose they're going to scour the place for that automatic pistol."

"What automatic pistol?" asked Vereker, with startling abruptness.

The directness and tone of his question seemed for a moment to disconcert Captain Fanshaugh. He parried with a cold glare, which was intended to show that he resented the manner of its asking, but replied quietly:

"The automatic pistol used by Sutton's murderer."

"Did he tell you that?" asked Vereker, unabashed.

"Well, no, he didn't. It was merely a presumption on my part. It seems to me to be the thing to find, if possible."

"Ah, yes, of course," said Vereker innocently; "but even if it's found it might be impossible to trace its owner."

"That's true," remarked Degerdon, and asked, "Have they found any further cartridge case?"

"One, I believe," replied Vereker casually, "but for the life of me I can't see the use of hunting for cartridge cases. What can they learn from them?"

"Oh, a great deal," replied Fanshaugh. "For instance, a private of a foot regiment, when we were in India, shot his company sergeant-major for kissing his wife. No one saw the crime committed, and dozens of men were under suspicion. But the culprit was discovered at last. They found out by the ejector marks on the rim of the cartridge and by the firing-pin impression on the cap which rifle that cartridge had been fired from. They taxed the walla to whom that rifle belonged, and he said, 'Please, sir, it was me as did it.'"

"Very smart," was Vereker's sole comment, and when he looked up, he noticed that Ralli's eyes were fixed on him with a strangely perplexed and questioning glance.

"To me the business looks like suicide," said Degerdon, stretching himself lazily.

"Not with a shot in the apron, Degerdon," replied Fanshaugh, "unless Sutton was camouflaging suicide to look like murder. There's the case of that chief of police in America who recently played the trick. He thought he'd fake a murder by gangsters and put bullet- holes into the walls and ceiling of his room with another revolver and then shot himself through the heart. I thought the heart shot was damned cunning. The police know that suicide by shooting through the heart is a very rare occurrence. Of course he did it so that the payment of his insurance policies might not be questioned."

"I remember it," agreed Vereker. "He even faked threatening letters to himself, and just before doing himself in called up the telephone operator and gasped out that he'd been shot by gangsters. But in Armadale's case," he added significantly, "there was no need for trickery over insurance policies and apparently no reason for committing suicide. Besides, the police definitely know it was murder."

"How did they find that out?" asked Degerdon eagerly.

"Well, the inspector didn't tell me how they found out that it was murder. Although I'm very friendly with him, he knows I'm from the *Daily Report*, and of course the police always keep the Press in the dark on certain points. To tell us everything might seriously hamper them in their work."

With these words, Vereker rose and, thanking Ralli for his hospitality, said that he would get back to the "Silver Pear Tree."

"Don't forget your shooting-stick and let me know how it works," said Ralli, as he accompanied Vereker through the house to the main entrance. "Also remember my words about your room here. Come up and see me at any time. Don't stand on ceremony. I'd like to know how your sleuthing goes. In this hunt, as 'Fruity' would put it, I'm only a foot-follower, but even he, if he's genuine, may be useful when hounds have checked. I suppose you would rather I said nothing about your detective work to anyone?"

"It would be better for the present," agreed Vereker. "Our having been up at Oxford together ought to allay an indefinite amount of curiosity if you're asked what I'm doing here. Besides, you can always fall back on the *Daily Report*. Au revoir."

Chapter Nine

On leaving the house, Vereker, when half-way down the drive to the main entrance gates, turned sharply to the right and, crossing the bordering lawn and flower-beds, made his way through a narrow belt of larches into an adjoining meadow. Here, by skirting the southern wall of the kitchen garden, he came round to the polo ground. Walking at a sharp pace, he reached the spot where Sutton Armadale's body had been found. Depositing his painting gear on the turf he went down on hands and knees and made a search for the small hole which he had discovered earlier in his investigations. After a few minutes, he located it, and reaching for the shooting-stick which he had laid at hand on the grass, inserted its steel extremity into the hole. It fitted exactly, leaving a circular impression with its terminal metal disc. At once a triumphant gleam lit his eye and he promptly commenced his search for the other hole which he had previously found. This hole he had "sighted" on the former occasion much as a beater or keeper marks down a wounded bird, and now traced without difficulty. Once more the steel shoe of the shooting-stick fitted into the aperture exactly. Then taking a tape-measure from his pocket he measured the distance between the holes and found it to be a little over twenty-six yards. At the moment he was quite at loss to work out a rational explanation of these facts, but stored them up in his memory as potential clues. At a later phase of his quest they might prove of paramount importance. Picking up his pack and easel once more, he set out for the Nuthill road. As he approached the gate leading from the meadow on to the highway, he was attracted by the sound of footsteps behind him. Turning round, he was surprised to see Captain Fanshaugh hurrying to overtake him.

"I was taking a short-cut home," he said, "and seeing you ahead I thought I'd catch you up. I've been riding on your tail for the last ten minutes."

"You live somewhere over at Nuthill?" asked Vereker.

"Yes. My sister and I set up house there when the army had no further use for me. War's an anachronism now they've disbanded so many cavalry regiments. We've got quite a nice little bungalow and compound. We call it 'Jodhpur.' My sister's a war widow and I'm a bachelor. If at any time you'd like to look us up, we'll make you welcome. Drop in any time after dinner for a peg and a chin-wag."

Vereker thanked him, and as they tramped towards Nuthill turned the conversation round to the subject that was uppermost in his mind.

"You were an intimate friend of Sutton Armadale's, weren't you, Captain Fanshaugh?"

"We'll not call it intimate. We were good friends, and I was a sort of guide and philosopher to him on polo, hunting, and shooting. Poor old Sutton, he wanted to shine as a sportsman. With his racing and yachting activities I'd nothing to do. He wasn't very successful in the former, and the latter he finally gave up altogether because he thoroughly disliked being seasick. On polo, hunting, and shooting he was the most ineffectual enthusiast I've ever met. He never was a pukka sportsman. Somehow, I always think that Big Business, as they call it, is dead against true sportsmanship. It makes bad losers and breeds a sort of win-at-all-costs spirit in its devotees. After a man has spent the best part of his years at the financial game, it's difficult to alter his fundamental outlook. In spite of all the trouble I took with him, I couldn't teach him to be even a fair polo player. He'd listen attentively to what I had to say and then go and do the damned thing all wrong. To hit a ball under his pony's neck he'd always ride wide instead of riding on a line with the ball. And he treated horseflesh as if it was machinery instead of soul stuff like himself. With a gun he was not only hopeless but a standing or rather acrobatic menace. In the hunting field he was an amiable nuisance. Those were old Sutton's faults. Yet he was always dead keen, and, after all, he was unconsciously damned funny. He was generally very good-natured and could stand a joke against himself. In fact, he loved one if it brought him into the limelight. He lived for limelight. And against those faults could be set any number of virtues. He was chock full of pluck; he was a loyal friend. He loved the aristocratic tradition, but he wasn't altogether a snob. He had a ready tongue, a hearty laugh, and a damned healthy body. He was a jolly companion and a good host."

"Had he a violent temper?" asked Vereker.

"People who knew him in the city said he seldom lost his temper, but when he did his face was one of the ugliest things imaginable—something you'd see in a cold pork nightmare. Of course a man at business is not the same man at home. I knew nothing about that side of his life. With me he was always very jolly. I've known him turn nappy, and the only way to treat him then was the way you'd treat a nappy horse."

"He was a good pistol shot, I believe," suggested Vereker.

"First rate, but target shooting's a rotten criterion in any case."

"You've seen him practise?"

"Times out of number."

"I believe he always shot with a Colt automatic of .45 calibre. Had he two of these pistols?"

"He never carried more than one," said Fanshaugh.

Vereker seemed to think there was a note of evasion in the reply. "As an enthusiast he'd be likely to have more than one."

"That's quite probable."

"Was he on good terms with Mr. Stanley Houseley?" asked Vereker, changing the subject.

"Now you're asking a difficult question, Vereker," said Fanshaugh. "It's generally known that Sutton and Angela were an ill-matched pair, so I'm not giving away any secrets. How long they were going to stick together was an open question. They lived as man and wife only for appearances' sake. 'Hell-for-leather' was a very old lover of Angela's. She had turned him down for Sutton, and from all one hears she seems to have come to the conclusion that Houseley ought to have been her man."

"What sort of fellow is he?"

"One of God's own. The words 'pukka sahib' may be a joke with your loose-gutted, sloppy-principled up-to-dates, whose very dancing suggests an Oriental bagnio, but they still mean 'pukka sahib' to me. 'Hell-for-leather' is one in every sense. Sutton always treated him in a very friendly way, but Houseley on his part was politeness with a hoar-frost on it. It's not human nature to love the man whose wife you love."

"Sutton Armadale wasn't jealous of him?"

"God knows. It was a Frenchman who said that jealousy was always born with love but didn't always die with it. In love and war they can still teach the world."

"But wasn't Armadale growing very fond of Miss Cazas?" asked Vereker.

"Ah, yes, I know he was. To put it delicately, there are women whom you can love passionately but with whom you'd hate to live. To simple folk loving and living with are synonymous; they make happy-for-ever-after couples. But when intellect begins to feel its strength in our difficult social life an oscillation is set up. Your reason tells you Lily, but your instinct cries for Rose, which, by the way, sounds like a music-hall song. All this intellect's damned disturbing and ought to be suppressed."

"What do you think of Miss Cazas?"

"She's a little devil; amusing, sprightly, game, but not my type. She lacks quality and has too small a girth to be a good stayer. I wouldn't marry her for worlds, and anyone who does will have to ride her with a gag snaffle. Still, she mesmerizes the youngsters. Both Degerdon and Winter are under her little finger."

"Who's she in love with?"

"With Edmée Cazas chiefly. She appeared to be passionately in love with Sutton, she professes to be genuinely fond of Ralph Degerdon, and she treats poor Winter as a Chinese Empress would a eunuch."

"Is there any truth that Sutton was the indirect cause of the Degerdon's failure?"

"There's no doubt about it. You can't blame Sutton. He might have bolstered up the Braby Group for a time, but he had a most sensitive nose. He smelt a stench from that quarter long ago and, when he found out that it came from a rotten swindle, he did the right thing; he left them to it. Young Ralph bore him no ill will on that account. He's not vindictive, and I for one am sorry for him. He's only a cub and, if I'm not mistaken, he has the makings of a man in him. Perhaps this crash is the best thing that can have happened to him. Some roughing it abroad will take the looseness out of him or break him up altogether. It's not a bad alternative in this world."

As Captain Fanshaugh finished speaking, the two men came to a halt in front of the "Silver Pear Tree." Here, after renewing his invitation to Vereker to drop in at his bungalow, Jodhpur, whenever he felt inclined, Fanshaugh took a short-cut across the fields to Nuthill. Vereker entered the inn and, having deposited his gear in his room, descended to the coffee-room and ordered tea. At this moment he heard Inspector Heather's voice booming outside the inn, and going to the entrance found him standing talking on the gravel pull-up with Sergeant Lawrence Goss. On seeing Vereker, the inspector took leave of his subordinate and sauntered towards the door.

"Just the man I want to see!" exclaimed Vereker.

"That's nice of you, Mr. Vereker. I'm as thirsty as a camel. We've had a big and disappointing day's work. I hope you've fared better."

"Had a most entertaining time, Heather. But come in and let's compare our spoils. I hope you're not in a hurry."

"I'm putting up here for a week or so," replied the inspector. "It's nice and handy, and the beer in Nuthill's not nearly so good. I like it better out of the barrel, if it's nicely nursed."

"Nothing could be more convenient, Heather. Although we work on different lines, our combined intellects ought to be invincible. What do you say?"

"The partnership ought to improve you out of all knowledge," replied the inspector dryly.

"Sit down and have some tea. No sugar, if I remember. It's a sure indication that your guest's a crank, a slimmer, or just a robust consumer of what is called 'malt liquors.' You're not a crank or a slimmer. But before getting to business, let's agree to put all our cards on the table. Our methods ought to be complementary."

"That's it, Mr. Vereker. United we stand, divided you fall. I'm quite agreeable to team work."

"Then I'll begin. I got an itch for painting this morning."

"Nothing to do with the bedding here, I hope," remarked the inspector, sitting up sharply.

"No, you'll find the place eminently clean and comfortable; but let me get on. I made my way into Wild Duck Wood at dawn and started work. I soon found that I wasn't alone in the wood. I heard some one on the prowl. I thought it might be Collyer. It wasn't. I spotted a stranger in a brown Harris Norfolk jacket and cap as he hurried through the tangle. I went to the spot where I had viewed him and found the bracken and undergrowth trampled in circles as if he had been searching for something. It wasn't one of your men, was it?"

"No, we didn't start as early as that. I know the exact spot you mean; we came across it later. By the way, do you smoke Fribourg and Treyer's cigarettes?"

"I had some on me this morning, but when I run out of them I usually take to something pernicious in the way of gaspers. You found one of my butts?"

"Yes."

"I found one of a different breed. It was one of Bogdanov's Russians. I thought I'd got a clue to the prowler because they're not commonly smoked in these parts. It didn't prove as good as I expected. A few minutes later I met Mr. Ralli in the wood, and he offered me a case full of them. He wasn't the man in the Norfolk jacket; he was wearing grey flannels. He doesn't smoke before breakfast; therefore we can safely assume that the fag end I picked up wasn't his."

"There's a box of those Russian cigarettes in nearly every room in Vesey Manor," commented the inspector. "It looks as if the stranger had access to them. Either he's one of the staff of servants or has been a recent guest."

"A guest, inspector, who doesn't hesitate to fill his case from his host's abundance."

"How do you make that out?"

"From the cut of his clothes. Savile Row it was or I'm a bad judge. There's sometimes a big difference between habit and customs—West End clothes with East End manners."

"Steady, Mr. Vereker," cautioned the inspector as he pulled forth his pipe. "You're a bit impetuous. Servants usually get hold of their master's cast-off clothes, and I knew one valet who, when his boss was away, used to meet his girl in his boss's latest togs. The guv'nor returned unexpectedly on one occasion and met his valet in the street. 'God damn, it's you, Francis,' he exclaimed. 'I thought it was my wraith. What the hell's the meaning of this?' 'I was going to see my best girl, sir,' was all Francis could say. 'Well,' cautioned his boss, 'if you don't get her into trouble or marry her, I'll stop the price of that suit out of your wages. Get out of my sight till to-morrow morning.' But forrard with the business, Mr. Vereker."

"I accompanied Mr. Ralli to the manor and breakfasted with him."

"What was he doing out so early?" asked the inspector.

"He'd been for a morning walk with Miss Collyer. He made no secret of the fact that he's engaged to her."

"That's news to me, though I'd found out that he was rather gone on her."

"I suppose you thought he was merely taking his fun where he found it."

"At first, yes. Then I found out something on the strict q.t. that's vastly more important. As you're covered by the strict q.t. I may as well tell you she's his cousin by blood."

"Great Scott, Heather, you're astonishing! How did you unearth that?"

"I've been making inquiries round about, and wanting to know the history of young Frank Peach, who was Armadale's under keeper until quite recently, I called at the Peachs' cottage. Peach is away for a day or two, under our watchful eye, needless to say, but I found his mother willing to talk. She's a fine, upstanding, handsome woman. She seemed a bit scared of me at first, but I made myself very friendly. She was in Armadale's service as a cook before she was married."

"Ha, then you know every inch of the country, so to speak, Heather."

"I'm not boasting when I say I have a way with cooks," said Heather, giving his moustaches an attention which evidently sprang from associated memories. "Anyway, I got on the right side of her. She found out that I was a bachelor and told me she was a widow, and one thing led to another. I probed her about her son's affairs and, having learned that he was another of Miss Collyer's suitors, I finally wheedled the information out of her that the late Mrs. Collyer was not Miss Collyer's mother. Mrs. Peach's sister, who was lady's-maid to the late Mrs. Armadale, was Miss Trixie's mother. So you see that Frank Peach and the girl are blood cousins."

"Tremendous, Heather! Did you find out anything about Peach himself?"

"Quite a lot. One thing's significant: he had a furious row with Armadale a few days before the murder and he was on the scene of the murder a few minutes after Collyer found Armadale dying. Armadale never liked the lad, and after giving him the sack wouldn't give him a reference unless he promised to emigrate. Whether Armadale's action had anything to do with the secret of Miss Trixie's parenthood I can't say. Possibly young Frank knew too much. Anyway, when Armadale refused that reference there was a shindy. Armadale had to ring for his servants, and Peach was forcibly chucked out of the house. His last words were a threat to do Armadale in. I'm dead nuts on Peach as my likely man."

"It looks plain sailing from your side of the game, Heather," said Vereker. "I suppose you'll search their cottage for the weapon?"

"I have an idea that young Frank knows where that pistol is, and I'm just waiting for him. We've got word that the cartridge case you picked up on the polo ground was certainly not fired from the automatic found in Armadale's hand."

"Good! That's something definite to work on. In my tour of the manor this morning, Ralli showed me into his uncle's bedroom. In a drawer of his writing- table there's the usual stout cardboard box which goes with an automatic when you buy one. There were two cleaning rods and brushes in the box. I have strong suspicion that Armadale had two automatics in his possession."

"Were there two boxes?"

"No."

"He might have got rid of the first pistol when he bought the second, but it's a good point. Still I don't see at present how it connects up with Frank Peach or a burglar."

"I don't think it ever will. My suspicion that we must look for the murderer in the house grows stronger and stronger. By the way, on the back of that Colt automatic box there are scribbled two words. They are 'Gastinne Renette.' That sounds to me like a French or Belgian name, and I can't help in the first flush connecting it with Miss Cazas. You don't know of anyone called Gastinne Renette?"

"Damn it, but the name seems familiar!" exclaimed the inspector, and for some moments was silent in the task of ransacking his really marvellous memory. Then he said, "No, it won't come back. Perhaps it was in connection with some French case we dealt with at the Yard some years ago. Anyhow, I'll have it run to earth if possible. The Surety in Paris may be able to help us. If Mr. Gastinne Renette has figured in any police business, it won't be very difficult to learn his history and perhaps to track him down."

"Besides the cardboard box I've mentioned there were two fifty boxes of .45 ammunition. One of these was intact; from the other, fourteen cartridges had been taken. I then ran quickly through all Armadale's correspondence, but struck nothing that tickled my fancy. You may have better luck when you cover the same ground, which I suppose you will."

"It may be unnecessary. I can almost rely on you now, Mr. Vereker," smiled Heather.

"Now I've got a poser for you, inspector. On Mr. Armadale's writing-pad, the following words were scribbled in pencil, 'It has a strange quick jar upon the ear.' Does that mean anything to you?"

"Yes, a lot. It's a description of what you get at boxing when you stop a right swing. But, to be serious, it sounds like a line of poetry."

"It's certainly metrical, and I've read it before. Where, I don't know. It won't be very difficult to place, but I doubt whether it has anything to do with our business. Here, however, is something which may be relevant. On the middle of the pad is the impression in reverse of an address. It's in Armadale's writing, and is obviously the result of blotting an envelope on the pad. It runs, 'Mr. J. Portwine, Learoyd St., W. Hartlepool.'"

"Good business, good business, Mr. Vereker. We want that address. Dunkerley, the butler, told me that a seafaring gent called Portwine turned up at the manor about a month ago to see Mr. Armadale. He put up at this inn for a few days, and was drunk most of the time, according to Mrs. Heaver, the landlady. He was a pretty rough handful, and Dunkerley says he could curse in every known language, including Chaldean. He drank port, too, and it's nasty stuff to get tight on."

"Literally drinking himself to death," commented Vereker quietly.

"I might have said that myself later on in the evening," laughed the inspector. "About this seafaring gent, who's probably only Lisbon wine after all, I've found out something that's important. He hitched up with Trixie's mother a year after Trixie's birth. Now, it's rather unlikely that before her marriage his wife owned up to an illegitimate child. Yet on the other hand she may. He might be one of those sailors who don't care. But suppose she didn't and he found it out afterwards. Put a bloodthirsty bos'n in such a position. He'd start sharpening his cutlass on the doorstep right away."

"That's certainly a promising line, Heather. What are you going to do about it?"

"We're on his tracks already, and when we lay hands on Mr. Portwine we'll decant him."

"Do you connect him in any way with the burglary?"

"Naturally. He probably got the geography of Vesey Manor from his wife, who knows every inch of it. As the first Mrs. Armadale's maid you can bet your shirt-studs she knew all about the safe in the library. From all accounts, the late Mrs. Armadale was an easygoing sort who trusted her servants implicitly, and it's more than likely that her maid frequently locked up her jewels for her at night."

"Rather risky, I should say, but the carelessness of women with their valuables is notorious. Every week you hear of one leaving a king's ransom in a taxi-cab."

"There's one little item still that I can't make head or tail of," remarked the inspector after a pause. "It's the suit of clothes Burton, the gardener, discovered in the laurels near the bathing pavilion. It may have no connection with our case, and yet something tells me it's part and parcel of it—no pun intended."

"Have you found out the tailor who made or sold it?" asked Vereker.

"Not yet. That's going to be difficult. It's a ready-made suit of a shoddy that's turned out by the mills at Batley in Yorkshire by the mile. By a process of trial and error we may find out the tailor in London who sold it. Then that tailor won't know the name of the customer who bought it unless it was sent on to his address."

"It was cleaned lately, but I believe that Sergeant Goss said there were no cleaners' marks."

"Not a trace. It seems a rather hopeless line at present, but I can't neglect it."

"You've interviewed all the servants in the manor, I suppose?" asked Vereker.

"Yes, but the servants' quarters are practically in a separate wing of the house. None of them heard or saw anything unusual on the night of the burglary. Dunkerley, the butler, told me all about Portwine, and Frederick, who unbolted all the doors on Thursday morning, found that a bolt of the side door near the gun-room had been pulled back. As this bolt fits very badly into its socket, there's a knack in pushing it home. He is absolutely certain that he shot that bolt home when he locked up on Wednesday night."

"Of course he may have been mistaken," said Vereker, "but it's an important item. When the guests left the house on Thursday morning for the scene of the tragedy, out of which door did they go?"

"The door leading out of the dining-room on to the back veranda."

"But the door near the gun-room leads out of the western end of the house and is certainly nearest the polo ground."

"That's true, but it's a door that was very seldom used except by Mr. Armadale himself. It has a specially constructed lock, very much resembling a Yale, but there's no handle on the inside, and it has to be opened by a key from both sides. Dunkerley has one key, and the other Mr. Armadale always carried on his own bunch."

"That explains it fairly satisfactorily," replied Vereker. "Did you interview the maid who was told to look after Miss Cazas? She didn't bring her own maid."

"Yes," replied the inspector, "but she's not a very intelligent girl and chatters like a magpie. She seemed very concerned that Miss Cazas had grazed both her knees in the swimming-pool the evening before, and told me at length what trouble she had in matching a button which the young lady had lost off one of her walking shoes. She wound up by saying that Miss Cazas wasn't the goods because she only tipped her half a crown on leaving."

"And what about Mrs. Armadale's maid?"

"She's too clever by half and as tight as an oyster. But, by gum, she's pretty—she'd make a robber's go- bang. She has gone with her mistress to Sutton Pragnell for a couple of days. I'll give her another twisting when she comes back. I'm rather fond of baiting a cheeky girl if she's really pretty. It's like trying to hit a butterfly with a baton. But did you see any of Wednesday's guests up at the manor to-day, Mr. Vereker?"

"Two. Captain Fanshaugh and Mr. Ralph Degerdon. Fanshaugh's a retired cavalryman. He knows a good deal about fire-arms and surprised me with his knowledge about the marks an extractor and a firing-pin leave on the brass shell of a cartridge. This may mean nothing, because the matter had been brought to his notice by a shooting affair in India. He's a downy bird with all his wits about him and of a very resolute temper, I should say. Still, I like him immensely. Degerdon is rather hard to place. He's younger and shows few marked characteristics. Oppressively good-looking and would make a first-rate lover in a musical show if he had a third-rate voice. He's cast in a softer mould and has a tendency towards being a 'good-timer'; but, as a horsy man would say, he has a generous eye. I'm going to interview him alone; he may yield something important. I shall also try to get in touch with the other two male guests of Wednesday; Houseley, who left early, and Mrs. Armadale's cousin, Aubrey Winter. I particularly want to meet Houseley."

"Still sticking to your old line, I see," remarked Heather. "Because Mr. Houseley's yum-yum with Mrs. Armadale. You may be right, but at a first glance none of the gentlemen you've mentioned seem to me in the list of possibles. They're not the kind to engineer a burglary and then pump lead into their friend and host. What we've got to do is find that damned automatic pistol!"

Inspector Heather glanced hurriedly at his watch and rose.

"My men will have stopped work by now," he remarked. "And, if any of them have found that pistol on the estate, you'll have to stand him a bottle of fizz and I'll present him with a packet of Player's. I'll go and see if I can find them. After that I must run down to the police station at Nuthill. I'll be back in time to have a night-cap with you unless something very important has turned up."

Chapter Ten

On Inspector Heather's departure, Vereker settled himself in the only easy-chair in the coffee-room, and lighting his pipe gave himself up to idle dreaming about the Armadale case. In this mood, which on subsequent analysis always appeared to him to resemble very closely the preliminary mood from which sprang his creative impulses in painting, his mind flitted inconsequently from one point to another. It was a pleasant, fluid sort of cerebration without any of the exhausting demands of purposive concentration, and yet from its idle ferment ideas suggesting a line of action frequently grew. He fell to thinking of the divergent courses taken by himself and Inspector Heather in their pursuit of a solution to the riddle of Sutton Armadale's violent death. Heather had proceeded from the discovery of trouble between the financier and his underkeeper, Peach, to inquire into the latter's history and movements. In this he was working on the very tangible basis of a threat to kill. The officer had also been considerably impressed by the intrusion of Jonathan Portwine into the fabric of the case. Here, again, were factors which might be sufficiently strong to drive a violent man to murder. He himself had from the very first been attracted by the marital differences between Sutton Armadale and Angela as the source from which the trouble had risen. What might have proved an eminently happy marriage had resolved itself into a complete severance except in outward appearance. And what bitter ferocity on both sides might underlie icy politeness and simulated endearments! He could imagine the deadening pain which Angela must have suffered on her discovery of Sutton's deception of her and in her swift disillusionment in him. Her aristocratic egotism must have received a disrupting shock on finding that love, which she had idealized and qualified with a nice discrimination, could be so capricious and catholic in taste as to lead her to the same couch as a lady's-maid! And in her revulsion she had flown back into the arms of her former lover, Houseley, whose passion apparently approximated her ideal of steadfastness and cultured appreciation.

Stanley Houseley! For a moment, in Vereker's mind, he was dramatically transfigured, and with swift transition slipped ludicrously into the sporting anticlimax of "Hell-for-leather." Thence arose the memory of Heather's remark about a Rover Meteor car, and at once Vereker jumped from his chair. He would go and interview Mrs. Burton, the gardener's wife, at the lodge at the manor gates. At the entrance to the inn he encountered a telegraph boy who had just propped his bicycle against the post from which hung the sign of the "Silver Pear Tree." The wire in the boy's hand was addressed to him. Vereker took it and tore it open. It ran:

Have got in touch with Edmée prospects look costly treasury depleted—RICKY

Procuring a telegram form from the messenger, Vereker scribbled the reply:

Lunch with me at L'Escargot one o'clock Monday—
ALGERNON

Handing it to the boy for transmission, he set out at a brisk pace towards the gates of Vesey Manor.

Mrs. Burton, the gardener's wife, was one of those comfortable women who take existence with a sane and versatile enjoyment. No note in its pleasant roundel was unduly stressed; there was a quiet, happy interest in birth, in love, in marriage, and even a funeral, though a gloomy emotional necessity, could yield its quota of sweet tears. Funerals had to stand the test of criticism from the point of view of successful functions. "Uncle Jim's funeral was pretty good, but I've seen better in our family," were her words on a recent occasion, and they are instructive. She and her husband had finished tea when Vereker arrived. Victor Burton, her husband, was a thin, weather-beaten-looking man of very few words. His vital juices seemed to have been sapped as a tribute to his wife's bland exuberance, but he had an air of complacency which suggested that the process had not been altogether unpleasant. When Vereker explained that he was a friend of Mr. Ralli and would like to ask a few questions about the car she had heard start up and pass the lodge on Thursday morning, Mrs. Burton shed any pretence at reserve and became affable, if not voluble. She was unable, however, to add much to what Vereker had already learned from Inspector Heather. In the midst of the conversation her son, Reginald Burton, entered, and hearing a discussion about a motor-car at once became alert. He was a fresh-looking youth of about sixteen, who had just got employment in a garage and petrol station at Nuthill. At this phase of his existence the world seemed to him to have been created as a fitting *mise en scène* for the internal combustion engine. With the superciliousness of youth and its pride in knowledge, he brushed his mother aside and took the matter into his own hands.

"I heard both cars, sir," he said, addressing Vereker.

"Then there were two cars?" asked Vereker, with surprise.

"Oh, yes. I'm nearly certain the first was a Rover Meteor and I know the second was a Trojan. Nobody could mistake a Trojan engine."

"At what time did you hear the first car?"

"I couldn't say exactly, but it must have been between two and half-past two. I was lying awake with toothache. When I heard the first car, I sat up and looked out of the window. You can see right down the Nuthill road from my window. The driver was larking about with his headlights, putting them on and then dimming them. Having a game with them, I suppose. It wasn't a pitch-dark night, and I could see fairly well across the meadow next to the road. A woman was in the meadow about twenty yards from the hedge when I looked out. She went through the gate and seemed to join the car on the road. I could see her quite clear in the light of the lamps."

"Was she tall or short?"

"Tall and wore a brown fur coat but no hat. To me it seemed the double of Mrs. Armadale, but of course it couldn't have been Madam. Then I heard the car start up, and it accelerated and went past here at about forty miles an hour."

"Did the lady enter the car?"

"I couldn't say, sir."

"You didn't by any chance see her in the meadow after the car had passed here?"

"I didn't look. I was too much interested in the car itself—which I was pretty certain was a Rover Meteor—to bother about the lady. My mate, George Barter, who had been over at Godstone and was getting back to Nuthill about that time, told me next day that a Rover Meteor had passed him on the road."

"What about the second car you heard?"

"I heard it about half an hour afterwards. It stopped at almost the same spot as the Rover Meteor had done. This seemed rather rum to me, and I got up and looked out of the window to see what was going on. This time I saw a lad leave the gate and run as hard as he could across the fields towards the polo ground. Then the second car started up and passed here. I knew by its engine that it was a Trojan."

"Thanks very much, Burton. I see you take a great interest in your job. Otherwise you wouldn't have been able to spot the makes of those cars."

"You get to know them all after a bit, sir," replied the youth, highly pleased with Vereker's compliment.

Vereker then drew Burton senior into conversation about the parcel of clothes which he had found under the rhododendrons near the bathing pavilion. Burton explained that he was hoeing and raking between the shrubs when he came upon the parcel.

"Could you say if it had been there any length of time, Burton?" asked Vereker.

"Mebbe a night, mebbe a week, mebbe longer, sir. We rakes and 'oes between them shrubs every Thursday. The weather has been bone dry all August, so that weeds haven't bothered us much. Next month's the month for weeds. Ted, my man, did the job last week, but, as he said, it didn't need anything more than a kiss and a promise, and he possibly missed the packet."

"Were there any footprints on the loose earth?"

"No, sir, or if there was, I raked 'em out without noticing 'em. The inspector from the Yard had a good look round to see if he could find footprints, and he remarked as how rakes was a blinkin' noosance and ought to require permits like fire-arms."

"I'd like to see the exact spot if you could spare the time just now, Burton," remarked Vereker.

To this Burton was agreeable. Slipping on his coat and a straw hat reminiscent of a past and joyous decade, he accompanied Vereker from the lodge to the rock garden behind the manor.

Here Vereker made a very careful search among the shrubs and rhododendrons bordering on the spot where Burton had picked up the parcel, but his quest brought nothing further to light. With an air of disappointment he stood mopping his brow when, looking in the direction of the bathing pavilion, he caught sight of a fragment of gauzy material held fast in the foliage of a daphne, a few yards away. Crossing to the evergreen, he plucked the material from its entanglement and found that it was a diminutive handkerchief of beautiful French lace. Instinctively he put it to his nose. It was still heavily scented in spite of its exposure, and there was no mistaking the perfume. "Stephanotis!" he exclaimed, and all at once his face lit up with a strange light. It had recalled a vivid memory, one of Vereker's very few romances, and it took him back to his work on the Bygrave case. Mrs. Cathcart had been passionately fond of the scent, and she—well, she and he had parted since then. For some moments Vereker stood in a mood of wistful reflection, and then with dramatic suddenness straightened himself. The air of romantic lover vanished in a flash, for he had recalled the scent that had almost overwhelmingly pervaded the room which Miss Edmée Cazas had recently occupied in Vesey Manor. Thrusting the handkerchief into his pocket, he crossed rapidly to the bathing pavilion, followed by Burton, who was apparently coming slowly to the conclusion that the young gentleman was a "bit batchy." In the pavilion, after an intensive search, Vereker found nothing, but just as he was about to return with Burton to the lodge he picked up on the loose gravel path leading to the swimming-pool a button that had become detached from a lady's shoe. This he carefully inserted in his ticket pocket and, after a further general survey of the rock garden, signified to Burton that he would return to the "Silver Pear Tree." As they walked slowly together down the drive to the gates, they were overtaken by Ralph Degerdon, who had just left the manor. He had stayed on after Captain Fanshaugh's departure to have a private talk with Ralli, and was now making his way to the Captain's bungalow for dinner. At the lodge they parted with Burton and, as they tramped westward, Vereker at once turned the conversation on the topic of the burglary at Vesey Manor.

"Did you hear any suspicious sounds during the early hours of Thursday morning, Degerdon?" he asked.

"Yes, I did," replied Degerdon, without any hesitation. "I was awake at several intervals during the night. If you remember it was poisonously hot, and it must have been between two and three that the sound of a window being opened attracted my attention. At first I thought it must be some one, either Edmée or Angela, on the floor below, who had pushed open a casement for air. The idea at once occurred to me to follow suit, and I rose and did so. I was feeling very wakeful and, as it was a glorious night, I lit a cigarette and stood at the window smoking and cooling off in my pyjamas. I casually leaned out to see whose window had been opened on the floor below, and to my surprise found that all the windows on that floor were closed. I at once concluded that either Edmée or Angela had closed a casement instead of opening it, and thought no more about the matter for the moment. Since then, of course, it has occurred to me that I must have heard the burglar entering by the library door. I finished my cigarette, flung the butt on the stone balcony below, and was just about to get back to bed when I heard a footstep on the gravel in front of the veranda on the ground floor. I at once rushed to the window and looked out. Unfortunately the gravel close to the veranda was hidden from my view by the balcony, and a burglar to avoid being spotted from the upper windows would naturally keep well in to the house. I stood and listened for fully five minutes, but heard no further sound. Just as I had returned to bed I once more heard footsteps on the gravel and, jumping up, hurried to the window. There wasn't a soul close to the house clear of the balcony, but I thought I caught a glimpse of a man's figure vanishing round a bend in the path that leads through the laurels to the rock garden."

"Tall or short man?" asked Vereker.

"I couldn't distinguish in the half-light, but I should say a short man."

"You didn't take any action in the matter?" asked Vereker.

"No. I thought it was damned funny," continued Degerdon, with a curious uneasy hesitation, "and at the moment I wondered whether I should knock up Sutton. On further consideration I thought I'd better not. I suppose I'm rather sensitive to ridicule and—well, you know what a bally fool I'd have looked if I'd waked the whole house up on a dud burglar scare. They'd have ragged the life out of me for weeks. I turned in and, forgetting all about the business, fell asleep again."

"You heard no further sounds in the house itself?"

"Oh, yes; I'm forgetting to tell you that before I actually fell asleep again I heard Sutton moving about in his room."

"But Fanshaugh's and Winter's rooms separated your bedroom from Armadale's," commented Vereker, looking disconcertingly into Degerdon's eyes. "You couldn't possibly know that it was Sutton who was moving about."

"Yes, I know that," replied Degerdon, smiling, "but I reached the conclusion that it was Sutton after I had learned what had happened next morning. At the moment, of course, I couldn't say who it was, though I was fairly certain that it wasn't 'Fruity,' who was separated from me by only one wall."

"I see," said Vereker dubiously. "You were wakened by Ralli, I believe."

"Yes. I thought for a moment I was at home and didn't jump to things very quickly. But when I heard my pyjama jacket tear, I thought it was time to sit up and ask questions."

"You accompanied Mrs. Armadale to the polo ground?"

"Yes."

"She was very upset, I suppose?"

"Less than I'd expected, but Angela's tempered steel. She wasn't in love with her husband, but she was horror-struck at his violent end."

"I hear that she'd got rather too fond of Mr. Houseley of late," suggested Vereker.

"Ah, well, perhaps it wasn't all her fault. I don't know much about their private affairs and don't like to talk about them. Sutton, I feel sure, wasn't quite playing the game. I like Angela, and I'm probably biased in her favour. If people marry they ought to try and do the right thing by one another. It may be difficult, but it's seldom impossible. I'm a bit dogmatic on the subject, but a man who mixes his drinks is generally a nasty kind of drunkard and people should cut him."

"They say that Sutton Armadale was paying too much attention to Miss Cazas," said Vereker blandly.

"I know all about that. I'm very much in love with Edmée, and the way he hung on to her skirts rather annoyed me. He did his best to dazzle her with his money, but Edmée told me she didn't care two straws for him. She was leading him on to give him a salutary lesson for Angela's sake."

"She's a very charming woman, I'm told," said Vereker sympathetically. "I hope your feelings are returned."

The words produced the effect which Vereker had intended.

"You've not seen her?" asked Degerdon, with surprise.

"No. You must introduce me."

"Certainly. I'm sure you'll like her. She's not like other women; there's something different about her," said Degerdon, with growing enthusiasm. "At times she's so sophisticated and at others so charmingly childlike. And she's so deuced clever. She can dance and sing and play exquisitely. I haven't got her photograph on me or I'd let you see it. She's as beautiful as she's accomplished."

"I hope your money troubles won't make any difference to your relations," remarked Vereker pointedly.

"Good heavens, you don't think for a moment she's one of the mercenary sort, do you?" asked Degerdon.

"I wasn't suggesting that," replied Vereker diplomatically, "but money makes the mare go, you know. Lack of it often means such a wearisome postponement. Love's generally impatient."

"Oh, Edmée and I are not a bit impatient. She's worth waiting for. We're not engaged yet, but I'm certain my being broke won't affect us in the slightest."

For some minutes the two men walked in silence. Vereker was lost in his own thoughts. His conversation with Degerdon had revealed to him an unsuspected ingenuousness in the man. He was doubtless very much in love with Edmée Cazas and had declared it with the courage and enthusiasm of youth. Vereker was all the more surprised because Degerdon's face did not altogether suggest such boyish candour. Lavater's conclusions on the science of physiognomy might not be infallible, but the face was unquestionably a basic index to character. With his habitual scepticism he decided not to accept Degerdon's simplicity as wholly sincere, and broke the silence with the remark:

"I've left my confounded cigarettes in my other pocket."

"Have one of these," immediately suggested Degerdon, producing a gold cigarette-case and pressing it open. "They're Bogdanov's Russians. 'Hell-for-leather' was the first to introduce them to me. I like them so much that I always smoke them now."

Vereker picked out a cigarette with almost exaggerated clumsiness, and during the process had sufficient time to read an inscription incised across the inner leaf of the case. —"To Ralph with love from Edmée." To him that sentence was a profound revelation.

"You like a country life, I suppose?" he asked, as if to change the tenor of his own thoughts.

"Not altogether. I'm too busy in town to be entirely a countryman. I try to make a judicious mixture of life."

"Do you ride to hounds?"

"Rather. Under 'Fruity's' guidance I've become awfully keen."

"What staggers me," said Vereker, "is the cheerfulness with which you all get up early in the country. As an experiment, I dragged myself out at sunrise this morning to paint in Wild Duck Wood. I thought I'd be absolutely alone, but I hadn't settled down to work ten minutes before I heard some one making his way through the covert."

"Men on the estate are usually about at dawn," said Degerdon casually.

"At first I thought it was Collyer," continued Vereker, "or, as you've suggested, one of the workers on the estate, but he was a well-dressed young fellow about your own height and build. The set of head and shoulders very much resembled your own."

"What was he wearing?" asked Degerdon. "Perhaps I can place him for you."

For a second Vereker hesitated. In a flash he saw or thought he saw the purport of the question. At the back of his mind he had stored away an evidentiary note concerning a brown Norfolk jacket and cap for future reference. He did not wish that note's potential usefulness nullified through any tactical error on his part.

"A blue flannel blazer and grey flannel trousers," he replied.

"It might be anyone," said Degerdon. "Ralli usually wears grey flannels for knocking about in, but I've never seen him sporting a blue blazer."

"It wasn't Ralli," remarked Vereker. "I met him in the wood a few minutes later. In any case, it doesn't matter."

"Talking about early rising," continued Degerdon easily, "cub-hunting commences next month, and that means showing a leg before the lark or, in any case, before I usually feel inclined to. This morning, I simply couldn't get up. 'Fruity' stayed with us overnight, and we sat up chin-wagging till all hours. I was waked at eight, but it was ten before I fell out of bed."

"Have you ever met this fellow, Raymond Braby?" asked Vereker, turning the conversation.

"Frequently. I never want to meet a more charming man."

"The investors in his companies wouldn't hold that view," remarked Vereker caustically.

"Doubtless, but in the struggle for money a man has a peculiar knack of shutting his eyes to the troubles of those outside his personal circle. He'll send a cheque to help sufferers from an earthquake in Italy or a famine in India, but if Cyrus T. Bodkin beggars thousands of his fellows in America over an oil swindle, I've never heard of anyone in this country crying his eyes out about it. In business the man who loses his cash gets about as much sympathy as a man who loses a bet. Braby'll be sorry for me because he knows me, but he won't shed tears over Mary Smith of Golders Green who is stranger to him and is wondering whether it's going to be the cemetery or the workhouse."

"The world's a bit too big and the human heart a bit too small," remarked Vereker thoughtfully. "Was Braby a man who might try to get his own back through an agent?"

"I don't think so. But there are others in the money scrum who might want to kick his shins. Then there's the lunatic who does delightfully unexpected things— Mary Smith's brother for choice," said Degerdon bitterly.

"Ah, yes," said Vereker, with an ironic smile, "but we've got a happy retreat for such people as Mary Smith's brother at Broadmoor, if by any chance they escape the gallows. Our ethics are a bit tricky, and all we can hope is that Progress is not, as Baudelaire put it, an invention of the Belgians!"

At the "Silver Pear Tree" the two men parted, and Degerdon continued his way along the Nuthill road. On entering the inn Vereker retired to his room and jotted down, as was his custom, all the particulars of his day's work on the case. On going once more over the ground and reconstructing his conversation with Ralph Degerdon, he was assailed by a peculiar sense of uneasiness. That uneasiness arose from his inability to draw satisfactory inferences from two of the most significant portions of that conversation. When Degerdon had remarked that he had heard Sutton moving about in his room during the early hours of Thursday morning, Vereker had seized upon the weakness of the statement like a hawk flashing on its prey. Seeing that Fanshaugh's and Winter's rooms separated his from Sutton's, how had Degerdon come to the conclusion that it was Sutton he had heard? His reply had been a frank avowal that he had formed his judgment in the light of subsequent events and not at the moment. If true, the explanation was simple; but, if concocted extemporarily, it showed an amazing readiness of mind. Again, when Vereker had probed him discreetly about the presence of a youth resembling him in Wild Duck Wood that morning, he had promptly asked, "What was he wearing?" Was it again the simple directness of innocence or the perspicacity of a man wide awake to the value of the information that the answer might supply? Vereker, suddenly alive to possibilities, had lied. It was necessary to allay suspicion in order to assure the possible reappearance of that Norfolk jacket and cap. Lastly, there was Degerdon's almost supererogatory information that he had not risen till ten. Vereker was acutely aware of the psychological significance of unnecessary statement given with an air of conversational diffuseness. It was a common resort of the liar or deceiver. Degerdon was indirectly stating that he was in bed at the hour when Vereker was hinting that he was in Wild Duck Wood. This indirectness, too, to hide the fact that he was conscious of being suspected. The exasperating factor in this instance was that the statement was artless enough to be true. If the statement were untrue, Degerdon had momentarily forgotten that its falseness might easily be detected by a tactful questioning of Captain Fanshaugh. The oversight seemed too glaring to be associated with the preparedness of a resourceful man. And at that moment Vereker exclaimed:

"Algernon, you're a clumsy fool! There's a possibility, a decided possibility—"

But his soliloquy was cut short by a loud knock on his door and the entrance of Inspector Heather.

"Well, Heather, found the Colt automatic pistol?" asked Vereker when the officer had taken a seat.

"Not a trace, but I haven't given up hope, Mr. Vereker. I've some good news. On having another good look at that suit of clothes which Burton found, Goss noticed a cleaners' mark which he had skipped on the first kit inspection. Poor old Goss! We call him 'Speedy' at the Yard. He lived up to his name on this occasion, but I've a notion God helped him. Tracking down the shop where a suit has been cleaned and by whom it was left for that purpose is about as dull and long a job as it is important. Sometimes it is as hopeless as trying to find out where a box of matches was bought. 'Speedy' put his fist on the right egg almost before he was sure what we wanted him to do. He explained his good luck by ascribing it to a species of inspiration which he persists in calling a 'hinkling.' However, we've got the name of the gent who left that suit to be cleaned. It's Raoul Vernet. He was at an address in Woburn Square a fortnight ago, but has since vanished. I dare say he's back on the Continent now, and probably with Mrs. Armadale's necklace in his pocket."

"So you've added a third suspect to your dessert of Portwine and Peach," remarked Vereker.

"I'm beginning to think that the murder of Mr. Armadale has nothing to do with the burglary," said the inspector thoughtfully.

"Unless the bold seaman, Portwine, has got in touch with a gang of Continental crooks," suggested Vereker.

"There is that possibility. We shall begin to get a better view of things once we've tracked down these two mysterious people—or rather three, if we count Mr. Gastinne Renette."

"One more point, Heather, before I forget it. When you next see Mrs. Armadale's maid, will you find out from her whether her mistress had occasion to wear a fur coat, probably sable, on Wednesday night or more likely very early on Thursday morning? She will doubtless remember having put the coat away."

"She tidied a fur coat away all right," replied the inspector. "In the course of my chat with the little minx, I found out that Mrs. Armadale had slipped on her old sable coat over her bathing costume when going to and returning from the swimming-pool."

"H'm!" muttered Vereker reflectively. "I've taken a sudden objection to the number of sable coats in England during a period of financial depression. Every clue in this case seems about as tenuous as gossamer."

"Never mind, Mr. Vereker, get your fingers and toes into it and hang on," encouraged the inspector, and with a broad smile added, "I shouldn't worry much about facts. Double up on the psychology stunt. It's so juicy!"

"That's just where you rule-of-thumb men in the C.I.D. fall short, Heather," chaffed Vereker. "You're all right with the Bill Sykes type of criminal. You'll catch him once in a while if he makes a bloomer at his job. But, now that man has practically conquered the world and even sport begins to be tame, the field of crime lies open to daring and original spirits. Your misfortune is that they've got brains and mean to use them. It's about time I read that *Daily Express* cutting to you again."

Vereker's hand went in search of his pocket-book, but before he could extract it Heather had risen and with a cheery good night had vanished.

Chapter Eleven

The next day being Sunday, Vereker rose rather later than usual, and pondered over his programme for the day as he sat in his dressing-gown leisurely smoking after breakfast. The morning was brilliantly fine, and he had a resurgence of that spirit to paint which even in the midst of his most exciting preoccupations with criminal investigation would occasionally exercise a Circean enchantment over him. He had hardly dressed, however, when a servant from Vesey Manor brought him a note from Basil

Ralli asking him to come up at once if possible. Mrs. Armadale and Mr. Houseley had arrived very early by car, and the former had expressed a wish to see him before they left at noon. It was an opportunity that couldn't be missed, and at once Vereker dismissed all thoughts of painting from his mind and set out for the manor with a growing sense of excitement. On his arrival he was shown up to the solarium, where he found Ralli, Mrs. Armadale, and Houseley sitting at ease and chatting with undisguised cheerfulness. Mrs. Armadale was, as he had expected, typically English. Tall, beautifully proportioned, with fair hair almost bleached by exposure to sun and wind and contrasting with her tanned complexion, she proved that the feminine product of our country life could vie in beauty with the womanhood of any race on earth. Her wide-set, bluish-grey eyes met Vereker's with a frankness and composure that were completely disarming. The whole face seemed alight with a new-born zest in life which lent it a girlishness that belied even her thirty years. Vereker at once noticed that she had assumed no trace of mourning in her dress as a sop to public opinion, and even in these reasonable days it seemed to reveal a dash of courageous individuality. Stanley Houseley, on the other hand, was not what anyone would at first glance call a handsome man. The face was prognathous, and a large brown moustache seemed too obtrusive an adornment in its broad expanse. His eyes were shrewd and observant, but with a cold and somewhat aloof glance. In stature he was tall, and his broad shoulders were set in a curious stiffness of carriage which lent him an air of stateliness which bordered on pompousness.

No sooner had Vereker seated himself after the preliminaries of introduction than Ralli rose, as if by prearrangement, and said:

"Come along, Houseley, I know you're simply dying to look round the stables."

"Ah, yes, that would be rather jolly," replied Houseley mechanically, and rose.

When the two men had left the solarium, Mrs. Armadale drew her chair closer to Vereker's and at once broached the subject that was uppermost in her mind.

"Basil was telling me this morning at breakfast that you're an old friend of his and were helping in an unofficial way to solve the mystery of my husband's death."

"As a matter of fact, Mrs. Armadale, I'm down here as a representative of the *Daily Report*," corrected Vereker. "This again isn't strictly true, because I don't represent them in any capacity. The editor's a very old friend of mine and, knowing I'm intensely interested in the investigation of crime, especially murder, he kindly despatches me as a sort of reporter 'without portfolio' to carry out my own plans. It's very useful in a way, because the Press is allowed privileges that would be denied a purely private individual."

"But Basil says you're quite famous as an amateur detective," interrupted Mrs. Armadale.

"It's very good of him to boost me so strenuously. I've had some experience in the business, but I'm an artist by profession and not at all famous in either line."

"You're very modest about yourself, and it makes me feel we shall be good friends. But to come to the point. My husband's death has put me in a very terrible position, and I naturally want the dreadful mystery surrounding it cleared up as quickly as possible. Basil told me he trusted you implicitly and took the responsibility of letting you know all the family secrets. I was frightfully annoyed at first, but I see now that it was absolutely essential if you were to have a free hand. Naturally, I don't want the whole wretched business broadcasted, and in this, perhaps, you can help me. If there's anything you want to know, you must ask me frankly. I will be perfectly candid even if it's painful— which it's sure to be."

"I'm afraid I shan't spare you, Mrs. Armadale," said Vereker firmly. "It's rather embarrassing to be taken so readily into confidence, but whatever happens I can't allow myself to be influenced by graciousness. It wouldn't do in this job. This may seem infernally rude, but I haven't sought this interview. Now you know my attitude, the remedy is in your own hands. Do you wish it to continue?"

For a moment a bright flush suffused Mrs. Armadale's cheek and a pugnacious light flamed in her eyes. Then, as if shaking herself free of some unpleasant mental encumbrance, she turned quickly to Vereker.

"I hope you're not prejudiced against me," she said.

"Certainly not. An open mind is frequently as distasteful to anyone suffering from a sense of injustice. I simply want you to understand my point of view."

"I understand it quite clearly now, Mr. Vereker. So please commence."

"Good. If I'm to help you, my services may be something like a dentist's. You must screw up your courage. I've no spiritual anaesthetic I can administer beforehand. In the first place, were you in love with Sutton Armadale when he married you?"

"To start with, that's what we call in the hunting field a 'bullfinch' with a slippery take-off. Let me pull myself together and take it at a canter."

For some moments Angela Armadale was silent, her brow knit, her eyes fixed on the blue distance into which the rolling country faded southwards.

"It's so difficult to explain," she began hesitatingly. "I was twenty-eight at the time and really ought to have known exactly where I was. They say a woman's desperate at twenty-nine, but that wasn't the case with me. I had had innumerable proposals of marriage, but my outlook was perhaps too exacting. I'm afraid my views on men had been too much influenced by my reading. Instead of treating the novelist as a showman I'd treated him as a high priest. Even to-day when they allow themselves to be realistic about love, they grow stupidly romantic about intellect. There was 'Ugly' Norton, who was so handsome. He wrote infantile verses to me sprinkled with 'dear heart,' but his conversation was limited by the four walls of a stable. He was a frightful bore. 'Tushey' Vaughan, though otherwise lovable, drank too much and was secretly very religious. I nicknamed him 'Gin and Jesus.' He heard of it and never spoke to me again. Jim Cresswell was very jolly, but sprayed saliva when he used to tell me I was 'weally the pwettiest gel' he knew. Lawrie Beresford was ardent enough to be in love with me and at the same time keep some drab in town 'on principles of hygiene.' I didn't care for those principles. Stanley Houseley's a dear, but when he first kissed me I felt as if I'd been flung into impenetrable bush. So you see I was always a bit difficult to please. Then I met Sutton. He was considerably older than I, but I was very fascinated in spite of the fact that his nose grew hair. He was so wealthy and overpoweringly persistent. I surrendered. The rest of the story you know."

"Are you in love with Mr. Houseley now?"

"Yes, but I'm afraid I shall never be passionately in love with any man. I have spasms of ardour which are always cooled by squirts of chilly criticism. I can't help it. Cupid fitted me with a martingale."

"He loves you?"

"I'm sure he does. Stanley's affections are so deadly constant. Once I used to think he had no fire. I was mistaken; his apparent calm is only a matter of habitual control."

"He's going to marry you?"

"Yes. We decided on that months ago."

"Ah, I see," said Vereker. "You were heading for the Divorce Court?"

"I had determined that Sutton and I should end our relations one way or another. If he hadn't given cause, I'd have steeled myself up to doing so."

"Had he given cause?"

"Yes. He wasn't aware I knew, but I had all the evidence necessary."

"He was very fond of Miss Cazas," suggested Vereker.

"You've guessed right first shot. As a matter of fact, Edmée came on the scene most opportunely. Sutton and I were irrevocably estranged when she appeared. I told him I was going to end matters, and asked him if he'd divorce me if I gave him cause. On this point he was obstinate as a mule. He was terribly conventional in an old-fashioned way and dreaded what he called 'the odium of divorce proceedings.' He was also a man of very violent temper when roused, and told me that, if ever he found out that any man had betrayed him, he'd shoot him like a dog. Things seemed utterly hopeless, and I'd come to the conclusion that I'd have to live with him for the rest of my life. I would never have consented to live with any man irregularly. I've always acted on the principle of head before hindquarters. Then Edmée shot across the ride. It may sound very dreadful, but I was so glad that I not only acquiesced but secretly helped her by keeping out of the way."

"What's your opinion of Miss Cazas?"

"She's an enigma to me. At first I thought she wanted to arrange things so that Sutton would eventually marry her. This may have been her intention. Subsequently she may have discovered that Sutton wasn't having any or wouldn't fit in with her idea of being ridden with a loose rein. I don't know. She then simply exploited him financially. It became a matter of kisses for cash. At this juncture I stepped in and consulted my solicitor about divorce proceedings."

"How long ago was this?"

"Just a fortnight to-day."

"Your husband knew?"

"I told him last Wednesday."

"The day before his death! Do you think he committed suicide?"

"I really couldn't say."

"Had you told Miss Cazas about your intention of divorcing your husband?"

"Yes, and said I hoped she'd be happier with him than I had been."

"Was she pleased or otherwise?"

"She didn't seem overwhelmed with joy. She asked me why on earth I wanted to divorce him, and explained that they managed these things much better in France. I told her we weren't in France, and she merely replied, 'Tant pis,' and went off at once to talk matters over with Sutton. It wound up in fireworks; they hardly spoke to one another for the remainder of the evening. I have a suspicion he told her that he had no intention of marrying her, but I don't know."

"Did you hear anything during Wednesday night, or rather Thursday morning, which made you think that everything wasn't all right?"

For some moments Angela Armadale hesitated before replying, as if carefully weighing her words.

"Yes," she said at length; "at about three o'clock on Thursday morning I heard Sutton's voice in Edmée's room. Her suite was next to mine. The walls are fairly sound-proof, so that I couldn't distinguish his words, but he was evidently blazing angry. He always bellowed on such occasions. The altercation was brief, and a few minutes afterwards I heard her door slammed violently and everything was silent."

"You can't explain why your husband was in Miss Cazas' room at such an hour?"

"Sutton always 'chewed the rag' when he was thoroughly angry. He had evidently worked himself up to such a pitch that he could stand it no longer, and probably came down to renew the battle and get it off his chest."

"Mr. Houseley didn't stay here overnight?" asked Vereker casually.

"No. After tea he and I went for a stroll, and Sutton came upon us unexpectedly. Stanley had just kissed me at the moment, and of course there were explanations. I then told Sutton I was going to divorce him. Naturally, Stanley returned to town at once."

"In his own car?"

"No. Medlicott, my chauffeur, drove him over to the station in my Hispano-Suiza."

"Mr. Houseley's car is a Rover Meteor, I believe?"

"Yes," replied Mrs. Armadale, with curious hesitancy and a swift glance at Vereker.

"Now, Mrs. Armadale, I want you to be very frank with me. I'm going to ask you a very pointed question. Did you see Mr. Houseley again before your husband's death?"

The question had the effect of an electric shock. Mrs. Armadale uttered a little exclamation of pained surprise, and sat for a few moments with a dazed expression on her face. Then, with a supreme effort, she replied in a voice husky with trepidation:

"Yes."

"Where?"

"On the Nuthill road not a stone's-throw from the entrance gates. You can see the exact spot from here."

Vereker's searching glance swept her face, only to find an expression of placid resolution thereon. With amazing swiftness, she had regained control of herself.

"By prearrangement, of course?" he asked.

"Certainly."

"At what time was this?"

"It was exactly ten past two by the clock on Stanley's car.

"Were you long with him?"

"Only a few minutes. You'll probably want to know the reason for our meeting, and I don't see why I should make any further mystery about it. Before Stanley left for town, we had a very serious discussion about my plans for the future, and I told him I was going to leave Vesey Manor for good next morning. He asked me where I intended to stay, and I said I'd go and live with my aunt in Brixtow. He hinted that though it was the loveliest hunting country, it was too far away from town for his liking, and suggested my going down to stay with the Thorolds at Eastbourne. 'Black' Thorold is his brother-in-law. I agreed, and he arranged to fix things up on his arrival in town, return as soon as possible in his car, pick me up, and drive me straight away to Eastbourne. On working it out, he reckoned he'd be back at Vesey Manor about two o'clock in the morning, and said he would signal to me from the road by dimming his headlights. It may sound childish, but I was delighted with the idea of an elopement—I'm at times foolishly romantic—and I consented."

"Subsequently the romantic touch faded, and you changed your mind?" asked Vereker coldly.

"Romance has always been a faith rather than a touch with me," replied Mrs. Armadale, with a suspicion of tartness. "You're inclined to take all your fences at a gallop, Mr. Vereker. My change of plan wasn't due to a change of mind. After Stanley had left on Wednesday evening, my solicitor rang me up and asked me to meet him next morning. As the interview was imperative and he's a very busy man, I agreed and decided to forgo the fun of an elopement. I tried to get on the phone to Stanley, but didn't manage it. There was nothing left for me to do but tell him of my change of plan when he arrived at two in the morning."

"You didn't go down to Eastbourne to stay, after all?"

"No. After a confab with my solicitor it was decided that I should go to some friends of mine at Sutton Pragnell. He was of the opinion that it would be more diplomatic in the circumstances not to stay with Stanley's relatives. I don't know the fine points of divorce etiquette, but I submitted to his ruling."

"After hearing of your change of plan, did Mr. Houseley go on to Eastbourne?"

"No, he went back to town immediately."

"Did he say what time he got back?"

"About eight in the morning."

"He took six hours to cover twenty odd miles," commented Vereker, in a tone of surprise.

"He had a breakdown on the way, and poor Stanley knows nothing about machinery. Talking of his car, he said the brute first went lame in the off-fore, and after he had attended to this it was seized with something damnably like colic and wouldn't budge. He didn't know what to do, and declared if he'd had any chloral hydrate he'd have popped an ounce or two into the radiator by way of an experiment. Finally, he got the thing to go by accident, and managed to keep it running as far as Purley. There he garaged it and taxied home."

"On returning to the manor, you went back to bed?"

"Yes, and slept soundly till Basil waked me on Thursday morning."

"By what door of the house did you go out and come back, Mrs. Armadale?"

"By the drawing-room door on the terrace below us, and thence across the lawn and drive into the meadow."

"Not by the door near the gun-room?"

"No. There are only two keys to that door. Sutton always carried one on him, and Dunkerley had charge of the other."

"When you returned you neither saw nor heard anybody about the house? I have a suspicion that the burglary took place between two and three o'clock."

"No; but there was one thing I really couldn't account for. On returning to my room, I found that my light was on. I'm sure I switched it off before leaving."

"You had switched it on while dressing?"

"I hadn't undressed, but before going out I went to get a fur coat out of my dressing-room wardrobe."

"In your excitement you may have overlooked the light," suggested Vereker.

"That's possible, but I'm almost certain I didn't. I was particularly anxious not to attract attention, and I rarely lose my head. This burglary wouldn't have happened if Sutton had followed my advice. I had always told him we ought to have a night-watchman or even two, as the Bravingtons have, but he didn't like the idea—said it turned a house into a bank or warehouse."

"After retiring to your room on the first occasion did you see any of the other guests in the house again?"

"No. Sutton opened my door at one o'clock and said good night very amiably for appearances' sake. I never saw him alive again," replied Mrs. Armadale.

Vereker was not slow to notice the slight catch in her voice.

"Did anyone else in the house know of your intention to elope during the early hours of Thursday morning?" "Yes. On Wednesday evening I asked my cousin, Aubrey Winter, to tell Sutton next day. I didn't want to give the poor chap any more pain or trouble than I could possibly help. It was bad enough as it was."

"Where did you keep your key of the library safe?"

"Usually in my purse. I sometimes hid it under my bedroom carpet when I didn't wish to carry it about with me."

"Has anyone ever seen you put it under the carpet?"

"No one to my knowledge. I always took jolly good care about that."

"Did you wear your pearls on Wednesday?"

"Yes; during the afternoon, at the Flower Show prize distribution, and I locked them up myself in the library safe just before I went to bathe in the swimming- pool."

"Was anyone in the library at the time?"

"Yes. Mr. Degerdon and Miss Cazas were hunting for a book. I asked them which one they were searching for, and Mr. Degerdon replied, 'Dekker's *She knew her Business*.' They both laughed heartily, but I couldn't see the joke. I think they were pulling my leg. Have you heard of such a book by a Mr. Dekker?"

"They were joking, I should say," replied Vereker solemnly, and asked, "After locking up your pearls, Mrs. Armadale, where did you put your safe key that evening?"

"I slipped it into my jewel-case on the dressing-table in my bedroom. There was nothing of any great value in that jewel-case, because I had put all the other jewellery that Sutton had given me in the safe, knowing that I should never wear it again. I had told Sutton I was giving all his presents back to him."

"You were being rather Quixotic, weren't you?"

"It's a matter of taste, I suppose, Mr. Vereker. I was doing my best to live up to my romantic faith."

"Miss Cazas would doubtless have admired your estimable tenets had Mr. Armadale lived," said Vereker dryly.

"Possibly," laughed Mrs. Armadale in reply, "but one never knows. Edmée is the funniest mixture of unexpected fineness and mercenary vulgarity I've ever met. If Sutton had offered them to her, she might have flung the lot at his head with contempt, or she might have taken them and pawned the lot to pay off her debts."

"Is she in debt?"

"Always. She calls them her 'financial scapular,' and says it's only when you owe tradespeople money that they're really courteous to you. You've not met Miss Cazas?"

"Not yet. I hope to very soon. A great friend of mine says she's very fascinating."

"She is. I warn you to be careful. And she's really beautiful."

"I'm very susceptible to beauty, Mrs. Armadale," replied Vereker gallantly, "but I don't think anything Continental can hold a candle to the dazzling fairness of our own English type."

"Neither do I," replied Mrs. Armadale, as a mischievous smile twitched at the corner of her lips and flickered in the shining blue depths of her eyes. "If there's anything more you'd like to know and that I can tell you, just ring me up at Sutton Pragnell 44; or if you want to be very careful, just let me know where I can meet you in town. I want to get this horrible business over and forget it for ever."

"Thanks, Mrs. Armadale. There may be one or two points on which you may be able to help me, but I shan't trouble you if I can possibly help it."

Ralli and Houseley now returned to the solarium, and conversation for a while became general. Later, Ralli and Mrs. Armadale excused themselves. The former had expressed a wish that his aunt should accompany him to the library and check the items of jewellery which the burglar in his haste had omitted to take from the separate drawer in which they had been locked. It was an opportunity for which Vereker had been longing, and he decided to make use of it.

"Mrs. Armadale and I have been discussing the events of Wednesday night and Thursday morning—" he began.

"I'm quite aware of that," interrupted Houseley, "and I've already expressed my opinion both to her and Ralli, that I think it's most inadvisable to chatter about this business to people who're not concerned. It's bad enough to have to go through a mauling by the police without being questioned by a lot of meddling outsiders."

"Your point of view's excusable," replied Vereker, ignoring this rebuff, "but you're a bit wide of the mark in calling me a meddling outsider. Mere politeness—"

"Then in what capacity are you acting?" asked Houseley, turning abruptly and facing Vereker truculently.

"Acting for the Press, I think I can spare you all a lot of pain by suppressing ail sorts of irrelevant family history. Again, I'm a great friend of Inspector Heather, who is in charge of the police investigations. The police don't always let the public know all their agents in such a business as this."

"You're a C.I.D. man in reality, then?" asked Houseley.

"I'd rather not answer that question," replied Vereker, with an air of profound mystery which immediately had the desired effect.

"Ah, I take your point, I take your point," said Houseley. "If there's anything in reason you'd like to know, I'll tell you—but with reservations, strictly with reservations, you understand."

"I think you'll be wise to leave out any question of reservations, Mr. Houseley," said Vereker aggressively. "Your own position in this business isn't exactly that of a popular hero. The police know that your relations with Mrs. Armadale, even before her husband's murder, were rather more intimate than those of a friend."

"I'm not the least bit ashamed of it, either. I don't want to be a hero to any smelly rabble," said Houseley.

"Love is the devil's own advocate to the lover, but his pleadings don't sound so irresistible in a court of law," remarked Vereker quietly.

"Unfortunately there's something in what you say," replied Houseley reflectively, and in a more amiable mood. "But, to get to business, what exactly do you want to know?"

"On Wednesday evening you returned to town after rather an unfortunate contretemps near Wild Duck Wood," commenced Vereker relentlessly.

"Who the devil told you that? Can Angela have been so damnably foolish?" exclaimed Houseley, with unconcealed alarm.

"You needn't blame Mrs. Armadale for being indiscreet. We knew all about the reason for your sudden return to town, Mr. Houseley, not long after we commenced our investigations. To put it very bluntly, you, a guest, were making love to your host's wife. He had caught you in an unguarded moment kissing her. You must have felt most uncomfortable and, I should say, rather small. I presume there were explanations and that you decided it was politic to return to town at once."

Mr. Stanley Houseley looked up at Vereker with a sense of growing uneasiness. At that moment the meticulous care of police methods and their comprehensive range gave him the sensation of being helplessly at the mercy of the law.

"I returned to town immediately after that unfortunate contretemps, as you choose to call it," he said sullenly.

"Shortly after two o'clock your car, a Rover Meteor, was seen by a Nuthill mechanic, who was returning home from Godstone, not very far from the entrance gates to this house," continued Vereker.

"That's so. I was there."

"I imagine you returned to town after your brief interview with Mrs. Armadale."

"How do you know Angela was there?" asked Houseley, with another start of surprise.

"She was seen talking to you. Everybody in this district knows Mrs. Armadale, I should say. When she left you to return to the house, you motored back to town by Godstone, Catherham, and Purley?"

"Yes, I took that road."

"The distance from here is, say, twenty-five miles, roughly. At what time did you arrive in town?"

At this question all Mr. Houseley's truculence returned. Turning sharply to Vereker, he said brusquely:

"I don't feel disposed to discuss that matter at the moment. If it's necessary for me to answer such a question later, say in a court of law, I'm prepared to do so. It's very easy to be tripped up by some clever counsel browbeating you on the subject of times. I'm not going to make inadvertent slips in such an important matter. Men have been hanged before now through trifling discrepancies in their statements of times."

"Of course you're not compelled to answer any questions put by me, Mr. Houseley. In this matter, I'm only doing all I can to help Mr. Ralli and Mrs. Armadale."

"I'm rather dubious of the nature of the help you offer. It's an old detective confidence trick. I'm not such a damned fool as I look."

"Possibly not," remarked Vereker, smiling at the doubtful nature of the compliment. "In any case you'd be home in an hour unless you had a breakdown."

"Why not admit that the police know all about it? You probably know from a garage proprietor in Purley that I left my car there to be overhauled."

"Well, Mr. Houseley, you must admit that the police are not such fools as they look."

"They're just too damned clever by half. This bally country is police-ridden. In another ten years it'll be as bad as Germany," remarked Houseley bitterly.

"That's more than likely, considering the unchecked increase of crimes of violence," said Vereker in a friendlier tone, and asked, "Did you know Mr. Armadale well?"

"I knew him less than I liked him—an atrocious bounder always! He couldn't even die like a gentleman."

"He was a very keen sportsman, I believe," suggested Vereker mischievously.

"A what, did you say? Sportsman? Great Scott! He didn't know the difference between a horse's withers and its gaskins, and for a long time thought a horse's frog was a euphemism for something unmentionable. At a meet he would coffee-house till the last minute, during a draw he'd chatter like a magpie, and he was the best man at overriding hounds I've ever met! Have you seen his mare, Proserpine?"

"No," said Vereker, pleased that he had turned the conversation into a congenial channel.

"Well, Armadale fancied himself at times as a judge of horseflesh. He bought Proserpine. All I can say is, see her and die in agony. I'm sure a well-bred pack would turn up their noses at her as meat."

"Still, you must admit he was a first-class shot," continued Vereker complacently.

"Who told you that? My hat! But I mustn't let myself go. *De mortuis—*"

"I thought it was generally admitted that there were few finer shots with an automatic pistol," suggested Vereker.

"Sorry. I took you up wrong," said Houseley. "That's quite possible. It's a crook's weapon."

"Have you ever handled one, Mr. Houseley? I don't know much about them."

"Oh, well, yes, I've done quite a lot of shooting with automatics. Some years ago we used to frequent a shooting-range between Leicester Square and Piccadilly Circus. I forget the name of the street, but it was quite handy to our club. For a time it was quite the rage among the younger members to challenge one another to shoot for a fiver. I used to win quite a lot of money at it. Just a lark to pass the time, you know. You can't dignify pistol practice with the name of sport."

"Do you think it possible that Mr. Armadale committed suicide?" asked Vereker suddenly.

"I've thought that from the very first," said Houseley, with conviction. "I don't think I'm letting out a secret to you when I tell you that Angela was going to divorce him. He knew it would hold up his scandalous behaviour with this unspeakable little Belgian cabaret girl, or whatever she likes to call herself, to the public eye, and he simply refused to take the fence."

"You were always very friendly with him?"

"I put up with him for Angela's sake. We were polite rather than cordial—until Wednesday evening. Then I gave him a bit of my mind, and I didn't mince matters, I can assure you."

"You're a friend of Captain Fanshaugh's, I believe?"

"Oh, yes, 'Fruity' and I have always got on well together. He's a white man—fine horseman, good shot, good polo player, and a gentleman. I like him very much, though he's inclined to measure everything with a 'jobbing' spear, if you know what I mean."

"You don't like Miss Cazas?"

"I can't stand her. Thinks herself the deuce of a success, mark you. Fanshaugh told me that she made them all laugh till they cried mimicking me on Wednesday night. Guttersnipe kind of humour I call it. She often mimics her mother walking to raise a laugh. Could low-bred vulgarity go further? She's pretty enough in a common kind of way, but has a price ticket tied to her charms. Young Winter introduced her into the Armadale circle. He's only a youngster and may be forgiven for running riot before having had blood. Angela didn't object, for subtle reasons of her own, but Armadale's choice of friends was notorious. He had a predilection for anyone who looked as if he had come up a drain-pipe."

For some moments both men were silent, and then Angela Armadale stepped out on to the solarium, accompanied by Ralli.

"Stanley, it's nearly twelve o'clock. I think we ought to get a move on," she said. "I'm quite ready, so come and start up your car."

"Right-o, dear," replied Houseley, and rose from his chair.

Chapter Twelve

On the departure of Houseley and Mrs. Armadale, Ralli took Vereker by the arm and led him into the drawing-room.

"Well, what do you think of old 'Hell-for-leather'?" he asked.

"I haven't quite made up my mind. Opinionated, with a turn for rudeness at unexpected moments. Not too subtle at first glance, but possesses a lot of native cunning. Thinks a sporting vocabulary sets 'the guinea stamp,' and certainly eats too much. Plenty of pluck and determination and very single-minded. A supporter of Church, State, and the Distilling Industry!"

"He annoys me," said Ralli, "with his confounded assurance on every subject under the sun. Dawn of intelligence with finality in words. Did he start on the worn-out topic of motor-cars being used as covert hacks?"

"No. I led him fairly well along the line I wished until I mentioned sport, and then I let him have his head."

"I bet he bolted! Poor Angela, I wonder how she'll get on with him. He's so glossily polite, and women only love politeness as they do chocolates—to be eaten with the latest from Mudie's; if it interferes with the passional life, it's an impertinent irrelevancy. Still, Stanley's not a bad sort on the whole. Let's forget him. I've some information that may be of use to you."

At once Vereker grew alert.

"I'm glad you're taking an interest in the game. What's the news?" he asked.

Ralli pulled a bunch of keys from his pocket and, picking out one of them, held it up for Vereker's inspection.

"You see that key? It's a key which Sutton always kept on this bunch, and used for letting himself in and out by the door near the gun-room. After you'd gone yesterday, I happened to be passing that door and suddenly decided to enter the house by it. You can imagine my surprise when I found the key was no longer on the bunch."

"Was it there when you took charge of the bunch?"

"It couldn't have been; the bunch hasn't been out of my hands since I took charge of it."

"How did it return?"

"Dunkerley brought it to me this morning. One of the housemaids had picked it up when cleaning out Captain Fanshaugh's room the other day."

"Whereabouts in the room was it?"

"Under the bed."

"That's certainly remarkable, Ralli! Perhaps Fanshaugh borrowed the key from Sutton for some purpose or other."

"Most improbable. But, if he had, why didn't he return it to me?"

"Let me have the key," said Vereker, "and don't say a word to anyone about it on any account. It may mean nothing at all, and it may mean the devil of a lot. Is there only one other key to that door?"

"Yes, and Dunkerley has it. I asked him about it when he returned this one."

Taking the key from Ralli and slipping it on his own key-ring, Vereker rose and took his leave. He was eager to see Inspector Heather, and hoped to catch him before he left the "Silver Pear Tree" on his day's work. On his arrival at the inn, however, the detective was out. Inquiry elicited that he had set out after an early breakfast and had not yet returned. He was expected back to lunch at one. There was nothing to do but wait, and Vereker went up to his room, where he poured himself out a whisky and soda and settled himself in an easy-chair. His mind was full of his morning's experiences, and his thoughts at once reverted to his interview with Mrs. Armadale. Her shining beauty disposed his susceptible nature in her favour, but there were one or two facts that had emerged from their conversation which were an interesting disclosure. That she could be coldly calculating to attain her ends was revealed by her allowing to go unchecked a friendliness between Sutton Armadale and Miss Edmée Cazas until it had ripened into a guilty liaison. Her attitude to a strict rectitude of conduct even in an unhappy marriage had been shown by her seeking divorce as the only escape from the spiritual disgust attendant on such a union. She was without doubt free from any mercenary taint and seemed to possess a warm and generous heart. Yet there was at the core of her nature something frozen, some gelid area which had never thawed under the glorious flame of a natural passion. Even of the man who had married her, she had admitted that the fascination he exercised was tempered by the peculiarity that his "nose grew hair." She was one of those who look at the theatrical scenery of life too closely.

From Angela Armadale, Vereker's thoughts moved by a natural transition to Stanley Houseley. He was a type, and not an uncommon type, whose opinions are formed for him by his "set." These opinions solidify into unshakable convictions in early manhood and obviate the pain of further thinking. The set has a code of behaviour which is inviolate and, after all criticism, offers a workable philosophy of life for minds that find abstractions intolerable. And the best of them, thought Vereker, cannot be bettered anywhere.

The arrival of Inspector Heather cut short his reverie. The police officer was all bustle and cheerfulness, which was a sure indication that he had struck an exciting trail.

"There's a sprightliness in the step, Heather," said Vereker, on seeing him, "a movement from the fantastic toe to the more fantastic buttock which tells me that things are going well. I know the meaning of that choreographic grace, and the fluttering of your moustache drives me to extempore poetical composition:

> 'And that cornuted hair you call moustache,
> Which hides your mouth—or is it just a gash?
> When coy cooks say it gives your kissing savour,
> You, foolish, think they're working up a 'pash'
> For you or for constabulary cash,
> When all the time it's for a beery flavour!

Help yourself to a Scotch, and report."

"Nothing definite, Mr. Vereker, but a general advance. We've got on the track of Mr. Jonathan Portwine, and I shall run up to London first thing tomorrow and listen to what he has got to say for himself. There's the inquest in the afternoon, which will simply be adjourned, but which I must attend. Peach has returned from his quest for a job, and his general demeanour shows he's in a very ugly mood. We're hot on the footsteps of Mr. Raoul Vernet. The yeast begins to work!"

"But, as a foreigner resident here, isn't Vernet registered?" asked Vereker.

"He's a bird of passage like many Continental criminals. They manage to land in England by a day excursion, get lost, and return to the Continent in the same way at a later date."

"Where did you find Portwine?"

"In Limehouse. In a boarding-house 'where sailor men reside and where are men from all the ports from Mississip to Clyde,' as Mr. Kipling puts it, or in words to that effect."

"Heather, I feel sure you'll spend your retirement writing verse—instead of reminiscences. Sonnets from Scotland Yard, eh?"

"I think 'Heather Honey' would be more poetical," replied the inspector, with ludicrous gravity, "but we're anticipating. Any news from your front?"

"Wait a minute. Have you traced that automatic?"

"The answer's in the negative, but I've an idea we'll lay hands on it yet."

"More anticipating! Have you found out who Gastinne Renette is?"

"Yes, Mr. Vereker, a very famous gunsmith in Paris!" replied the inspector, and burst into hearty laughter. "I'm sure Mr. Gastinne Renette is not the man we want."

"Well, I'm damned!" exclaimed Vereker, with disappointment. "Never mind, it's only another refractory piece that didn't fit into the picture puzzle. I must pin my faith to Raoul Vernet as a suitable alternative. He's known to the Sûreté, I suppose?"

"They've an idea who the gentleman is. He's not French but a Belgian, and hails from Louvain. We shall probably hear more of him later. He was a jeweller's assistant who turned crook, and is an expert on pearls!"

"That looks promising, Heather," said Vereker, with enthusiasm.

"In connection with Portwine it's a good line, because Vernet is very friendly with seamen of many nationalities. He's a 'man of infinite resource and sagacity,' as some one has said."

"Your pal Kipling again, Heather, if I'm not mistaken. Still, I'm going to complicate matters now. Did you get the number of that Rover Meteor, which you located on the Nuthill road on Thursday morning?"

"Yes. That car is still in a garage in Purley and belongs to Mr. Stanley Houseley. I shall call on him for a little explanation."

"It's not in a garage in Purley now, Heather. It turned up at Vesey Manor with its owner and Mrs. Armadale this morning. I've seen them both."

"And had polite conversation. What fruit?"

"He was on the Nuthill road at two o'clock on Thursday morning for the purpose of an elopement with his lady-love. I should like to elope with her myself, but let that pass. The lady changed her plans at the last minute because she had to interview her solicitor next morning about divorce proceedings against her husband."

"Good Lord!" exclaimed Heather. "That's news, if you like."

"One moment, inspector. Mr. Houseley said goodbye and went back to town."

"What time did he get back?" asked Heather.

"Eight o'clock—six hours to cover twenty-five miles. There's something about that which requires explanation. I tried to get one from Mr. Houseley, but he suddenly grew truculent, though he indirectly admitted he'd had a breakdown."

"Of course the breakdown may have been faked. On the other hand, he may be telling the truth, especially if he's one of those owner-drivers who boast they're born motorists and drive by instinct."

"Another point, Heather. This Mr. Houseley knows a good deal about automatic pistols, and in his younger days was, as he admits himself, a very fair shot!"

"The devil he was! But no, Mr. Vereker, I can't feel that you're on the right track."

"On the contrary, I'm certain I'm somewhere near it. By a process of elimination, I hope I shall get there. Again, there's the clue of that side door of the manor, near the gun-room, which Frederick is positive he bolted securely on Wednesday night. An incident has happened in connection with the key of that door which is mysterious, to say the least of it. When Mr. Ralli looked for that key on his bunch yesterday, he found to his surprise that it wasn't there, and he's convinced it hasn't been on the bunch since that bunch came into his charge. It was found on Thursday, the day of the murder, under the bed in the room which Captain Fanshaugh occupied on Wednesday night."

"But you don't suspect Captain Fanshaugh of having any hand in this job?" asked the inspector.

"I suspect anyone and every one. Now you've thoroughly questioned the servants in the house, do you think they're all right, Heather?"

"Right as rain! Dunkerley, the butler; Frederick and George, the footmen; Parsons, Mr. Armadale's valet; Ted, the pantry boy; the grooms, stablemen, cooks, maids—every one is above suspicion."

"Well, I'm leaving that end of the business to you. Mr. Armadale was rather a gay bird, and from his past history we know he was not above paying attentions to a pretty maid. You've made sure that history hasn't repeated itself and roused jealousy?"

"I've thrashed that out pretty thoroughly. There was nothing that gave me a single clue. We're left with seven possibles among the men: Portwine, Peach, Ralli, Degerdon, Fanshaugh, Winter, and Raoul Vernet; among the women, Mrs. Armadale and Miss Cazas."

"You've forgotten some one, Heather, and that's Miss Trixie Collyer, his illegitimate daughter."

"I took her into consideration very early in the day, but couldn't spot a strong enough motive."

"You're forgetting, Heather, that Armadale objected very strongly to Ralli's entanglement with her. The young lady knew that Mr. Armadale stood in the way of a very desirable marriage for her. Now that he's out of the way, her dream is going to come true."

"I figured that all out, but working on the principle that women very rarely use fire-arms, I'm rather inclined to suspect Mr. Ralli than her."

"It's a shaky principle, Heather. You remember Mrs. Caillaux, who shot the editor of the *Figaro*; and recently in France and on the Riviera similar shootings have taken place. Miss Collyer, brought up as a game-keeper's daughter, would almost instinctively turn to fire-arms as a means of accomplishing her ends."

"You're casting too wide a net, Mr. Vereker. In your inquiry you must try and keep in view that the murder is connected with the burglary until you've definitely proved it isn't."

"I've worked up a nice little solution of the burglary, Heather, but I must make one or two more moves before I can confidently disclose it to you. It may be connected with Mr. Armadale's murder. If it is, you'll have to do your damnedest to lay M. Raoul Vernet by the heels as quickly as possible. By the way, a second car, a Trojan, stopped on the Nuthill road on Thursday morning. Any news of it?"

"Oh, yes; a stolen Trojan car was found abandoned by the side of the road near Whyteleafe. Our lines seem to be converging, Mr. Vereker," said the inspector, rubbing his hands briskly together, "and I think the fact entitles us both to one more toothful of your excellent Scotch before lunch."

After this meal, Inspector Heather set off for Nuthill Police Station, and Vereker, feeling rather at a "loose end," thrust his sketch-book into his pocket and made his way to his sketching ground in a clearing of Wild Duck Wood. The spot, apart from its pictorial value, drew him on account of the mysterious incident that had occurred there on his last visit. Clear-cut in his visual memory was a brown Harris Norfolk jacket and the set of a young man's head and shoulders. On encountering Ralph Degerdon, some hours later at Vesey Manor, that vignette had been recalled with startling vividness. Degerdon was then wearing light grey tweeds and a soft felt hat, but the carriage of head and torso were similar, if not the same. Subsequent conversation had gone far to invalidate Vereker's surmise that it was Degerdon he had seen, but an uneasy doubt haunted his mind. He had brought with him the shooting-stick which Ralli had given him, and found it a fair substitute for a sketching-stool. As he was making his rapid charcoal studies on tinted Michallet, he was struck a sharp stinging blow on the ear by a missile which, on investigation, proved to be an acorn. As there was a complete absence of wind, he was at first rather surprised, but absorption in his work soon erased the incident from his mind. A second acorn, which hit his sketch-book squarely in the centre and bounded into the air in front of him, caused him to rise and glance swiftly round. There was no one in sight; but, guessing that the marksman must be some practical joker in concealment, he thrust his sketch-book into his pocket and was about to beat the surrounding covert. At that moment, from a clump of guelder, there appeared the grinning face of Captain "Fruity" Fanshaugh.

"Not a bad shot, Fanshaugh," said Vereker, laughing.

"You were a sitter, Vereker," replied Fanshaugh, and emerged into the open.

"I didn't expect to meet you here," remarked Vereker.

"I lunched with a friend over at the Guards' Depot at Caterham, and, as I felt like exercise, I thought I'd make a cross-country journey back to Nuthill. There's nothing like trudging to give a man an accurate knowledge of his country. The best man to hounds I ever knew regularly spent some days foot-following during the cub-hunting season. I see you're sketching. Ralli told me you were a painter, not a 'real one as climbs up a ladder,' but a High Art walla. Have you seen him lately?"

"I saw him this morning. He asked me to run over to the manor and meet Mrs. Armadale and your friend, Houseley."

"Ah, it does a man good to see Angela. There's my ideal of a woman, plenty of bone and full of quality. How's she standing the strain of this affair?"

"Admirably, I should say."

"Glad to hear it. And her *cavaliere servente*, Houseley? More attentive than ever now there's hope, I'll bet. By the way, I hear you're very friendly with the Yard inspector whose down here on this Armadale job. Has he got any nearer to a solution of the puzzle?"

"He doesn't say very much, but I gathered from his cheerful manner this morning that he's hot on the trail."

"Has he found the pistol yet?" asked Fanshaugh casually.

"I'm almost certain he has; he's so chirpy. They've been scouring these woods and fields very thoroughly," said Vereker, with an observant eye for the effect of his words.

"Very disturbing for game," remarked Fanshaugh, with a note of uneasiness which did not escape the alert Vereker.

"I suppose so," he agreed, and added, "From what I gathered in our chat this morning, one of the principal clues in the case has something to do with the side door to the manor—the one near the gun-room."

"By Jove!" exclaimed Fanshaugh, with ill-concealed surprise. "But what's the clue?"

"I couldn't say exactly, but there's some question about the bolts," replied Vereker cautiously. "Have you ever used that door or noticed anything peculiar about it, Fanshaugh?"

"Never been through it in my life. Sutton had a weakness for that door. He used to call it his own particular postern, and always carried the key to it on his person."

"Do you know if there were other keys to it?"

"I've never heard of one, but there are sure to be others. Angela would be certain to have a duplicate."

Producing the bunch from his pocket, Vereker picked out the key which Ralli had given him that morning and said:

"I wonder if this key's one of them."

"That's one," said Fanshaugh eagerly. "Where the devil did you find it?"

"I didn't exactly find it," replied Vereker, with a mingled sensation of surprise and satisfaction. "Has one been lost?"

"How the devil should I know?" exclaimed Fanshaugh clumsily.

"Of course not," agreed Vereker amiably, "but you feel certain that it is a key to the side door near the gun-room?"

"I'm almost certain," assured Fanshaugh, with painful hesitation, as he looked shrewdly at Vereker. Had he been sufficiently observant and had he known his companion better, he would have noticed a slight tension of the masseter muscles—the only indication in Vereker's face of the sudden thrill of excitement which he was rigidly suppressing.

"I must hand it to Ralli when I see him again," said Vereker, with well-feigned calm, as he returned the bunch to his pocket.

"It may have an important bearing on the case. How did you get hold of it?" asked Fanshaugh, with continued interest.

"It was lying on an occasional table in the room which Ralli has put at my disposal at the manor while I'm knocking about this neighbourhood," replied Vereker unabashedly.

"I'm calling at the manor on my way back. Shall I hand it over for you?" came the polite inquiry.

"If you'd be so good," said Vereker, detaching the key from his bunch.

For a few seconds he stood hesitant, and then handed the key to Fanshaugh who, remarking that he must be back in Nuthill for tea, took his departure and was soon lost to sight.

"Not very complimentary to my intelligence," muttered Vereker reflectively, and dismissing the subject from his mind glanced curiously round.

"There's something mysterious about this spot!" he exclaimed. "It's a spot that wishes to be visited, but I'm afraid there's no Celtic rock-a-by-baby spoof about its uncanny attraction. First an unknown with a close resemblance—a shaving-mirror resemblance—to Degerdon; then came Ralli, and now Fanshaugh!" He glanced round and noticed the trampled state of the bracken on all sides. Heather's minions had evidently done their work thoroughly on the off-chance of finding a weapon that had been flung away by the man who had shot Armadale. On thinking it over, Vereker was struck by the amount of labour expended on such an uncertain assumption. Still, experience had evidently proved to the police that in a case of murder the culprit's first idea was to get rid of the deadliest link connecting him with the crime. If Sutton's murderer had followed such a course, what more likely place than this covert with its dense undergrowth in which to bury the instrument for an indefinite length of time. Vereker's interview with Captain Fanshaugh had completely driven all desire for sketching out of his mind. Leaving the wood, he made his way up to Collyer's cottage with the intention of having a talk with the gamekeeper. Collyer was out, but Trixie Collyer came to the door, clad in a white overall and with palette and brushes in her hand. She asked Vereker into the little sitting-room of the cottage, which served as her studio and where she was busy at a flower study composed of pale yellow dahlias and Michaelmas daisies.

"You mustn't be too critical, Mr. Vereker," she said, as he examined her work. "Mr. Ralli has been telling me about your fame as an artist, and it rather frightens me."

Vereker suggested a slight alteration in tone values and was diplomatically encouraging. During this conversation, he took the opportunity of having a good look at Basil Ralli's fiancée and was struck by her extraordinary beauty. Her jet black hair, worn short and waved, reflected pale blue in the high lights from the general colouring of the room, and in contrast her skin shone almost luminously white. Scarlet lips, rather sensuous in their fullness, almost suggested artifice by their natural brilliance, and her eyes were the large liquid eyes so often seen in Turkish women. As Vereker talked, she stood gazing at her painting with a frown of dissatisfaction on her face.

"It's no good," she exclaimed at last, as she flung down her brushes on her painting table. "I'm too upset to work."

"All our nerves are a bit on edge at present," commented Vereker, "over this terrible business at the manor."

"I'm not worrying very much about that, Mr. Vereker," she hastened to inform him. "Mr. Armadale was my father, and in a way I think he was genuinely fond of me, but I can't say I returned his affection. Until recently I didn't know he was my father, and, when I found out, the little affection I had for him vanished. Unknown to anyone, I went up to Hartlepool to see my mother. My curiosity was very natural, I think. I found her a very unhappy woman, a drudge degraded by her life with a drunken sailor who beat her regularly. Indirectly my father had brought her to this. She confided in me that she had been passionately in love with him and still loved him. Not once did she blame him for his seduction of her, for that's what, in plain words, his conduct amounted to. He had pensioned her off with three pounds a week, and left me to be brought up by his gamekeeper's wife. For myself, I didn't care two raps, and I'm grateful to him for my education, but his wretched treatment of my mother I couldn't forgive. So you see, Mr. Vereker, if I'm not greatly upset by my father's death, some of my callousness may be forgiven."

"He was rather unhappy about your friendship with his nephew, I believe," said Vereker, and was surprised at the effect produced by his words.

At once the girl's whole frame grew rigid, her fingers were clenched in anger, and her large eyes lit with dangerous fire.

"Beast!" she exclaimed vehemently. "Not only had he made a mess of my mother's life but he was determined to spoil mine. He told Basil when he discovered he was growing fond of me that I was his illegitimate brat by a little trollop who had been his first wife's maid. He spoke of my mother as if she were a common street woman!"

For some seconds the girl's beauty was convulsed by the ugliness of an overwhelming anger, and then, conscious that she had let her feelings carry her away, she suddenly ceased talking and recovered her self-control with amazing swiftness.

"I'm sorry, Mr. Vereker," she said calmly, "but my paddy gets the better of me when I sense an injustice. I must try and forget all about it now."

"The only thing to do," remarked Vereker sympathetically.

"There's still a fly in the ointment," continued Miss Collyer. "Now that everything looks more hopeful for me than ever it has done, I'm being pestered by another suitor whom I don't care two straws for. His name is Frank Peach, and his mother is my mother's sister. I've done my best to be friendly and decent towards him, but we're worlds apart, and there's something strange about him which gives me the creeps. I'm really horribly afraid of him. When I found that his feelings towards me were growing warmer than I cared for, I tried my hardest to choke him off. It only made matters worse. He simply wouldn't be choked off. He grew jealous and sulked. As long as I remember, he has been subject to morose fits, during which he moons about alone and speaks to no one. There's a trace of insanity in his family on his father's side. However, since I told him that I was in love with Mr. Ralli, he has begun to threaten us both. This morning he met us on our walk before breakfast and created a terrible scene. It was all I could do to prevent the two men from coming to blows. So you see why I'm upset, Mr. Vereker."

"I can quite understand your feelings," remarked Vereker.

At that moment Collyer came into the cottage. He was looking worried, and on Vereker's tactful reference to the fact, he smiled.

"You see, Mr. Vereker, I don't know from Adam what Mr. Ralli's going to do about the shootin' this year," he said. "He don't seem to be terrible keen on shootin' at all; partridges is very poor, and all this trampin' about coverts ain't doing a heap of good. I wish they'd find that dratted pistol and go back to London first train. My pheasants ain't had no peace of mind for the last week."

"I'm afraid I'm one of the offenders, Collyer."

"That you ain't, sir. You don't do no harm sitting quiet like and painting portraits of trees and such. Birds don't mind that. It's all this rampaging about and 'ollerin' to one another. There's too many people allowed about, and if I had my way I'd stop Captain Fanshaugh and Mr. Degerdon makin' a right-of-way through Duck Wood on to the Godstone road. I've just seen the fust-named gent paradin' about the estate as if the place was his. Mr. Armadale was easy-going, but Mr. Ralli's going to be sloppy."

"I met Captain Fanshaugh on my way here through Wild Duck Wood. He said he was returning from Caterham and cutting across country to Nuthill."

"Then the gentleman ain't particular about the truth," said Collyer. "He hadn't been to no Caterham. I saw him coming up from Godstone way through my glasses, and that's just opposite direction."

"You don't seem to like Captain Fanshaugh, Collyer," said Vereker, with a laugh.

"Well, sir, he's meddlesome, that's what he is. He got on the soft side of Mr. Armadale, and not content with running the stables he wanted to run my job as well. I told him straight, sir, that he'd better mind his own business, which was shootin' when the season came round, and leave the keepin' to me. We had words over the partridges. He asked me one day, 'Do you know the chipped-egg system, Collyer?' and I says, 'Yes, sir, and I could teach you how to suck 'em.' He was mad with me for a bit, but I heard him tellin' the guv'nor about it later as a joke. The guv'nor gave him too much rope, and as I reckoned left him a tidy bit in his will."

"Oh, I didn't know that, Collyer," said Vereker, with surprise.

"It's true. I heard Mr. Armadale givin' the instructions to Mr. Pettifer, his solicitor, when that gentleman came down for a day's pheasant shootin' last winter."

"Do you know how much he left him?"

"That I couldn't say, sir. They was walking in front of me on the way to Hanging Covert, and as we was going downwind I couldn't catch all as was said, but I heard the word thousand. 'May it do him good,' says I to myself; 'I dessay he needs it, for he's always tryin' to make a bit for hisself at horse-coping.'"

"Have Mr. Degerdon and Captain Fanshaugh always made Wild Duck Wood a short-cut on to the Godstone road?" asked Vereker.

"No, sir, only since Mr. Armadale was shot. As I was saying, Mr. Ralli's soft with them." Turning to his foster-daughter, he said, "If so be as you marry him, Trixie, girl, you'll just have to put a bit o' that temper of yours into him. He needs a bit of wiring up. I don't see why they should be helping the police to find that pistol," he said, addressing Vereker once more. "The inspector has more than enough men of his own to trample down covert."

"They're helping the police, are they?" asked Vereker to make sure that he had heard aright.

"That's the yarn they spun me, sir, when I came upon them unexpected yesterday morning just after sunrise in Duck Wood."

"I was in Wild Duck Wood yesterday morning about that time. I didn't see you, Collyer, but I thought I saw Mr. Degerdon. He was wearing a brown Norfolk jacket and cap."

"That was him, sir. I saw you all right making your pictures quiet as a lamb under them old oaks. Thinks I, it would be better if more gents would take to paintin' landshapes, as they calls them, instead of trapesin' about helpin' bobbies to do their job."

"Like you, Collyer, I wish they'd find that automatic pistol. It would help to clear up the mystery. Do you know if Mr. Armadale ever had more than one automatic in his possession?"

"He used to have three, sir. He gave me one which is lying about the house somewhere at the present moment."

"It's in the small right-hand drawer of the chest in your bedroom," said Miss Collyer.

"Ah, that's where I put it when Mr. Armadale give it to me. It were no use to me. Whether the guv'nor kept the other two or only one, I couldn't say."

"Would you lend me yours for a few days, Collyer? I'd like to make one or two experiments with one."

"Certainly, sir," said Collyer, and went upstairs to get the weapon.

On his leaving the room, Trixie Collyer asked Vereker . he would like a cup of tea. At the moment, Vereker was longing for tea, and as he looked up at her to thank her for her opportune thought he noticed a strange look of uneasiness on her face. The fact at once fired his interest, but excusing herself, she disappeared into the kitchen to make the tea. A few minutes later, Collyer returned to the sitting-room and Trixie brought in a laden tray.

"You be wrong this time, Trixie," said Collyer, addressing her. "I can't lay hands on that Colt pistol. It's not in the drawer you said."

"That's where it was when I saw it last," replied the girl, with an air of preoccupation, and turning to Vereker, asked, "Milk and sugar, Mr. Vereker? It's most annoying; we haven't a drop of cream in the house!"

"It's somewhere about the house," said Collyer, trying to recollect when he had last handled the weapon. "I'll have a good rummage round for it later, and let you have it to-morrow, sir."

"Thanks very much, Collyer," replied Vereker. "I hope you'll come across it. You're certain it hasn't left the cottage?"

"Oh, yes, sir, I'm sure of that. I cleaned and oiled it not long ago, and mebbe I put it away careful somewhere else. I don't like American pistols lying about handy. If you don't know 'em, they're nasty things for accidents. It's easy for anybody careless to leave a cartridge in the barrel without knowing it."

After tea, Vereker thanked the Collyers for their hospitality and, leaving the cottage, started off across the estate for the

Nuthill road. On his way he met Basil Ralli making his way up to the cottage.

"Now, Vereker, you mystery-monger, what's the meaning of this?" asked Ralli, laughing and producing a Yale type of key from his pocket. "Fanshaugh handed this back to me about an hour ago and said you had asked him to deliver it to me."

"So I did. It's Sutton's key to the side door near the gun-room. What did he say? I'm particularly anxious to know."

"He told me some cock-and-bull story about your finding it on an occasional table in your room at Vesey Manor."

"I kept him in the dark about the manner and place of its discovery."

"I know; but the joke is that this is not the key to Sutton's private postern."

"You've tried it?" asked Vereker eagerly.

"Of course I did. These keys are all very similar to an unpractised eye, and before Fanshaugh left I thought I'd make certain, because the key didn't look like the one I gave you."

"He underrated my intelligence. I half expected this result," said Vereker gravely.

"You're sure you've made no mistake?" asked Ralli.

"Certain. I know my Yale key, which is as familiar to me as my own nose—rather more so. Are you perfectly certain you gave me the correct key?"

"Absolutely!" replied Ralli emphatically. "There's no other key of that type on Sutton's bunch."

"What did Fanshaugh say when you pointed out to him that it wasn't the key of the side door?"

"He simply roared with laughter and said you'd probably given him the wrong key off your bunch."

"He had no other key like it on him?" asked Vereker.

"No. I suggested that possibility at once, but he said he had no other keys on him at all. There the matter ended, and we both concluded that the error lay with you."

For some moments Vereker stood silently reviewing the matter. At first glance it had appeared to him that Fanshaugh knew more about that key than he had admitted. It had been discovered in his room by the housemaid who had cleaned the room after his occupation. He had obviously lost it, because it had been found under the bed. His conversation with Vereker on the subject had disclosed his uneasiness, and Vereker had led him into an unwitting but very startling admission. He had denied ever having used the side door himself, and yet he had been perfectly certain about the identity of the key. This, of course, was possible and might be explained quite easily by some peculiar conjuncture of circumstances, but it was highly improbable. It pointed to palpable and clumsy lying in an effort to conceal the fact that he had entered the house by that door at one time or another. The only valid reason for such a deception was that he was trying to hide the fact that he had used that door during the early hours of Thursday morning! And now, as if to confirm Vereker's suspicions, he had by a very simple ruse got possession of the key, disposed of it, and handed Ralli a substitute. By so doing, he had deftly removed an important clue, but he had committed an astounding blunder, of which Vereker determined to take full advantage when the moment was opportune. Asking Ralli to keep the whole matter secret and refrain from discussing it further with Fanshaugh, Vereker proceeded on his way.

It was at this point in his investigations that certain vague suspicions which had all along lurked in the crannies of Vereker's mind now became obtrusive. They were all the more insistent because he had from the beginning tried to repress them as irrelevant and without any foundation. He now boldly faced these suspicions and bluntly asked himself the question—had Ralli engineered the whole incident of this key to the side door? The only reason for such a course was to divert suspicion from himself to a quarter where it would eventually prove innocuous. His subtle and penetrating mind had evidently weighed the vital importance of Frederick's disclosure that there had been egress and entry by that side door on Thursday morning, for the footman had discovered that a bolt which he had firmly shot home on Wednesday night had been withdrawn and not properly driven into its socket again. It was a refractory bolt and would prove a serious obstacle to anyone in a great hurry. The direct bearing of that clue was its fixing of suspicion on the inmates of the manor. This new train of thought filled Vereker with a sense of dissatisfaction because it wakened him to the realization that he had perhaps been altogether too confident and somnolent. Perhaps he was dealing with a brain infinitely subtler and readier than his own, and the thought filled him with sharp misgiving. From the very first, Ralli had gone out of his way to be friendly and win his trust. He had discreetly made appreciative remarks about Vereker's talent as an artist to Angela Armadale, to Trixie Collyer, to Captain Fanshaugh, probably hoping that those encomiums would return to Vereker. It was an astute method of flattering, and on a point which Vereker had to admit that he was peculiarly susceptible. Had the suggestion that Ralli's offer of hospitality was prompted by ulterior motives been a brilliantly correct guess by that cunning and experienced officer, Heather? It was extremely difficult to say. If pecuniary gain were a sufficient motive for a man like Fanshaugh to remove Sutton Armadale, the same incitant was infinitely stronger in the case of Basil Ralli. With Ralli the power of that motive had struck Vereker from the very first as overwhelming and, though he always attempted in his work to keep an open mind, he was obliged to admit that in this instance he had allowed his usual watchfulness to relax in a dangerous manner. The realization had the tonic effect of a cold douche and, as he walked slowly back to the "Silver Pear Tree," Vereker reviewed his latest theory from every angle. In a flash he connected motive with the all-important question of weapon, and it came home to him with a curious shock that Collyer's automatic might be the very instrument by which the murder had been committed. That weapon was at the moment missing; it was a weapon to which Trixie Collyer, and therefore Ralli, could have had easy access. It was a Colt .45. At once Vereker recalled the curious look of uneasiness that had crossed the girl's face when Collyer had gone upstairs to find the pistol. Under the warm impulse of roving imagination the theory became feasible, and little incidents bearing thereon which had at the moment of their occurrence appeared trifling now took on a portentous significance. He hurried back to the "Silver Pear Tree," eager to communicate the whole of his recent experiences and conjectures to Inspector Heather. That officer, with his cold and solid practicality, would bring the acid test of experience to bear on amateurish enthusiasm. From the clash of their methods and temperaments some valuable residuum of truth would surely emerge. But on Vereker's arrival Heather had not returned, and the landlady of the inn had no information as to when he might be expected. Vereker dined alone, and afterwards waited patiently in his room for the inspector's reappearance. To pass the time, he took from an old bookcase a musty and ancient copy of Locke's *Essay on the Human Understanding*. He became immersed in the chapter on the "Reality of Knowledge," and ploughed steadily on until he reached the chapter dealing with "Enthusiasm." There he fell sound asleep, and woke to find that it was nearly midnight. He rose and went to Inspector Heather's room. There was no response to his knock and, on quietly opening the door and striking a match, he discovered that the room was unoccupied. Heather had not returned. Doubtless something of great importance had occurred, and with a feeling that events were now shaping towards a startling revelation, Vereker crept noiselessly back to his own room and undressed. Before he fell asleep his latest theory concerning the possibility of Ralli's connection with the murder of Sutton Armadale seemed to suffer a painful shrinkage. The first warm glow of enthusiasm had dissipated in a mysterious way, and as he reviewed the matter he began to wonder why he had been so fired with its possible importance some hours previously. Thence his mind rambled on to the subject of the extraordinary vagaries of that very thing the human mind, of words as the medium of expression of ideas—a conversion of soul to sound—of the relations between human thought and reality, until the very idea of his own existence seemed to acquire a strange tenuity, and he slipped away into the restful oblivion of sleep.

Chapter Thirteen

Next morning, Vereker was roused by the quiet opening of his door and the slow, smiling appearance of Inspector Heather's broad face as he peered into the room.

"You're awake at last!" said the inspector.

"I needed a decent sleep after waiting up till all hours for you, Heather. Where the devil did you get to yesterday? You look tired."

"I am. I've been up all night, and now I'm going to turn in."

"What business kept you out of bed?"

"I'll let you know later. See that they wake me about tea-time; it's deadly important."

"I believe you've been night-clubbing as a relaxation."

"Night-watching's more in my line. The landlady told me you were rather anxious to see me last night, so I thought I'd have a word with you before I went to bed. Is it anything important?"

"It looked frightfully important at the time. Now I'm not so sure."

"Has it anything to do with the automatic we're looking for?" asked Heather, with a note of eagerness.

"Well, yes, it may possibly be the very weapon," said Vereker very quietly.

"You've found it?" asked Heather excitedly.

"Don't jump to hasty conclusions, inspector. I've discovered that Sutton Armadale used to have three Colt .45 automatics. He gave Collyer one, and kept one or possibly both of the others. Now, as either Miss Collyer or Ralli could easily have laid hands on Collyer's pistol, I thought I'd borrow it for your inspection. After firing a couple of cartridges out of it, you'd be in a position to say whether it was the weapon which discharged the cartridge case I picked up on the polo ground."

"That's sound work, Mr. Vereker! Where's the weapon?"

"God knows. Collyer went to look for it, but couldn't find it in its customary drawer in his bedroom. He's going to search for it and let me have it to-day. If he can't lay hands on it—and I've a suspicion he won't—the result will be a clear line on Miss Collyer or even Mr. Ralli. There's sufficient motive in either case, don't you think?"

"Blithers, Mr. Vereker, blithers! It points to my first suspect, Frank Peach. He used to visit the cottage daily, being one of Miss Trixie's best boys, and I hear he has been threatening both Ralli and the girl quite recently. This is excellent. Now we shan't be long!"

"If that's all you can offer as a suggestion, Heather, I'm not interested. Go to bed and be damned to you!"

"I'm going, and the same to you with gravy. See you later."

"I'm lunching with a friend in town, but I'll be back for tea if possible. At that time I hope I'll find you a little brighter intellectually."

Outside L'Escargot, Vereker met Ricardo accompanied by a tall, rather lanky young man who was a stranger to him and whom Ricardo introduced as Aubrey Winter —Angela's cousin. Ricardo, in morning coat, silk hat, light gloves, a buttonhole, and a cravat tie that seemed to dominate the ensemble, was resplendent enough for a wedding. Vereker eyed him up and down critically.

"A bit shrill, Ricky! I'm surprised at this reaction from Bohemia. It's a great compliment to me, or rather to my lunch."

"Sorry, but I'm not lunching with you. You didn't give me sufficient notice—I've to sardine my engagements nowadays."

"Then what's the gay occasion?"

"I'm taking Laura Hardinge to Prince's."

"Am I to gather that you wish to float a loan?"

"I shan't issue the prospectus to-day. An unexpected cheque arrived this morning. The *Report* has accepted my serial, *The Cost of Loving*. I can hang out for a very brief period."

"Quite a good title," remarked Vereker, with a smile.

"Struck it by accident. A French pal of mine came over for a month's holiday, but he returned to Paris after a fortnight. He said the 'cost of loving' was too high in London."

"Would it trouble you to return that tenner?"

"Seriously. It can't be done to-day, Algernon. Some other day, perhaps—on a more auspicious occasion, we may discuss reparations. Then I shall probably suggest some sort of moratorium."

"I shall be at my club during the afternoon. Shall I see you later?"

"It's just possible. I have lots of news. In the meantime I thought you'd like to regale Aubrey. He's at a loose end and always looks like a cartoon of Famine in Russia, so I brought him along as a substitute. He'll do you justice. Try their *crêpes de volatile*—they're most entertaining. Bye-bye."

With a flourish of his cane, Ricardo hailed a taxi, jumped in, and disappeared. Aubrey Winter and Vereker entered the restaurant. Vereker had all along been anxious to see Aubrey Winter, and was secretly grateful to the tactful Ricky for arranging the meeting. He found Winter an ingenuous and good-natured youth, and soon drew the conversation round to the subject of Sutton Armadale's murder.

"Your bedroom was next to Fanshaugh's, I believe," said Vereker.

"Yes, on one side, and on the other was Armadale's suite."

"Can you recollect hearing anything unusual during Thursday morning?"

"My dear fellow, it was a night of alarums and excursions. I seemed to be hearing rumblings on all sides at all hours. I'm a wretched sleeper. The night was putridly hot, and, besides, I was rather troubled by a personal affair."

"I hope you won't think me impertinent if I suggest that it was on account of Miss Cazas," said Vereker.

Aubrey Winter blushed rather refreshingly.

"Ricky has been talking about me, I see. I must admit that Edmée gives me many sleepless nights. I'm desperately fond of her, and I'm afraid I'm in the rotten position—"

"I understand these things, Winter; I've had some experience," interrupted Vereker tactfully. "Did you hear Armadale moving about during the night, or rather morning?"

"Yes, at about three o'clock I heard his door open and close, and I feel sure he went downstairs. He must have been downstairs about a quarter of an hour. I thought I heard him come up again, and I feel pretty certain he entered Fanshaugh's room before he went back to his own."

"That's very strange," commented Vereker.

"What's stranger to me is that 'Fruity' makes such a bally mystery about the whole thing. He asked me particularly not to say anything to the police about what I'd heard, because it would only confuse the issue unnecessarily. Frankly, I hate any hole-and-corner sort of business, and if the police question me I shall tell them the truth. There's nothing to be gained by any sort of hanky-panky in such matters."

"I think you're right, Winter. Moreover, it's dangerous."

"It has nothing to do with Sutton's murder, or suicide, or whatever it is, so I can't see why there should be any mystery-making."

"No, no, certainly not; there's nothing like being frank in a case like this. Did you hear Sutton go downstairs when he is supposed to have heard the burglar, say between four and five o'clock?"

"No, I must have been asleep, but about half-past five old 'Fruity' was astir. I heard his door close. I thought I'd heard him come upstairs, but he denied this when I mentioned the matter to him. He said he had left his door open for air, and rose about that hour to close it, because the dawn breeze was blowing his curtains about and keeping him from sleeping."

"Sutton Armadale was a great friend of Miss Cazas," remarked Vereker, filling Winter's glass.

"He was awfully decent to Edmée. She was dreadfully cut up by his death. As she says herself, he was just a big, kind uncle to her. Being in love with her, I'm inclined to be stupidly jealous of every one. I do my best not to be. Jealousy makes a fellow look so small, don't you think? Of course, when she explained to me that Sutton, knowing she wasn't very well off, made her very tactful presents and called her his extravagant little niece, I understood perfectly. She always called him 'Nunky,' you know. Edmée gets rather cross about my jealousy, and tells me I should be proud that other men admire my girl. It's difficult, but I suppose one really ought. Fellows can't help falling in love with her, and she's so kind-hearted and sympathetic that she hates to hurt them. Poor old Degerdon's also very much in love with her. She says she doesn't admire his sort, and is leading him on just to teach him a wholesome lesson. I'm sorry for him, but as Edmée says, it does a man good to learn that every woman isn't at his feet. Deg is a bit cocksure with the fair sex."

"You think Miss Cazas' relations with Sutton were purely Platonic?" asked Vereker.

"Oh, purely, purely. Edmée told me it was one of those great big friendships between man and woman that are very rarely possible. 'A friendship made in heaven' is her rather beautiful way of expressing it."

"Was there anything in the nature of a quarrel between them on Wednesday night?"

"You couldn't call it a quarrel. Sutton was rather annoyed at the way she was leading Degerdon on, and she resented his dictating to her how she was to behave. Edmée is very touchy and can be spiteful with her tongue. She retaliated by being worse than ever. Sutton was awfully strait-laced in many ways, and the cause of the trouble was that he came upon them larking in the bathing pavilion. He always hated mixed bathing. Edmée was sitting on Deg's knee in her bathing costume, I believe, but she denied this to me."

"Did he speak to Degerdon?" asked Vereker.

"Oh, yes, and Deg got very huffy. He said if Sutton was going to disguise Vesey Manor as a nunnery, he for one was going to give the place a miss in balk. Sutton told him it was necessary to draw the line somewhere, and that those guests who liked mauling and clutching one another should choose Hampstead Heath on a summer's night. Edmée, of course, capped it by adding 'and before they've cut the grass.' There the matter ended, but they were very cool to one another for the rest of the evening."

"Were they always good friends on other occasions?" "I don't think they hit it off together at all well. Deg always thought Sutton a bit of a humbug."

"After going to bed on Wednesday night, did you hear or see Degerdon again before you saw him on the polo ground on Thursday morning?"

"Strange that you should ask me that! I have a hazy recollection of hearing Sutton and Degerdon having a hell of a row together long after I turned in. Of course I must have been dreaming, and my dream must have been prompted by what had occurred earlier in the evening. At least, that's the only explanation I can offer, because they couldn't possibly have been quarrelling again in the early hours of the morning."

"It would hardly seem possible," said Vereker, and asked, "Your cousin, Mrs. Armadale, told you that she was going to elope with Mr. Stanley Houseley?"

"Yes, and I advised her very strongly against it. She and Sutton didn't pull together, but after all he was her husband and rather a marvellous chap altogether. Few men can become millionaires in a lifetime. But Angela and I don't always see alike. She doesn't like Edmée, and has often tried to make me throw her over altogether. Angela thinks me a bit of a fool and says I'm what the Americans call a 'sap.' Anyhow, I should never be such a big 'sap' as to leave a decent chap like Sutton for that pompous old ass, Stanley. Now she's going to marry him and, as he dislikes Edmée, I shall see less of Angela than ever. I threatened to punch his head not long ago when he called Edmée a cabaret girl, and he's not likely to forget it in a hurry. Tried to be sarcastic at my expense, but I fairly scored when I asked him if he'd like to find that pet moustache of his growing out of the back of his left ear. Stubborn ass, old Stanley!"

"Did you tell anyone else in the house about this elopement plan of your cousin's?"

"Yes, I mentioned it in strictest confidence to Edmée, who agreed with me by saying that Angela was really qualifying for bibs and pinafores again. Edmée's such a finished product that she has no patience with women who, as she says, look shy and suck their thumbs when a fellow wants to kiss 'em."

From this point the conversation drifted into generalities, and after lunch Aubrey Winter left Vereker to keep an appointment concerning the purchase of a Burnley car. Vereker made his way to his club and had not been there long before Ricardo arrived. Thence they repaired to Vereker's flat in Fenton Street, where they could discuss affairs without restraint.

"Miss Hardinge enjoy her lunch?" asked Vereker as soon as they had settled themselves comfortably in his studio.

"Algernon, I didn't lunch Laura at all. That was what I call a lubricating lie. I took Edmée to Prince's; only I didn't want that tendril, Aubrey, to know. Neither did she, because of late she says he seems to have changed his toys from dolls to guns. I've been put to a lot of trouble on your account. Edmée's as elusive as a bluebottle at all times, but recently I've found it almost impossible to get her by herself for five minutes together."

"Did you get any information out of her about the Armadale affair?"

For a few seconds Ricardo was silent. Then, shaking his head gravely, he said:

"I don't like the look of things. There's something rotten about the whole business. From what I can gather, Vesey Manor on Wednesday night was like a thieves' kitchen. Every one seemed to be ready to slit throats on the slightest provocation."

"Your lady friend seems to be a bit of a damned nuisance wherever she goes."

"I'm disillusioned, Algernon; she was only sugar- coated after all. I've been obliged to strike her off my list. The worst of it is, she'll never realize the degradation, and I get as much satisfaction as the Pope would get in excommunicating the Devil. It had to be done. I find she associates with all sorts of undesirables of her own nationality. The other day I met her in company with a worm whom she introduced to me as Raoul Vernet. He was unacquainted with soap, blackleaded his shoes, and wore a compass on his watch-chain! He's a typical—well, the French call such a man *maquereau*.

I went and had a Turkish bath after being in his company for about a quarter of an hour."

"Where does he hang out?" asked Vereker.

"God knows, and I'm sure He'd rather not. Edmée seemed to be very intimate with him. He insisted on discussing something with her in French in spite of my declaring that I didn't speak the language. But I have a working acquaintance with the lingo and kept my ears open. He seemed to be in a great hurry to get back to France, and eventually Edmée lent him some money for his passage—which, by the way, she borrowed from me. I lent it almost gladly in such a good cause."

"Poor old Ricky!" exclaimed Vereker, laughing.

"Don't be sorry for me, Algernon, I've put it down on my bill for expenses incurred on your behalf."

"Anything else you picked up from their conversation?"

"Not much. Vernet seemed very upset about a friend of his, called Hippolyte Ferray, who had somehow got into trouble with a Trojan car, but what it was all about I couldn't quite gather. He seemed most anxious to shake me off, but, as you know, Algernon, on business I'm perfectly prehensile. I wanted to get Edmée alone, and finally I did. She was in a highly nervous state about this affair at Vesey Manor and talked rather incoherently. She seemed more upset about the loss of Angela's pearls than she did about Sutton's death. I told her not to worry about things and that we had a very clever inquiry agent who was looking after the interests of the guests. I arranged that you should meet her and have a quiet talk."

"When am I to meet the lady?"

"You're to call at her flat at five this afternoon and have tea."

"Damn! I rather wanted to get back to the 'Silver Pear Tree' about five."

"Edmée was anxious to see Ralli this afternoon because she's going back to Belgium as soon as possible, and has run down to Vesey Manor to say good-bye. She also wanted to see about a diary which she left behind on her last visit."

"Then there's nothing for it but to keep the appointment," remarked Vereker. "I wanted to see Heather at five o'clock, but I can phone him a message to be sent down from Vesey Manor. Any other items of interest that may bear on my job, Ricky?"

"I'm afraid not, old pickle. You've given me rather an arid patch to cultivate on this occasion. No meat in my part, but I've played it with as much *brio* as I could.

"One minute," said Vereker, with sudden eagerness, "here's a point on which you may be helpful. Have you ever read or heard the words, 'It has a strange quick jar upon the ear'? Seems to have a Shakespearean run about it."

At once Ricardo rose to his feet, and the look of depression which had settled on his features, at the thought of his ineffectual services for Vereker, vanished.

"My dear Algernon, I'm sorry for you. Of course you can't help being illiterate; all painters are. Here's where I bourgeon. Let me recall those lines to you:

'It has a strange quick jar upon the ear,
That cocking of a pistol, when you know
A moment more will bring the sight to bear
Upon your person, twelve yards off, or so.'"

"Heavens, Ricky, you've a marvellous memory for some things. Who wrote the stuff? Can you remember the versifier's name?"

"Versifier, my dear Algernon? Poet of the first water—well, perhaps water is rather inappropriate to Byron. No mixer of ice-cream sodas for sloppy souls wrote those lines. You'll find them somewhere in 'Don Juan.'"

At once Vereker pulled out a slip of paper from his wallet.

"Ah, yes, D.J. C.4, S.41," he said. "I read the riddle: 'Don Juan,' Canto 4, Stanza 41. This is remarkably interesting!"

Vereker relapsed into silence and sat deep in thought; his face grew pale, and his breath came quickly.

"I think that deserves a drink, Ricky," he said at length, and in a strangely calm voice. "You've been a really helpful assistant. I thought Byronism was buried in Russia ages ago."

"Possibly it was, but before we go further and you forget, let's have the drink. I suggest something long and strong. I'm a bit depressed, and at the moment agree with Byron when he sang:

'Man being reasonable must get drunk,
The best of life is but intoxication:

Glory, the grape, love, gold, in these are sunk
The hopes of all men and of every nation'—

so hand me the keys of your cellarette and I'll wait on us both!"

While Ricardo was busying himself in the direction of
refreshment, Vereker was excitedly pacing up and down his
studio. He was eager to meet Miss Edmée Cazas, and he was
anxiously debating in his mind the line he would take in his
interview with that lady. He felt that it would be no occasion for
gentle persuasion, but a time for directness and, if necessary, a
certain amount of judicious bluff. At last the work of sifting the
information he had laboriously gathered seemed to promise a
solution to the mystery of the happenings at Vesey Manor on
the fateful morning of Sutton Armadale's death. Little by little
a theory had shaped itself from the seemingly inchoate mass of
detail, and he was eager to put that theory to a final test. If Miss
Cazas proved amenable to reason, he might be able to acquire the
finishing touches which would crown his work with success. He
was sanguine, but his hopefulness was tempered with caution.
So often before had a promising edifice of theory been razed to
the ground by some unexpected and disruptive fact. With fretful
impatience he passed the time chatting with Ricardo, who, with
characteristic changefulness, had forgotten his depression and
was once more in exuberant mood. At half-past four Vereker left
his flat and, hailing a taxi, asked the driver to take him to Francis
Street, W., the address which Ricardo had given him.

Miss Edmée was in and awaiting him. On seeing her, Vereker
remembered Ricardo's description of her as a wisp of provocative
feminine gossamer, and it struck him that, as a thumb-nail
sketch of her, his words could hardly be bettered. On entering
her drawing-room, he was at once aware of the prevailing odour
of stephanotis. Tea was brought in by a highly coloured French
maid, and, as Miss Cazas attended to the business of serving
him, Vereker took the opportunity of studying her face. She was

undoubtedly beautiful, but her rather prominent nose, typically Gallic, was displeasing to his taste, and her toilette, finished to the last degree of art, gave her the semblance of something unreal, so far was it removed from the robustness of English health and freshness. Her eyes had that extraordinary veiling of the lids and lashes suggestive of languor and passion which has appealed so strongly to artists at all periods of luxury and over-refinement. Her figure was admirable in its proportions, and she moved with the grace and sophistication of the danseuse. In spite of his prejudice and a determination to be hypercritical, Vereker was obliged to admit that he was decidedly impressed. With eminent practicality she brought the conversation at once to the business on which she knew Vereker had come.

"You're busy on the investigation of the Armadale affair," she said, speaking with hardly a trace of accent. "I'm glad you've called on me, Mr. Vereker. I can help only a little perhaps, but I will answer all your questions as clearly as possible. Poor Sutton" (she accented the name on the final syllable), "his tragic death has been a terrible blow to me. I have behaved rather wonderfully under it. I was one of his very great friends."

"Your friendship was one of those that are made in heaven," suggested Vereker, with a difficult simulation of sincerity.

"Exactly," she replied, with a swift, penetrating glance. "You have used my own words."

"You were born lucky, Miss Cazas; such friendships are naturally rare on this earth. But before we talk about this business I'd like to return you something you've lost." With these words Vereker produced the dainty lace handkerchief which he had picked up in the rock garden of Vesey Manor and handed it to her.

"Oh, thank you so much," she replied, with a disarming smile; "but how did you know it was mine?"

"A happy piece of guess-work, Miss Cazas. Your scent is stephanotis, and the rest was rather easy."

"You're a wonderful detective, Mr. Vereker; but, again, how did you know I used stephanotis?" she asked archly.

"More guess-work, Miss Cazas. Your bedroom at Vesey Manor retains a delightful memento of you and simply won't forget your stay there."

"Now that is very clever, Mr. Vereker. You deserve full marks, and I put you at once to the top of the class," she laughed, as she tucked the handkerchief away in her dress. "Now how can I help you in your investigation?"

"By answering my questions very frankly, Miss Cazas. It's the only way you can help me. Let me begin. At what time did you all go to bed on Wednesday night?"

"At twelve o'clock, or perhaps it was a little later."

"I believe there had been some unpleasantness between you and Mr. Armadale earlier in the evening?"

"Ah, but no. It was just a slight tiff about nothing. Mr. Armadale was a very generous man, and occasionally he gave me very acceptable presents. I'm very extravagant, and I get into debt. I used to tell him my troubles, and sometimes he would scold me and tell me I was his naughty little niece. It was such an occasion."

"But I thought the tiff rose out of your behaviour with Mr. Degerdon?"

"*Sacré nom de Dieu!* Who told you that silly nonsense? Ah, I know—it was Aubrey. He is an impossible fool. He is very fond of me, and I tease him by making him, oh, so jealous. I told him a big fib about it."

"I see. How're the knees, Miss Cazas? I hear you hurt them rather badly when you were larking about in the swimming-pool."

"Oh, I grazed them very severely. I should like to show them to you, but it would not be quite proper— eh? They're not thoroughly healed yet."

"Most unfortunate. I hear Aubrey Winter told you all about Mrs. Armadale's little elopement scheme. She was going to run off with Mr. Houseley at two o'clock in the morning."

"Perhaps he did. I'm not quite sure. I was not very interested in her childish way of making love, so I do not remember."

"You knew, of course, she was going to take out divorce proceedings against her husband?"

"Yes, I knew. She told me so herself. I advised her not to be foolish, but, there, I cannot understand your English point of view on such matters."

"If Mr. Armadale had lived and Mrs. Armadale had been granted a divorce, would you have consented to become his third wife?"

"That is an impossible question to answer, Mr. Vereker. I liked Sutton, but I cannot say I loved him. Still, he was immensely rich, and to be his wife would not have been unpleasant if he had consented to being sensible. I am young—need I explain?"

"I understand, Miss Cazas. You're in love with some one?"

"Yes, and why not?"

"Is the gentleman's name M. Raoul Vernet?"

"Oh, no, certainly not. He's an old friend and a countryman of mine. But who told you about Raoul?"

"Mr. Ricardo happened to mention his name when we were talking about you. I think Mr. Ricardo's a bit jealous."

"Ah, no, Ricky is not jealous. Once upon a time, perhaps, but not now. He doesn't love me any longer."

"Is M. Vernet in London at present?"

"No, he has returned to the Continent. I think he has gone back to his home in Louvain."

"To return to Mr. Armadale, after going to bed you did not see him again alive?"

"No," said Miss Cazas, wiping away tears which at once rose to her eyes.

"Mrs. Armadale told me she heard him in your room about three o'clock. She says he was talking loudly to you as if he were very angry."

"Angela must have been dreaming—nightmare, I think you call it. After going to my room I never saw Sutton again," replied Miss Cazas emphatically.

"Did you see any of the other guests?" asked Vereker pointedly.

"But, Mr. Vereker, how could I? I don't permit gentlemen to come to my room, as you suggest."

"I'm sorry if my suggestion implied anything improper, Miss Cazas. As there was a burglary in the house and a certain amount of commotion, I thought you might have got up to see what was the matter."

"No; I sleep very soundly and heard nothing till Aubrey hammered on my door on Thursday morning. Then I heard of the shooting of Sutton, and afterwards it was discovered there had also been a burglary and Angela's pearls had been stolen."

"M. Raoul Vernet is an expert on pearls, isn't he?" asked Vereker, and glanced shrewdly at Miss Cazas to see the effect of his question.

"He ought to know something about pearls because it is in his line of business," she replied, looking Vereker boldly in the eyes and smiling confidently. "But what prompted your question?"

"To be frank about the whole matter, Miss Cazas, the police in charge of the inquiry into Mr. Armadale's murder are pretty certain that M. Raoul Vernet was indirectly connected with the theft of Mrs. Armadale's pearls."

At this information, Miss Cazas threw back her head and gave vent to a really hearty outburst of laughter, on the subsidence of which she exclaimed:

"But that is an excellent joke! Your English police are so stupid; they ought not to be entrusted with criminal investigation. Their duties lie in the direction of traffic and the safeguarding of the morals of cooks!"

Miss Cazas' gay abandonment surprised Vereker considerably. He was at a loss to know whether it was genuine or a remarkably clever simulation. He decided to play a trump card.

"I don't think the police suspect M. Vernet without reason, Miss Cazas," he continued amiably. "The morning of the burglary a parcel containing a suit of clothes was found hidden under some shrubs in the rock garden at Vesey Manor. On that suit of clothes was a cleaners' mark, which gave them a clue to work on. They traced the establishment at which the clothes had been left, and they discovered that the man to whom they belonged was a M. Raoul Vernet, who, at the time of the cleaning operation, was living at an address in Woburn Square. Perhaps M. Vernet will be able to explain everything satisfactorily, when asked how his suit of clothes managed to get to the grounds of Vesey Manor on the morning of the burglary and murder. To me it presents rather a fascinating problem."

"But I can solve the puzzle for you, Mr. Vereker," said Miss Cazas enthusiastically. "That suit of clothes was stolen from a car in which Raoul was travelling two months ago. It was tied up in a brown paper parcel, and when the car pulled up at an inn on the Eastbourne road the parcel vanished from the back seat where Raoul had left it. But I cannot explain how it got to the rock garden at Vesey Manor."

"Was it M. Vernet's car?" asked Vereker.

"Oh, no, the car belonged to a friend. Raoul told me all about it. He was very hard up at the time, and I lent him some money to buy another suit of clothes."

"Was his friend's name Hippolyte Ferray, and did he drive a Trojan car?" asked Vereker quickly, and for the first time in their conversation he noticed a look of swift dismay on Miss Cazas' singularly fascinating face.

"I think that was the gentleman's name, but I'm not sure. I don't know myself," she replied, with complete composure.

"M. Hippolyte Ferray was driving a stolen car, I should imagine," suggested Vereker simply. "I hear there was some trouble about it subsequently."

"M. Ferray was only a casual acquaintance of Raoul's," said Miss Cazas, with a suspicion of tartness. "If there was trouble about his car subsequently, you can hardly blame Raoul for that."

"No, of course not," replied Vereker. "Casual acquaintances are very misleading at times. I once remember meeting a very charming man in the train when travelling from Manchester to London. We lunched together, and the journey passed very pleasantly. He was arrested on his arrival at Euston."

"What had he done?" asked Miss Cazas, as if relieved by this digression.

"Cut his wife's throat a few days previously," replied Vereker.

"Ah, how terrible!" exclaimed Miss Cazas, with a dramatic shudder.

Vereker had been lost in admiration at the deft way in which his thrusts had been parried, but he was not yet going to admit defeat at the hands of this astute and pretty little Belgian. He promptly altered his tactics, and asked in his pleasantest manner:

"But why doesn't your friend, M. Vernet, register, Miss Cazas? So far he hasn't done so, and you know the police are rather hot on such remissness on the part of foreigners resident in this country."

"Raoul is the most forgetful man I've ever met. It must have completely escaped his memory. I will remind him on a future occasion."

"He must be terribly careless, Miss Cazas. Two months ago he was travelling in M. Ferray's car, and his parcel containing a suit of clothes was stolen. Only three weeks ago he left that suit to be cleaned at a valet service depot, and a fortnight ago it was sent to his address in Woburn Square. Is he careless about his dates?"

"Most careless, Mr. Vereker," smiled Miss Cazas, with complete nonchalance. "It is probably only a fortnight ago or less, as you've been good enough to point out."

"His forgetfulness'll get him into serious trouble one of these days, Miss Cazas. But, with regard to the theft of Mrs. Armadale's pearls, the police have bit by bit built up an extraordinary theory. Of course it's purely theory, but it's most interesting."

"If you're not in a hurry to get away, Mr. Vereker," said Miss Cazas, glancing at the clock on the mantelpiece, "I should be so glad to hear it—that is, if you're at liberty to tell me."

"I'm not in any hurry, Miss Cazas," said Vereker, with the determination that if this was a tactful hint to depart, it was going to be sternly ignored. "I don't quite know whether I'm at liberty to divulge the theory, but as you're eager to help me to safeguard the interests of the guests I'm sure I can safely take you into my confidence. You may even be grateful to me for taking the risk. On the morning of the burglary, as I've already told you, the police found a parcel of M. Vernet's clothes in the rock garden of Vesey Manor. They promptly took the trouble to inquire who M. Vernet was, and found that he was an unregistered alien. The Sûreté in Paris say he's a Belgian from Louvain, a jeweller's assistant, whose attitude to other people's property is not very orthodox. Mind you, this is the police story, and they're possibly mistaken, seeing that M. Vernet is a great friend of yours. Still, I give it you for what it's worth. I saw M. Vernet's clothes, and from their general appearance I should say they'd fit you. He must be an undersized man and elegantly slim. Strangely enough, to me the clothes smelt very strongly of stephanotis, especially the waistcoat. Naturally the police jumped to the conclusion that these garments must have some connection with the very charming occupant of the suite next to Mrs. Armadale's on the first floor. Those were your rooms, Miss Cazas, and I think it very rash of the police to formulate any theory on such a slight basis of scents. The obvious inference to draw was that stephanotis is a scent which many people like, and that there was no connection whatever. Then they found your handkerchief in the rock garden very close to the spot where the clothes were hidden, and foolishly deduced that you had placed the parcel under those shrubs. Why, I cannot say, but put a detective on a theory and he'll ride it to the devil. Having started, they meant to go on at all costs. It's quite an interesting study in speculation from their point of view. Of course the entry into the library would be made from outside, because your door opened on to the same balcony as the library door, and such a method of entry would lessen the chances of your meeting any of the servants or other guests in the corridor or being heard by them. To do this the library door would have to be unfastened beforehand. Just before going to bed you went into the library for a book."

"Yes," said Miss Cazas, "I always read before going to sleep."

"You can remember the book you borrowed?"

"Yes, it was André Maurois' *The Silence of Colonel Bramble*. I finished it."

"A charming book by a perfect artist. As it happens, Miss Cazas, you took a book by Mr. Sherard Vines, next on the shelf to that of M. Maurois. Possibly in your haste you made a mistake, but it's quite irrelevant. The police didn't pay much heed to the actual book you borrowed, but they thought you made the visit to the library a pretext for opening the library door. Foolish of them, wasn't it? The next difficulty was how to get the key of the safe. This proved quite simple in theory, because Mr. Winter had told you that Mrs. Armadale was going to elope about two o'clock in the morning. To enter her room and get the safe key from her jewel-case would therefore present no difficulty. After the key had been taken, the electric light in Mrs. Armadale's bedroom was accidentally left on. Now a professional burglar always carries a small hand-torch and never, if he can help it, switches on a light in an occupied house. As you're not a professional burglar, they thought it must have been you who had forgotten to switch off that light. They also thought it was quite possible that you didn't trouble to enter the library from the balcony, seeing that Mrs. Armadale was out of her room, but this is perhaps an unnecessary piece of embroidery. Now, however, comes the wildest flight of detective fancy imaginable. Having deduced that you, Miss Cazas, had burgled Mrs. Armadale's pearls, they were obliged

to connect you somehow with the suit of clothes belonging to
M. Vernet. But no obstacle could now impede their headlong
rush. On the discovery of the burglary next morning it would
be a very suspicious affair if by any chance it came to light that
the missing pearls were in the possession of one of the guests.
Ergo, you had to get rid of them at the earliest opportunity. A
phone call to your accomplice, M. Vernet—they had already
promoted him to this rank—to send down a car with some trusted
person to take delivery of the pearls had already been previously
arranged. M. Vernet knows a discreet fellow, Hippolyte Ferray,
another unregistered alien, who commands the use of a stolen
Trojan car, and he appears on the Nuthill road at the appointed
hour. A youth was seen by young Burton, the gardener's son, at
the lodge, actually to meet this car at about the right time, and,
having delivered his package, to make his way back to the manor
via the polo ground. Of course the difficulty of explaining away
the presence of a youth in the scheme of things was overcome *à
premier coup*. You were the youth, and you had dressed in M.
Vernet's clothes to play the part. Ludicrous flight of fancy, I should
say, but the police always like to make facts fit a preconceived
theory. They agreed that there must have been some reason for
the masquerade, and they accounted for it rather tortuously to
my mind. They surmised you'd find it easier to negotiate balcony
pillars in trousers. Flimsy skirts hanging about the ankles don't
lend themselves to climbing. Then you might not wish to make
yourself known to this casual acquaintance of M. Vernet's, this
M. Ferray, who was probably a member of a gang and likely to
add blackmail to his other accomplishments. Again, if you'd been
surprised in the library, you could have dashed back to your own
room via the balcony. The entrance to the library being some
distance from the safe would have helped you in your neat escape,
because a pursuer would promptly imagine the burglar had
descended from the balcony to the ground by one of the pillars.
He would certainly not look for a young man in a charming lady's

bedroom two doors off without reflection, and reflection takes valuable time. Taking every circumstance into consideration, the disguise might have proved of vital importance if you'd been seen escaping and had avoided capture. It was a weapon in your armoury against detection. As I've mentioned, the police love to fit facts to a theory, and when they heard that you had hurt your knees in the swimming-pool they were discourteous enough to suggest that you had simply grazed them when climbing the stone pillar of the balcony. They even went the length of saying that a button, which eventually became detached from your shoe, had possibly been loosened in the same act. Personally, I'm very sceptical about neatly constructed theories; life rarely bears them out, and I wanted to know why on earth you'd taken the trouble to get rid of M. Vernet's clothes. But it seems that Mr. Degerdon admitted having seen a man leave the house and disappear into the rock garden at the time of the burglary. You were not certain, or perhaps you were, that he might be able to describe the clothes to the police, and, had there been a search at the manor for a weapon soon after Mr. Armadale's murder, that suit of clothes would have been discovered among your belongings. Don't you think that a strange story, Miss Cazas?"

"It's simply marvellous, Mr. Vereker," came the reply, with a sigh such as a child utters after listening to an absorbing tale, "but, of course, it's sheer fudge from beginning to end. Why didn't they go further and construct a theory which would make me out a murderer as well as a thief?"

"Perhaps they were exhausted by their first effort, or possibly they wanted to keep the two crimes strictly apart. Their ways are always a bit inscrutable. They've got another charming theory on the murder, purely hypothetical stuff, but I really haven't got the time to tell you about it just now. But before leaving I should like to give you a little friendly advice, Miss Cazas."

"I always like friendly advice, Mr. Vereker. I know I shall do right by completely disregarding it."

"The occasion may prove an exception. You're thinking of returning to Belgium?"

"That was my intention. In fact, my things are being packed for the journey."

"Then hasten your departure. It may save you a lot of pain and annoyance."

"Are they going to arrest me, Mr. Vereker?" asked Miss Cazas, with the first real show of fear in her remarkable eyes.

"No, I don't think they've got as far as that, because the story I've told you is my own fabrication, and I haven't breathed a word of it to a soul up to the present."

"Suppose for a moment it was true, what is your reason for sparing me, Mr. Vereker?"

"For one reason, I always admire a clever and daring, if foolish, woman; but the real reason—well, I can't disclose it at the moment. Perhaps at some future date—"

"How generous of you, Mr. Vereker, but I'm not in the least bit alarmed! I shall tell my maid as soon as you've gone to unpack my things. I'm dining out with a friend to-night, and as I take hours to dress, I must commence at once."

Miss Cazas extended her hand to Vereker.

"You can take it from me that it's not the hand of a thief," she said, with a ravishing smile.

"I accept your word, Miss Cazas," replied Vereker, taking the proffered hand and bowing courteously, "but—but—No, I won't be so ungallant as to finish the sentence. Good evening!"

Chapter Fourteen

On leaving Francis Street, Vereker telephoned to Ricardo.

"I'm not returning to Fenton Street to-night, Ricky. I've further business down at Vesey Manor."

"How did you get on with Edmée?" asked Ricardo. "Did she liquefy under your scorching interrogation?"

"Ricky, she beat me to a frazzle! I drove her step by step into a corner and was about to give her the *coup de grâce* when in a flash my rapier was out of my hand, and I was disarmed and helpless!"

"Of course she resorted to tears. Edmée is the most accomplished weeper I know, and her eyes after the warm shower are like dew-wet violets instead of the usual poached eggs," commented Ricardo.

"No, I must give my adversary her due. I was confident, but she was assurance incarnate. I thought I was invincible when I was just a child in her hands. She defeated me without any appeal to tears. Cold, sure, deadly mentality—a fine example of 'l'audace et toujours l'audace!'"

"Possibly she started with an unfair advantage," remarked Ricardo consolingly.

"No, I won't crab her victory. To use a military metaphor, she brought up reserves that I hadn't suspected. She never even employed them directly. I at once detected the threat and beat a strategic retreat to avoid an absolutely crushing defeat. A born artist, she refrained from pressing her advantage, and thereby saved a needless and distressing carnage on both sides. We saluted each other gracefully and parted."

"Is there anything more I can do to help?" asked Ricardo, with something that sounded to Vereker like sardonic laughter.

"No, not at present. Send in your account when convenient."

"I won't charge for my services on this occasion, Algernon. It would be like a doctor sending in a bill for a bungled operation on your wife—if you had one. I'm still at your service. So-long!"

On leaving the telephone box, Vereker made his way down to Charing Cross Station, and caught a train for Nuthill. As he sat in the corner of his carriage there was a look of quiet determination in his eyes and a wry smile on his lips. His interview with Miss Cazas had not yielded the results he had expected, and with swift intuition he had guessed the reason why. His mood was combative, and he had decided to give battle on the other issue of murder in another quarter at the first opportunity. He would return to the "Silver Pear Tree," discuss the situation with Inspector Heather, and then drop in at Jodhpur to see Captain Rickaby Fanshaugh. On his way to Charing Cross Station, he had called at a bookshop in St. Martin's Lane and bought a copy of Byron's poetical works. As the train drew out of the station, he turned to Canto 4, Stanza 41, of "Don Juan" and read it. The stanza was merely a typical Byronic soliloquy in the poet's description of the melodramatic meeting between Don Juan and Haidee's father, Lambro, when the latter drew his pistol and was about to stop "this Canto and Don Juan's breath." It seemed to have little connection with the murder of Sutton Armadale, except that it touched on the subject of pistol shooting and was perhaps an index to the character of the financier's literary taste. After some consideration, Vereker came to the conclusion that the words written by Sutton Armadale on his blotting-pad had probably been scribbled there for some purpose completely irrelevant to the issue of the murder. Closing the book, he thrust it into his pocket and gave the matter no further thought.

On arriving at the "Silver Pear Tree," he found that Inspector Heather had left an hour previously, and it was uncertain when he would return. This was disappointing, because Vereker was eager to see the inspector and give him a full account of the result of his further work on the case. Surrendering philosophically to the inevitable, he ordered his dinner, ate it listlessly, and retired to his room to wash and change. He would call at Fanshaugh's bungalow at about nine. Even if the Fanshaughs dined as late as eight this would allow a reasonable interval after the meal. Having about half an hour on hand and being in an unsettled state of mind, Vereker thought he would pass the time in reading. Casting about for a book, he suddenly remembered the two small volumes which he had found in a drawer of Sutton Armadale's writing-table. They were Walter Winans's *The Modern Pistol and How to Shoot It*, and the same author's *Automatic Pistol Shooting*. He picked

up the former of these and settled down in a chair. As he glanced
through the volume, his eye suddenly caught the words, "'Don
Juan,' Canto 4, Stanza 41," and at once all his faculties became
alert. The words occurred in the author's chapter on the subject
of *duelling*, and in a flash their whole significance became clear
to him. Could it be possible that Sutton Armadale had met his
death in a duel? The question was unavoidable, and as he swiftly
reviewed all the curious incidents that had come to his knowledge
in his painstaking inquiry the idea of a duel fitted into the fabric
like the keystone to an arch. He had remarked to Ricardo that
the spirit of Byronism had died in Russia years ago, but did it not
survive in an emasculated form even in these less romantic days?
As for duelling in England, he remembered that a British Code
of Duelling had been published during the Duke of Wellington's
time, and had been approved by the Duke and others; that among
English army officers this method of settling private differences
had been favoured and resorted to until fairly recent times, and
was mentioned in an Army Act of 1879. Glancing at the author's
text, he found complete instructions for the carrying out of a duel,
even to the distance apart at which the contestants must stand.
That distance was twenty-six yards, one foot, two inches—the
very distance between the two small holes he had examined on
the polo ground. The points at which the combatants had stood
facing one another, pistol butts touching their thighs and waiting
for the critical "Attention! Feu! Un, deux, trois!" must have been
marked by the first things to hand, namely, the two shooting-
sticks which he had subsequently found in the gun-room. At once
his mind reverted to the round leather surveyor's tape-measure
lying on Sutton's writing-table, and its presence there, which at
the moment had appeared singular, now became clear. Once more
he referred to Mr. Winans's text, and as he read with strained
absorption he came upon the words, "M. Gastinne Renette of
Paris generally supplies the pistols, but in an out-of-the-way
place where you do not know the gunmaker and do not trust your

opponent or his seconds, it is advisable to instruct your seconds to be very careful what gunmaker is chosen, and if they are the least bit dubious to insist on M. Gastinne Renette being telegraphed to, asking him to send a representative with pistols."

"Well, I'm damned!" exclaimed Vereker. "So M. Gastinne Renette's connection, or rather want of it, with this affair is explained at last!"

Reading the paragraph again, he was assailed by the curiously dispassionate style of the author; its cold practicality savoured almost of the technical calm of an instructor telling a pupil where to buy a lawn-tennis racquet. It was a vivid disclosure of the author's settled conviction as to the moral rectitude of such an arbitrament.

Thrusting the book into his pocket, Vereker began to probe the less evident contingencies to which his discovery had given rise. The first point was the question of duelling pistols. If a duel had taken place, the weapons used had been Colt automatics of .45 calibre, fully loaded with magazines of seven cartridges. This was altogether contrary to any code of duelling, but suggested a combat *à outrance* arranged on the spur of the moment and carried out with the only weapons to hand. But one startlingly significant fact combated this supposition of a hastily arranged fight. Why had Sutton Armadale scrawled the name of a famous Parisian gunmaker, renowned for duelling pistols, on his writing-pad? The intention of seeking this method of composing difficulties must have been in his mind long before Wednesday night or Thursday morning. The whole matter had evidently been pondered on carefully. He had even taken the precaution to make himself a deadly marksman with a pistol, and skill with this fire-arm is not acquired in a few days. Premeditation on Sutton's part was clearly apparent. Then the question of time fitted in admirably with the supposition of a duel, for these contests were nearly always held at dawn, and Sutton Armadale had met his death about that hour. Having reviewed these facts rapidly, Vereker came to the vital

question of Sutton Armadale's opponent. Fanshaugh, being a
soldier, would be the likeliest man to accept a challenge to duel,
but Fanshaugh, as far as Vereker knew, had no quarrel with Sutton
sufficiently bitter to warrant the matter being put to such a deadly
settlement. Degerdon's differences with the financier were of the
sort to invite such combat, and the fact that in a pistol duel years
would be no disadvantage to the older antagonist might have been
a deciding factor in the choice of this method of wiping out scores.
Aubrey Winter, Vereker dismissed as an unlikely man, with the
reservation that he might not be an impossible man. Sutton might
have taunted him into an anger violent enough to rouse even
his sluggish temperament. Ralli, in spite of his amiability, had
that subtlety of mind and disposition which forbade the drawing
of conclusions about him. These were the four men resident in
the house on that fateful morning, and the clue of the side door
near the gun-room pointed clearly in their direction. Whichever
of them had gone out with Armadale to the polo ground had,
after the combat, returned by that door and used Sutton's key
for the purpose of letting himself in. The fact that the key had
been detached from Sutton's bunch, its subsequent discovery
in Fanshaugh's room, and his cunning method of causing it to
vanish once more clearly indicated Fanshaugh. Lastly, there was
Stanley Houseley. Nearly every factor in the case declared him
to be the most likely man of all to settle a quarrel with Sutton
by duelling. He was in love with Sutton's wife; he had been
discovered by Sutton kissing Angela on Wednesday afternoon; he
was a good pistol shot; his return to the neighbourhood of Vesey
Manor at two o'clock in the morning, and the fact that he had
not reached his own home again till eight were weighty evidence.
His mentality lent colour to the view that he would consider a
duel an honourable and gentlemanly way of settling a difference,
especially where a woman was the cause of the dispute. His
very nickname, "Hell-for-leather," hinted at an impetuosity and
violence of temperament favourable to such a conclusion. Against

this supposition stood the clue of the side door near the gun-room. There was no evidence to suggest that Houseley had re-entered the manor after his departure on Wednesday evening. For some minutes Vereker wrestled with this refractory point, and then with a violent start jumped from his chair.

"Eureka!" he exclaimed, for he had suddenly remembered that in a duel there must be seconds. Seconds in this instance had probably been dispensed with, but in that case some sort of director would be essential, and who could have been a more suitable claimant for such a post than Captain Rickaby Fanshaugh? He was a soldier; he was probably acquainted with the etiquette of duelling; he was a staunch friend of both men and a man of disinterested and scrupulously honourable nature. Seizing hat and stick, Vereker hurriedly left the "Silver Pear Tree" and was soon well on his way to Captain Fanshaugh's bungalow.

Fanshaugh was delighted to see him, and when Vereker remembered the incident of the key he wondered how much of the cordiality was forced. Miss Fanshaugh had retired for the night, partly owing to a headache and partly to an extraordinary persuasion that hours which suited larks also suited human beings. This was opportune from Vereker's point of view. His interview with "Fruity" was going to be of a direct and confidential nature. Seated in the Fanshaughs' drawing-room, the wall decoration of which declared a passion for photographic groups of polo teams and of the officers of his own regiment at different times, Vereker came straight to the point.

"I've dropped in, Fanshaugh, to ask you a few questions about this Armadale business. I think you can help me considerably."

"Only too pleased, Vereker. I don't think I can be of much use to you, but here I am at your service. Walk march!"

"You know I've been making a private investigation of the case?"

"I guessed something of the sort, but I thought it was almost a semi-official one. You've compared notes with the C.I.D. johnny, haven't you?"

"Only up to a certain point. Our methods have led us along widely divergent lines."

"You'll let him know your results, I suppose?"

"I shall use my discretion on that point. I'm not the least bit interested in the punitive results to any individual concerned in the crime. Immediately a problem's solution is clear to me, I'm done with it as a rule."

"Stout fellow! I'm with you there. But tell me, what is it you're not clear about?"

"After a devil of a lot of thinking, I've come to the conclusion that Sutton Armadale may not have been murdered at all."

"You're backing the suicide theory?" asked Fanshaugh.

"No," replied Vereker, and added in an even voice, "I've discovered that Armadale was killed in a duel."

"That's damn smart of you, Vereker," said the soldier, without a trace of surprise. "I hope you don't think I fought him."

"No. I think I know the man all right, but I'm convinced you took some part in that duel—say, as a director."

"You're wrong, Vereker. I can emphatically deny that allegation, and I'm not a liar—if I can help it."

The words were spoken with such quiet sincerity that for some moments Vereker was badly shaken. Could his cherished theory, so carefully worked out, be only a fantastic dream? The thought was humiliating.

"You'll admit that a duel was fought?" he asked bluntly.

"But you say you've discovered that!" exclaimed Fanshaugh, with a hearty guffaw. "The truth is, you're only working on suspicion and trying to bluff me. Am I right?"

"I'm convinced that a duel was fought," retaliated Vereker firmly, "and, if you'd care to hear how I came to such a conclusion, I'll be pleased to tell you."

"Fire away, old chap, it'll be devilish interesting," said Fanshaugh, settling himself pleasantly in his chair and lighting a Trichinopoly.

Detail by detail, Vereker narrated how he had built up his theory, and while he talked, Fanshaugh's face, which had at first worn an expression of superior reserve, thawed into the warmth of whole-hearted admiration.

"Ripping, Vereker, ripping! As 'Fuzzy' Waterton used to say, 'you got the pig out of that jheel' very cleverly. I'll now frankly admit there was a duel!"

"I'm rather disappointed you had nothing to do with the directorship of that duel, Fanshaugh," continued Vereker calmly. "It's the only way I can explain your little bit of legerdemain with the key of the door near the gun-room."

Captain Fanshaugh was obliged to laugh heartily at Vereker's thrust.

'I was appointed director, but I never officiated, Vereker. Before I go into that story, however, may I ask you the name of Sutton's opponent?"

"I've hesitated all along between two men, Degerdon and Houseley, but I'm inclined to think it was your friend 'Hell-for-leather.'"

"It would be deuced interesting to know how you tumbled to that," remarked Fanshaugh.

Vereker, thereupon, gave him a pithy account of how he had arrived at his conclusion.

"The factor that makes me give preference to Houseley," he said, "is that he's the only man among my suspects who can claim to be a good shot with a pistol. Otherwise I couldn't explain to myself why Sutton, who was a first-class marksman with a pistol, hadn't bagged his man."

"Luck enters into everything to some degree," remarked Fanshaugh critically. "Sutton was a deadly shot with an automatic at a target. Targets, on the other hand, don't shoot back, and it takes the hell of a good man to look into another man's pistol and keep his own from wobbling. But I'm going to disappoint you, Vereker, by telling you that your guess is wide of the mark. The man who fought Sutton Armadale was not Stanley Houseley but young Ralph Degerdon."

"Well, I'm hanged!" exclaimed Vereker. "I fancied that horse at first, but, as often happens, backed the other!"

"Now the cat's properly out the bag, Vereker, you may as well have the whole yarn. I've warned Degerdon that he must look out for trouble, and he's quite prepared. In the first place, the *casus belli* was Miss Edmée Cazas. Degerdon and she were a bit too intimate for Sutton's liking. The fact of the matter is, they're very much in love with one another. Sutton, you must understand, was absolutely infatuated with the woman and terribly jealous if any other man paid her attentions. To be fair, he had good reason, because Edmée played him up rather shabbily. She used Sutton as a sort of human Aladdin's Lamp. She rubbed him the right way, and the genie with the cash-box appeared. I think Sutton must at last have twigged that Edmée was in love with Degerdon. In any case, he took every opportunity of quietly insulting the lad, and the latter only stood it so long for the woman's sake. Things, however, fairly came to a head on Wednesday night. Over some trifle that occurred in the bathing pavilion Sutton was damned rude to Degerdon, and soon there was a regular scrap, in which all three participated. Vesey Manor was like an ice-house for the remainder of the evening. Early on Thursday morning, about three o'clock, to be precise, Degerdon went down to Edmée's room. He said he couldn't sleep, and as he heard her moving about he went down to have things properly out with her. He loved the girl, and he was determined to have a straight deal. He had begun to suspect from the row earlier in the evening that Edmée's relations with Sutton weren't quite as innocent as she would have liked people to believe, and he had decided to have a clear statement of the situation. While they were politely discussing their troubles, who should walk into the room but Sutton. He had somehow heard their voices and promptly gone down to inquire into the nature of the palaver. Jealous as he was of Degerdon, he put the very worst construction on his presence in Edmée's room at that otherwise unromantic hour. Degerdon put the whole matter very clearly and succinctly to him, but he refused to accept such an innocent explanation. He told Degerdon that he must leave first thing in the morning and never cross the threshold of Vesey Manor again, adding the words, 'You can do what you like elsewhere, but you're not going to turn my house into a lupanar.' Degerdon replied that if it wasn't for his age, he'd give him the biggest thrashing he ever had in his life for daring to suggest that his presence in Edmée's room had been prompted by anything dishonourable. This was evidently what Sutton wanted, and from his previous baiting of Degerdon it looks as if he had carefully worked up to it. He reminded Degerdon that a gentleman, if he were not an utter coward, could, if he felt insulted, demand satisfaction by challenging to a duel. Degerdon, furious at the implication of cowardice in addition to the previous insult, immediately challenged him. Sutton accepted the challenge, chose automatic pistols, and said he would gladly meet him on the polo ground at dawn, when he hoped to let a little clean daylight, if not decency, into him."

"Is Degerdon a good shot?" asked Vereker.

"He had never used an automatic in his life, and though he'd had a little practice with a service revolver during the latter part of the war he was certain he had never hit a man except with the butt of it. To resume, after the challenge and its acceptance the two men came up and asked me to act as a kind of director. When I heard that they intended to duel without seconds and to use automatics, I said it couldn't be done; it wasn't the thing at all. But they insisted, and I asked if I might have a referee's whistle to blow half-time. I thought a little cheerful banter might pour oil on troubled waters. At this they both got rather wrathy, and Degerdon asked me to cut out the low comedian stuff and either take on the job or leave it. Naturally, I couldn't officiate at a duel with automatics; I'd just as soon referee a boxing match where biting and kicking were considered stylish, so I gave them both a bit of my mind. Just to encourage them, I also told them that in English law the man who kills another in a duel is counted a murderer, but that if they'd wait and arrange things like gentlemen with seconds and duelling pistols, I'd only be too glad to be present. It was no use. Neither would listen to reason, and each went to his room. At half-past four they set out for the polo ground. I tried to dissuade them once more, but in vain. They went, and after a while I dressed as hurriedly as I could and followed. I was too late. As I was going through the stableyard a shot rang out, and when I reached the polo ground, I saw Sutton had bit the dust and Degerdon had completely vanished. Without worrying about him, I rushed up to Sutton. He had been pinked in the abdomen, and it had made a beastly mess of him. He had thrust the middle finger of his right hand into the hole to try and staunch the blood that was gushing out. I could see from the look of things that he was *in extremis* and suffering annihilating agony. The pain must have been terrible, for though Sutton was as full of pluck as you could make 'em, he began to scream like a badly wounded hare. As I had picked up the automatic which he had dropped on being shot, he caught hold of my legs and begged and prayed me to put him out of his misery. I had once seen a favourite horse of mine in pain; he'd been frightfully injured by a spear when we were out pig-sticking, and there was nothing for it but to destroy the dear old chap. I don't know if you've heard of the best way to destroy an injured horse. You rest the muzzle of your revolver above his eye and shoot for the base of the opposite ear. I'm a duffer at human anatomy, but I thought something like it would be the best plan with my old friend Sutton. His screaming was a bit unnerving, but I screwed up my courage, and kneeling down fired at him from about two feet distance. At the moment I didn't consider consequences; I'm a man who acts first and thinks about things afterwards."

Captain Fanshaugh was silent for a few moments as he drew his hand reflectively across his bronzed brow.

"I don't exactly know why pain has been sent into this world, but I'll bet for some jolly good reason," he remarked, as if in soliloquy.

"It can't be meaningless, Fanshaugh," said Vereker, "or this mystery we call life would seem a pretty futile business."

"There's something in what you say, but there must be times when it's utterly unnecessary. The whole problem's insoluble. In any case, I only did what I hope some good comrade will do for me if ever I'm in such a godless mess as old Sutton was."

Vereker sat speechless, overcome by the terrible significance of this dramatic statement, told in the plain, blunt language of a soldier, and at that moment Ralli's evidence about the lapse of time between the shots became clear. Fanshaugh poured himself out a nip of whisky and swallowed it.

"The business was over in shorter time than it takes to tell, and then I saw for the first time the possible consequences of my action. I wasn't overwhelmed because I was determined, if the worst came to the worst, I'd simply tell the truth and ask 'em politely to do their damnedest as far as I was concerned. But mine was only a sort of last act to the drama. There was Degerdon to consider. I might possibly be hanged for my humanity, but he would certainly be strung up for murder. After wiping Sutton's automatic with my handkerchief to remove finger-prints, I thrust it into his left hand—he was left-handed, you know—and looked round for Degerdon. I saw him at last, white as a sheet, peering out of Wild Duck Wood like a scared rabbit. He's young and unfinished and wants a lot of toughening. Picking up the shooting-sticks which they'd used to mark their stances, I legged it for Wild Duck Wood like a good 'un. There was no time to lose. Some time before, I had spotted Collyer in the distance running from his cottage towards Hanging Covert, and knew that those shots would soon rouse other people to a certain amount of curiosity. On my way, I'd been doing a bit of rapid thinking, and at such a moment you burn up a pile of philosophy while you're covering a hundred yards or two. I hadn't reached Degerdon a few minutes before Collyer seemed to appear out of the blue near the north wall of the grounds. He made a beeline for Sutton and began to administer first aid to the old boy. As we now know, Sutton was still alive when his keeper reached him, but I'm certain he was almost unconscious and completely out of misery. The first thing I asked Degerdon was what he had done with his automatic. He could only say he had flung it away in the wood. He then explained how, after having shot Sutton, he hared it for Wild Duck Wood with the intention of bolting home. He had completely lost his head. In the wood he straightened himself out a bit, and hearing a second shot from the polo ground, dashed back to the fringe of the covert to see what had happened. He came to the conclusion that Sutton had put himself out of pain, and then he saw me dashing at top speed towards him. I think pretty rapidly when I'm keyed up, Vereker, though I may not look built for speed in that line. Knowing that we must get back to the manor unseen if possible, I had detached the side-door key from Sutton's bunch, and after using all my English vocabulary and most of my Hindustani on Degerdon to bring him up to scratch, we beat it back like greased wireless waves. We let ourselves in as noiselessly as possible and slipped up to our respective rooms. There I did some more rapid thinking. I could see that the question of suicide would soon be discarded for that of murder. There was that cartridge shell of Degerdon's which would probably give the show away even if neither of us had been seen by Collyer. Its absence bothered the police for a bit until you found it. However, as there was no possibility of making out Sutton's death as suicide, the only alternative was to try and make it an unsolved murder mystery. If the formalities of duelling had been strictly adhered to, we could both have faced the music and taken whatever gruel the law apportioned to us. This was out of the question. A duel without seconds and with fully loaded automatics would have sounded like nothing but a silly and bloody murder. After hasty consideration, I decided it must be an unsolved murder mystery if we could possibly make it one, and when I heard later that a burglary had also taken place at the manor during the early hours of the morning, it seemed to me we were getting all the ruddy luck that was going. But I had all my wits on that second automatic which Degerdon had used. After the house had been roused and every one was on the polo ground, I took Degerdon and a party to beat the woods for a possible assailant. Having spread out the searchers to catch the presumptive murderer, well clear of the spot where Degerdon had flung away his automatic, I accompanied Degerdon to that spot and we hunted high and low for the pistol. We never found it, and though we've made several surreptitious searches alone and together, we haven't laid hands on the blamed thing yet. That's the story of this case, and now you know all the particulars perhaps it would be better to clear the whole darned thing up. Your investigations have pretty well run us down, and I reckon the police will do so sooner or later. It might be wiser for us to forestall them and own up. We may both be hanged for our parts in the show, and at the least we shall get a stiff term of imprisonment."

For some minutes Vereker was silent, and as he pondered his face assumed an air of unusual gravity.

"You've told Degerdon of the part you played in putting Sutton Armadale out of pain?" he asked at length.

"Yes, I saw no reason for hiding it from him," replied Fanshaugh frankly.

"You're perfectly certain that Sutton Armadale always shot with his left hand when using a pistol?"

"Absolutely certain. I've seen him practise on innumerable occasions, and he never used his right hand. His right eye was useless even behind plate-glass, and he was naturally left-handed."

"Then I'm sorry to say, Fanshaugh, after what you've told me, that I've very grave doubts about that duel of Degerdon's. It seems pretty clear to me now that no duel took place at all!"

"Good God!" exclaimed Fanshaugh, with marked trepidation. "How on earth do you make that out?"

"You will remember that Sutton Armadale was shot in the abdomen. The bullet entered on the right side and, as Macpherson the expert on gunshot wounds said, came to rest behind the left iliac crest, or in plain English behind the left hip bone close to its upper edge. Now if Sutton fought a duel with Degerdon, how could the bullet enter the right side of the abdomen? If Sutton faced his opponent, as the majority of duellists do—that is, chest and stomach to the front—it would have been a sheer impossibility for Degerdon's bullet to hit him on the right side. If Sutton had been right-handed, he might have turned sideways to Degerdon so as to present a narrower target and been wounded as he was; but a practised duellist would never do this, because a bullet entering the body might then traverse the whole width of the trunk and have a terrible chance of proving fatal. Sutton was left-handed, and, if he had adopted the sideways method of presenting himself, it would have been equally impossible for him to be shot on the right side of the abdomen. Have you got me? Is it clear to you?"

"Perfectly clear, old chap. I hadn't thought of that. That's where brains count, and I haven't got more than my share. But how the devil do you explain things?"

"It looks uncomfortably like murder to me," remarked Vereker gravely.

"Lord above, this is serious!" exclaimed Fanshaugh, deeply perturbed.

"Another damning piece of evidence against Degerdon is the fact that Sutton never fired his automatic," continued Vereker solemnly.

Captain Fanshaugh's face at once assumed a look of amazed incredulity.

"But Degerdon said that Armadale was quicker than he was and managed to loose off a good second before himself. I think you're talking poppycock now Vereker!"

"Perhaps Degerdon's a liar," replied Vereker quietly. "I don't know the young man well enough to say so definitely, but how do you account for the fact that there were six live cartridges in Sutton's automatic when the police took charge of it? The magazines of both pistols were fully loaded, you say?"

"With seven cartridges each," replied Fanshaugh emphatically.

"If Sutton fired one and you fired another out of the same pistol, how could there be six cartridges left in Sutton's automatic when it was found?"

"Phew!" exclaimed Fanshaugh, wiping perspiration from his forehead. "That damned point never entered my calculations. I've never bothered about the number of cartridges left in the magazine!"

"It was a bad oversight, but, of course, mistakes are frequently made by taking things for granted. There's another part of your yarn, Fanshaugh, which strikes me as weak. It may be all right, but it doesn't sound quite feasible to me. Is it likely that Degerdon would get up at three o'clock in the morning to carry on a quarrel with a young lady in her bedroom, seeing that they were both guests in another man's house?"

"Well, it looks rather fishy, but even after your pointing out the discrepancies in Degerdon's story of the duel, I can scarcely bring myself to think he's such an abominable liar."

"Perhaps it was something altogether different," remarked Vereker, and in his own mind there arose a strong suspicion that Degerdon's presence in Edmée Cazas' bedroom had some connection with his theory about the stolen necklace. He noted it for further inquiry and, turning to Fanshaugh, said:

"You've not thoroughly cleared up the mystery of that key to the side door, Fanshaugh."

"Plague seize that key! It has cost me some sleepless nights. In my excitement I lost it. It must have been when I was dressing or undressing on Thursday morning. I was afraid I'd lost it in the house, but I wasn't certain. When the bally thing turned up in your possession, I got the shock of my life. I had a suspicion you were jinking when you told me where you'd found it, and I decided to get rid of that key if possible. I was a bit surprised when you handed it over so confidingly. For a moment I thought you'd handed me a dud, but on looking at it afterwards I was glad to see that it was the right key. I handed Ralli a substitute and buried that key darkly at dead of night. *Requiescat in pace!* But what are you going to do about all this business? I want to know, Vereker. I'd like to settle up my affairs and leave all tidy if the worst comes to the worst."

"I'll let you know in good time, Fanshaugh. I've not got to the end of my investigations yet, and when I do it will be time enough for me to decide on future action—if any."

"I appreciate your frankness, old chap, and thank you. At the same time, I might as well tell you I don't care a continental either way now. I never stand looking at a 'rasper,' and the sooner you wind up this affair the better I'll be pleased!"

"There's one more question, Fanshaugh. Did you tell Miss Edmée Cazas about this duel business?"

"Oh, yes, Degerdon told her all about it afterwards in my presence."

"How did she take it?"

"There was a positive gleam of triumph in her eyes, and I've never seen a woman more beautifully flushed with life. They had fought for her—her favours. She was the prize; her beauty had been a matter of life and death. She kissed Degerdon passionately.

A human life had been sacrificed for her charms. To paraphrase some poet fellow—'But oh, the dismal mockery of the winning when she's won!'"

When Vereker arrived at the "Silver Pear Tree," it was close on midnight. He was surprised to see a light in Heather's room and hoped that the inspector was still up. Knocking cautiously at the officer's door, he heard a thoroughly disgruntled "Come in," and entered to find the inspector sitting at a table on which lay his note-book and papers scattered in untidy array. There was a worried look on his usually cheerful face.

"What's the matter, Heather? You look thoroughly peeved," remarked Vereker.

"I've a good mind to send in my papers and give up the game, Mr. Vereker," replied Heather wearily.

"This is heart-breaking news, Heather; let's cry together. I'm in a similar mood. There seems no end to this tangle. As soon as you feel you're on top of your man, you discover you've made an almighty bloomer and have got to start all over again on another tack."

"Have you anything to report?" asked Heather more cheerfully.

"Stacks! I think I've solved the mystery of the burglary. I'm going to ring up Ralli first thing in the morning and tell him to have Mrs. Armadale's room searched again for the missing pearl necklace."

"What makes you think it's there?" asked the inspector eagerly. "The room has been properly ransacked already."

"I've a suspicion amounting almost to a certainty that it returned there early this afternoon!"

"This sounds like beefsteak and onions! Let's have the yarn!" said Heather, considerably brighter.

Vereker then carefully related to the inspector the whole of his theory of the theft of Mrs. Armadale's pearls, winding up with the story of his interview with Miss Cazas that afternoon.

"You see, Heather, I was confident that I had her in a corner. I thought she'd capitulate when I let her know we practically had our hands on her accomplices, Vernet and Ferray, and that with luck that necklace was as good as back in Mrs. Armadale's safe. She wasn't even badly shaken. At first glance I was inclined to think she was putting up a superb bit of bluff. Feeling that my theory was fairly unassailable, I at once began to wonder where the wrong link was. Then I suddenly remembered she'd gone to Vesey Manor to say good-bye to Ralli after lunching with my friend, Ricardo, and I saw everything in a blinding flash. Ricardo's interview with her had evidently fairly put the wind up her, and she must have been pretty well scared already by thinking the police were connecting burglary with murder. As she herself is not a professional thief to our knowledge, she must have decided to return the stolen property before things got too hot. Probably she and her accomplices had already settled on this plan. To men like Vernet and Ferray there's always a pleasing difference between a prison cell and a hangman's rope. Her last shaft at me when she shook hands on parting gave me the cue, and I felt that I was once again on the right rail."

Heather, who had listened to Vereker's story with profound interest, now rose and held forth his hand.

"Shake on it, Mr. Vereker. I can say sincerely, 'Well done, good and faithful servant.' The necklace has been found. Mr. Ralli came here about five o'clock to tell me the astounding news. After this I must see about a Chief Constable's job for you."

"I suppose one of the servants found it in Mrs. Armadale's room," suggested Vereker, beaming with satisfaction.

"No. Miss Edmée Cazas herself found it quite accidentally when hunting for her lost diary. She had lent her diary to Mrs. Armadale to amuse her and didn't remember getting it back. First she searched her own room and then looked in Mrs. Armadale's. Thinking that that good lady had probably left it on a chest of drawers, whence it might have been brushed off in the excitement

of Thursday morning, she glanced behind the chest of drawers near
her dressing-table and there, sure enough, was her diary. Getting
one of the servants to help her, she moved the chest of drawers,
and behind it, to the amazement of both, was Mrs. Armadale's
necklace as well! It takes a lady with brains to find lost pearls, and I
suppose we must admit she has fairly licked us hollow!"

"I'm sorry the burglar found the safe empty," said Vereker,
laughing. "I'd have liked to see his face when he found that all his
trouble had been in vain. But how about the murder issue? I can
see from your face, Heather, that you've struck a nasty snag."

"Hit it good and hearty, Mr. Vereker. First, let me say Portwine
has been questioned and gave a clear and truthful explanation of
his movements. He has a perfect alibi for Wednesday night and
Thursday morning. He had only called on Sutton Armadale to tell
him that his wife was dead and ask him a question or two about his
wife's pension. He's such a mellow wine that Mr. Armadale, out of
the kindness of his heart, told him not to worry about the pension,
because he had decided to continue its payment to Portwine in
grateful memory of Mrs. Portwine's faithful services to his first
wife. So Portwine is out of the picture, and that reduces my line of
attack to young Peach, and I'm having him closely watched."

"Any trace of the automatic?" asked Vereker.

"We found it day before yesterday," admitted the inspector
rather shamefacedly.

"You barefaced scoundrel, Heather! You've kept that vital
information from me for two days. As my father used to say, 'this is
not strictly according to Cocker.' It isn't cricket anyway, but never
mind, I'll bowl you out with a 'sneak' yet. Where did you find it?"

"It was stuck in a guelder bush—I think you call it guelder—not
twenty yards from your painting ground. It was just by chance I
came upon it as I was beating about."

"Was it one of Mr. Armadale's?"

"I haven't the vaguest idea. We'll make inquiries and see if
we can trace where it was bought. It wasn't bought at Cogswell

and Harrison's in Piccadilly, where Mr. Armadale always bought his guns and equipment. I'm afraid it may have been purchased abroad. If so, the outlook's pretty hopeless."

"Is it the pistol Armadale gave to Collyer?" asked Vereker eagerly.

"No. Collyer is absolutely certain of that. The weapon he possessed had his initials, S.C., scratched on the side of the blued steel barrel."

"Well, I'm hanged!" exclaimed Vereker. "You've proved, of course, that it's the automatic which fired the cartridge case which I picked up on the polo ground?"

"That's where I'm bally well clean bowled, Mr. Vereker. From the micro-photograph of the shell it fires, it's almost as certain as certain can be that it's not the pistol which discharged that cartridge."

Vereker sank back in his chair with a long-drawn, low whistle.

"Well, if that doesn't simply beat creation!" he exclaimed. "Heather, it looks to me as if this job has got the better of us both. From what you say it's clear you're all wrong about Peach, and, as for me, my man simply couldn't have shot Armadale. But I think the time has come to talk of most important things. While trying to solve the mystery of that burglary, I've naturally kept a skinned eye on the worse issue of murder. I was certain from the first that they presented two distinct lines of inquiry, and up to this moment I was cocksure I'd unravelled the murder puzzle as well. And now you tell me this astounding yarn about the cartridge shell which completely shatters my whole theory. Listen while I tell you the sorry tale."

Lighting another cigarette, Vereker settled himself in his chair and recounted to the inspector his startling discoveries in the Armadale murder case, finishing his narration with an account of his recent interview with Captain Fanshaugh, but carefully omitting any mention of the part Fanshaugh had taken in the shooting of the financier.

"You see, Heather," he concluded, "I was certain from the evidence that this story of a duel was all bunk. It simply couldn't have taken place. It was clear to me that Degerdon had funked things at the last moment or had shot Sutton with malice prepense. He had plenty of time to think things out on Thursday morning and, coming to the conclusion that he was simply going to offer himself as a target to a deadly shot, he decided that targets weren't exactly in his line. It seems probable to me that he saw his chance immediately after Armadale had handed him his pistol for the fight and promptly took it. If it had been a square duel, why did he run away? When all the circumstances of the case had been made known, he'd have stood a sporting chance of dodging the hangman's rope, to put it at its worst. Instead, he bolted, and with a guilty man's conscience at once decided to get rid of the pistol. He declares he was unmanned, and in his distracted state flung away the pistol in Wild Duck Wood at the very spot where you found it. And now we face the shattering discovery that his pistol was not the one which discharged the cartridge I picked up on the polo ground! In the name of all that's good, read me the riddle!"

"Perhaps the cartridge case you picked up was put there purposely to tie us in a knot. Strange that I didn't find it on the first search, Mr. Vereker," suggested the inspector.

"It's possible, Heather, but it sounds a bit too complicated to be true. One more point. There's still that second wound—the one in Armadale's head—to be accounted for. Now you know my story of the bogus duel, what's your idea about that wound?"

"That's easy, Mr. Vereker. I've thought all along that that wound might have been self-inflicted. The terrible wound in the abdomen must have been hellish painful, and Mr. Armadale just did what many a man would do in similar circumstances. He put himself out of mess."

"Ah, well," yawned Vereker, "I'm going to bed to think things out. There's a gap somewhere that I've overlooked in my eagerness. I'm going to go over the ground and find that gap. Let's hope that to-morrow we'll see things a bit clearer. We're about to breast the tape, if I'm not mistaken!"

For some minutes Heather sat looking gloomily into space, and then with a shrug of his broad shoulders remarked: "To-morrow I think I'll take out a warrant for Peach's arrest. He has threatened to murder Ralli, and that'll do to go on with in any case. Good night!"

"I'm going up to town to-morrow, Heather," replied Vereker, as he made his way to the door. "I shall apply for an order in lunacy. You're getting dangerous, and the kindest thing we can do is to 'have you put away,' as it is called in the best circles. Good night!"

Chapter Fifteen

Next morning Vereker did not rise at his usual early hour for breakfast. He lay awake in bed trying to find some solution to the puzzle which now confronted him in the Armadale case. He had met with one of the set-backs inseparable from this kind of pursuit, but the occasion of its occurrence seemed to have been arranged by something saturnine in that mystery we call Chance. At the very moment when he had thought that an answer was imminent and the whole sequence of events had appeared to be to him as clear as daylight, something cataclysmal had happened and the carefully reasoned structure which he had raised threatened to crumble to irreparable ruin. The more he pondered on it the more convinced he was that one vital link was missing in the chain of evidence, but he was utterly at a loss to know where to seek it. If only Heather had discovered that the automatic pistol found in Wild Duck Wood was the instrument which had fired the cartridge case which he had so luckily picked up on the polo ground, his task would have been satisfactorily completed. It would then have rested with Heather to arrest Degerdon as the murderer. As for Captain Fanshaugh, if he chose to confess to his shooting of the financier as an act of mercy, he must be prepared to accept the interpretation that an English judge and jury might care to pronounce thereon. It was, thought Vereker, completely outside his province to hold the scales of justice on such a debatable point. On thinking over the matter, he suddenly decided to call on Captain Fanshaugh and let him know the strange story of the automatic pistol which Degerdon had flung away and which was now in the hands of the police. Rising, he hurriedly dressed, breakfasted, and made his way down to Jodhpur. On passing Heather's room, he found the door open and that everything within had been cleaned and tidied up by the inn chamber-maid. It was evident that the inspector was astir early and had already started off on some mission of his own, possibly to interview Degerdon. The officer had made some cryptic remark about getting out a warrant for Peach's arrest when Vereker had left him the night before, but Vereker had dismissed his words as part of Heather's usual playful banter.

On arriving at Jodhpur, Vereker found Captain Fanshaugh seated on the veranda of his bungalow quietly enjoying one of his strong Indian cigars and looking the picture of healthy contentment.

"Come and sit down and have a peg of whisky, Vereker," he exclaimed, on seeing his visitor. "By the Lord Harry, I'm sorry, I forgot I finished the whisky last night after you left. Norah has gone down to Nuthill in her Austin and will bring some back with her, but Heaven knows when she'll return. In any case, it's too early for detectives to drink. What's the news? You look as if you'd seen a ghost."

"I'm fairly up a gum tree, whatever that may mean," replied Vereker, flinging himself into a deck-chair beside Fanshaugh.

"Always sounds a jolly salubrious spot to me," remarked the captain, "but let me know the worst. Are they going to put us through the ruddy hoop?"

"Look here, Fanshaugh," said Vereker calmly, "there's something gloriously cock-eyed about this yarn of Degerdon's."

"So you averred last night and proved to your own complete satisfaction. I simply fell in love with your reasoning. It seemed unanswerable at the moment, but now, do you know, I simply can't swallow it. It sticks half-way down my gullet. I know Degerdon fairly well, and I cannot think he told me just a bally pack of lies. Of course he's in a tight corner and may purposely have foiled the line for my benefit, but I'm still feeling loyal to him. What's the latest?"

"The police have found his automatic in Wild Duck Wood," said Vereker.

"At last! I thought it would happen. Where on earth did they pick it up?"

"It wasn't on earth, it was in the air, caught in a tangle of guelder."

"Ah, well, the correct thing to say, I believe, is, 'The game's up. It's a fair cop.' I suppose the next thing will be to fit Degerdon with a pair of bracelets."

"I'm not so sure about that now," said Vereker. "Last night I thought I'd wound up the business and put up the shutters. To-day the end seems as far out of sight as ever. Heather has had the automatic examined, and fired some shots out of it. They are still trying to trace where and by whom it was bought. That will take time. But the bombshell Heather flung at me, after telling me all this, was that it's not the weapon which fired the cartridge case picked up by me on the polo ground!"

"They've found that out under the microscope, I suppose, but can they be certain?"

"Well, as certain as it is possible to be in such cases."

"Would they hang a man on such evidence?"

"That's a moot point, but I should say not solely on such evidence. The result of their examination, however, seems to prove that the weapon found in Wild Duck Wood is not the weapon Degerdon used. If it is Degerdon's automatic, then where on earth did the cartridge case I picked up come from? To me it doesn't seem reasonable to assume that some one has been faking clues to jigger up the circumstantial evidence."

"I can truthfully say that I haven't faked those clues, and as I've said before, I don't think Degerdon is wily enough to do so. I asked him about his spent cartridge case, and he hadn't the vaguest idea that it was a matter of any importance. There's another point, Vereker, which has puzzled me since yesterday. What's your opinion of the number of shots fired? I wouldn't be positive, but I thought I heard two reports before I arrived on the scene. They were in very quick succession, as one would expect, and I'm rather observant on such matters—army training, I suppose. If Armadale didn't fire his weapon, as you seem to have proved, how do you account for that?"

"It's very difficult to be certain. You may have heard the echo of the shot Degerdon fired. With these surrounding woods the place abounds with echoes. Collyer and Ralli both say they heard only two reports. It seems to be getting a more intricately tangled mystery than ever."

"Well, I'm nearly certain that there were two shots apart from my own, and that was why your statement about Sutton not having fired a round fairly took the feet from under me. But I'm getting hungry, and it's tiffin-time. Norah left it all ready. It's cold fodder but filling. Will you join me?"

Vereker accepted the invitation, and the men were just about to leave the veranda and enter the bungalow when a car swung into the gates at a dangerous pace and pulled up on the gravel square in front of them. The door opened and Ralph Degerdon sprang out of the driver's seat and joined them. He looked pale and in a highly nervous state.

"What's the matter, Ralph?" asked Fanshaugh, eyeing him with kindly concern.

"The most amazing thing on earth has happened, 'Fruity.' Have you anything to drink?"

"Plenty, boy. There's no whisky, but there's water. It's good enough for lions and it's good enough for you. But never mind drinks, tell us what's happened."

"There has been a double shooting tragedy on the Vesey Manor estate this morning. The C.I.D. inspector was walking with Basil Ralli on their way up to Collyer's cottage, when Peach, who used to be Sutton's underkeeper, stepped out of Wild Duck Wood and, whipping out an automatic, plugged Ralli and then made a run for it. Jealousy, you know, over that rather lovely wench, Trixie. The inspector doesn't look like a greyhound, but he gave chase. He must be a damned good sprinter and as tenacious as a bulldog. Peach blazed at him, but he hung on like a good 'un and was just about to grapple with his man when the fellow put the pistol to his own head and shot himself. It was a bungled job, and he didn't die outright. He lived long enough to make a hurried confession of his sins. He said he had settled Ralli because the chap had pinched his girl, and then confessed he had shot Sutton Armadale on the polo ground last Thursday morning for interfering in his relations with the young lady, giving him the sack, and refusing to give him a reference to get another job. After getting this off his chest he apparently died quite happy."

"My God!" exclaimed Fanshaugh fervently. "This is about the rummest news I've ever heard in my life! But, Degerdon, before you begin to congratulate yourself, let me tell you the secret of your duel is out. Heather knows the whole story, if I'm not greatly mistaken."

"Oh, heavens!" groaned Degerdon. "I thought I was well out of the wood."

Sinking into a chair, he sat dazed—like a man who has received a staggering blow.

"But how can Peach's story about shooting Sutton Armadale be believed?" asked Vereker quietly. "The fellow wasn't on the polo ground at the time."

"You're mistaken, Vereker," replied Degerdon slowly, recovering his composure. "Peach came on the scene just as we were about to fight. Although I was determined to go through with it, the more I thought of that duel after we'd arranged it, the more I disliked the look of it. For some time Armadale had had his knife in me over Edmée, and on several previous occasions had insulted me openly. I stuck it for Edmée's sake until I could stick it no longer. There's a limit even to my good nature. Finally, between two and three o'clock on Thursday morning, when he found me in her room and at once accused me of improper conduct, I cut loose and had the greatest difficulty in restraining myself from striking him. He pointed out that there was a way in which a gentleman could demand satisfaction, and on the spur of the moment we arranged a duel in a manner which wouldn't give my youth any advantage."

"Excuse my interrupting you, Degerdon, but would you mind telling us the real reason for your going down to Miss Cazas' room? Had you seen her entering her room from the balcony?" asked Vereker.

"Is it necessary to bring Miss Cazas any further into this rotten affair?" asked Degerdon coldly.

"It may be quite unimportant now, Degerdon, but I have a pet theory which I should like to substantiate, and I'm only asking you as a personal favour," replied Vereker tactfully.

"Strange that you should mention the point, but when I was standing at my window early on Thursday morning—I have already mentioned the occasion to you, Vereker—I saw a young man clamber over the balcony balustrade and enter the house by Edmée's door. I was flabbergasted and could scarcely believe the evidence of my own eyes. About this time, let me say, I was getting rather fed up with Edmée's treatment of me. In fact, I had seriously begun to question her good faith in a certain matter which I would rather not mention, so I made up my mind to go down and investigate. I pulled on a dressing-gown and slippers and descended to her room. To my great surprise, I found her all rigged up in a man's togs, and asked her what the devil she was up to. She simply burst out laughing, and having changed into her pyjamas in her dressing-room, came out and explained that she had been playing a prank on Angela next door. She said that as Angela was so frightfully proper she had often wondered how an English girl would deal with a handsome male intruder…"

"A remarkable sense of humour! Thanks, Degerdon, that's all I want to know. Go on with the main story," interrupted Vereker.

"Well, after Sutton and I had fixed up the fight, I began to see that I had practically condemned myself to death. He was a crack shot with an automatic; I had never handled one before and, what was particularly galling, he had practically driven me into this duel against my will and common sense. It was then I suggested that 'Fruity' should witness the combat to see that everything was above board. Sutton rather bucked against this, but couldn't very well refuse my request. 'Fruity,' as you probably know, refused the job, and there was no one else in the house I cared to call on to act as director. I was bally uneasy about the whole business and had really begun to doubt whether Sutt was going to play fair. However, I was determines not to show the white feather, and we went grimly through with our plans. My good faith in Sutton was not strengthened by a curious little incident which occurred just after we'd marked off our stances and he had handed me my automatic. I had previously examined both pistols, rather ineffectually, I admit, and now I discovered that the safety-catch of mine had been locked. A man used to revolvers isn't on the look-out for such a device on a pistol, and it was just by accident that I spotted this peculiarity. Lucky for me that I did! Otherwise it would have been impossible for me to fire the pistol at the crucial moment. This safety-catch incident was disturbing, and I was now perhaps unduly suspicious of Sutton, whom I had never really distrusted before. At this juncture, just as we were about to take up our positions, Frank Peach, who used to be Sutton's underkeeper, came across the polo ground on his way to Nuthill Station. In my nervous state and being determined to ensure perfect fairness in our fight, I called upon him as a sportsman to act as director. Sutton was agreeable, and we gave Peach careful instructions to shout, 'Attention! Fire! One! Two! Three!' and told him that either combatant might shoot after the word 'fire' and keep on shooting until, but not after, the word 'three.' After taking it all in, Peach consented to act on condition that, whatever happened, neither of us would divulge the part he had played in the business or drag his name into any subsequent proceedings, should any arise. We both swore on our honour as gentlemen to keep our lips sealed, and walked to our positions. We had tossed for ends and I had won. Thinking that there was nothing in it either way, I took up my ground nearer the house and facing west. The sun hadn't risen, so there wasn't much advantage in the choice. Peach told us to get ready, and we stood facing one another with our pistol butts on our thighs, mine on my right and his on his left. I discovered in that moment that Sutton was left-handed. I had never noticed this peculiarity previously. Also I saw that his right ear stuck out from and his left ear hugged the side of his head. Strange what irrelevant trivialities bulge out on your vision as something terribly important in a crisis! We were ready. Peach glanced first at me and then at Sutton. He was standing about two yards from Sutton at the most. 'Attention!' came the shout, and my whole soul seemed to be located in my trigger finger. I had never felt life rush to a point like that before. It was the wildest exhilaration I had ever experienced. I seemed to be waiting hours for the word 'fire' when Sutton all at once loosed off without raising his pistol from his thigh. Instantly I pulled my trigger. I don't remember Peach ever shouting the word 'fire!' but I wasn't going to stand like a deserter to be shot down without replying. The next thing I knew was that Sutton was lying on the ground writhing in pain, and Peach was running like the wind for Wild Duck Wood. Panic seized me. and without giving Sutton a thought, I simply bunked and followed Peach into the covert. I didn't overtake him, and when I reached the wood he had completely vanished. I have never seen him to speak to since that moment. That's the unvarnished story of what happened on Thursday morning."

Turning to Fanshaugh, Degerdon added:

"In describing events to you subsequently, 'Fruity,' I purposely omitted all mention of Peach. I had given my word of honour to him and couldn't possibly break it even for you, old boy. I think I'm absolved of my oath now that the poor fellow's gone."

For some dramatic moments the men looked at one another without speaking. Then Vereker, in a curiously even voice, said:

"The missing link in my chain of evidence at last! Your story, Degerdon, makes everything clear to me now. Let me heartily congratulate you on having completely missed your man!"

"I never could understand how Ralph ever hit him at twenty-six yards," remarked Fanshaugh, with a grim smile.

"Missed my man? What do you mean?" asked Degerdon in a bewildered tone. "I've been wishing to God ever since that awful morning I'd missed him and he'd hit me instead!"

Vereker clearly explained to the dazed Degerdon that, standing as they did, it would have been an impossibility for him to inflict the wound which Sutton had received on the right side of his abdomen. Then he asked, "Of course you didn't see what Peach was doing after he had shouted the word 'Attention!'?"

"Good heavens, no! my eyes were glued on Sutton, and I was in such a frenzy of excitement that he seemed to have shrunk to something ludicrously small. All I could distinguish was his automatic pistol, which had suddenly swelled to the size of a Big Bertha. I could have walked down the muzzle!"

"It's absolutely conclusive," continued Vereker, "now that he has confessed, that Peach, after the word 'Attention,' must have drawn an automatic, possibly the very one that is missing from Collyer's drawer, and shot Sutton when both your attentions were riveted on one another. He had already threatened to kill Armadale and was only waiting for a favourable opportunity.

The gods could not have sent him an occasion better suited to his purpose!"

"But what about poor Ralli?" asked Fanshaugh, with a sudden start. "Full of our own damned affairs, we've completely forgotten to ask about him."

"He's badly but not fatally hurt," replied Degerdon. "The shot passed through the upper part of his left shoulder well clear of anything vital. Collyer, the keeper, happened to be near and ran to his assistance, while Heather dashed off in pursuit of Peach. On the inspector's return, Ralli asked him what had happened to Peach. 'Put a bullet through his own brain, sir,' replied the inspector. 'Remarkably good shot, Heather!' was Ralli's sole comment."

"Thank God, Basil's not badly hurt!" remarked Fanshaugh. "It's damned bad for horses to be changing masters every week. He's just the man we want at Vesey Manor. I don't know any youngster who's shaping better in the hunting field."

"Look here, 'Fruity,' since I've learned that I haven't killed a man, I'm feeling tons better; but what about you, old boy?"

"Well, that's a secret between the three of us. We know that Sutton put himself out of pain by proxy, but it will be sufficient for the world to know that he simply put himself out of pain," replied Fanshaugh, and after some minutes of silence he asked, "Will you both stay to lunch? There's no whisky, so we'll just have to behave like lions—not the British variety, I'm afraid!"

After lunch, Vereker left Degerdon and Fanshaugh together at the bungalow and returned to the "Silver Pear Tree." Inspector Heather was resting after a hearty meal and seemed at peace with the world.

"Well, Heather, I suppose I'm to congratulate you on successfully clearing up the Armadale murder mystery. First one for a long time too!" said Vereker.

"Well, it was such a simple affair that I blush at congratulations," replied the inspector smugly. "I was on top of my man from the word 'go,' and I'm glad I didn't leave him. This will do me a heap of good. The *Evening Bulletin* has already got a reporter on the job, and the captions are rather interesting. 'Millionaire's murderer shoots himself on eve of arrest after abortive attempt on nephew!' I thought it sounded as if the murderer had had a go at his own nephew, but the journalist simply said that it wouldn't do any harm if the public read it that way for a start. 'Full Confession Before Death'; 'Smart Detective Work by Inspector Heather of Scotland Yard'; 'Inspector shot at but Missed!'"

"The last sentence is about the most astonishing of all," remarked Vereker, glancing comprehensively at his friend. "I suppose an abortive burglary came into the story?"

"You bet. 'Burglar Baffled'; 'Misses £20,000 Necklace'; 'No Connection with Murder!'"

"What's it to be, Heather?"

"I'll let you off with beer this time, Mr. Vereker; besides, I don't care for champagne. I had a lot of luck, a lot of luck. I'm jolly sorry you went so far off the track, but you're young and romantic. Instead of going on hard facts, you will keep taking a swig at that psychology bottle, and you persist in getting tied up with all sorts of sugar stuff about lovers and duels and elopements and unhappy marriages!"

"Lots of luck, did you call it, Heather? Pure luck from beginning to end! Even that burglary simply took its hat off to you and faded out of the picture exactly at the right moment. No, Heather, you didn't beat me this time, old boy. You were simply the darling of the gods, and it's your turn to stand the champagne."

"Two halves of bitter, madam," called the inspector to the landlady.

"All right, Heather. I've got a nice little report here about the duel, and how Peach, acting as director, drew an automatic and shot his late employer. The *Daily Report* will simply make a scoop with exclusive news about the whole grim tragedy of robbery, jealousy, and murder."

"Perhaps you'd prefer whisky to beer," suggested the inspector.

"No, Heather. Paradoxically enough, it's champagne for silence this time, and not wedding champagne either. Special cuvée or nothing!"

"It's a bad attempt at blackmail, but I'll pay up. Can you lend me a couple?" said the inspector, and as he thought he suddenly burst into loud laughter and shook till the tears streamed from his good-natured eyes. "It was the luckiest case in all my career!" he added.

"By the way, Heather, was the pistol used by Peach the one Collyer missed from his drawer?"

"It was, and had his initials, S.C., scratched on the barrel."

"What are you going to do about the one you found in Wild Duck Wood, the one Degerdon flung away?"

"I shall rule out that evidence as inadmissible. It had nothing whatever to do with our case, Mr. Vereker."

"There were three shots, Heather, as you first suspected," continued Vereker thoughtfully.

"There are only two now," replied the inspector laconically, "and there's still a cartridge case missing, according to your high-falutin story. I really think you ought to go and look for it."

"I would if it were necessary, but I don't require any further evidence at this solemn hour. I've finished with the Armadale case. My feelings are not quite those of unmixed satisfaction, but then we foolishly ask for perfection in the world, in our fellow-men, in police inspectors, without troubling to seek it in ourselves. Some day I hope to paint a picture without a flaw, to solve a mystery without making one wrong deduction, without taking one false step. Vain hope! I've always thought it strange, Heather, that we may be conscious of the futility of our aspirations and yet be driven relentlessly on by some secret urge which regards us personally as if we were merely insignificant factors in some fantastically majestic scheme! You and I, Heather, you and I—rather remote, rather disparate, altogether inexplicable, wholly insignificant—simply nothing in a world of unintelligible symbols…"

The inspector coughed noisily and said, with a note of complaint:

"Why don't you drink comfortable like? Here am I happy as a little bird in spring, just about mating-time, and you start mooning about like a chap who's about to commit suicide because his pension's going to die with him. I won't let you help me in any more of my cases if it's going to upset you like this. Here's to your future improvement. Fill up and drink comfortable like!"

Chapter Sixteen

Early in the evening, Anthony Vereker retired to his own room. He was in a thoughtful mood, and his preoccupation arose from the fact that his work on the Armadale case had proved completely unsatisfactory. He had convinced himself in the closing stages of his investigation that Ralph Degerdon had fired the shot which had killed Sutton Armadale. Degerdon had told a convincing enough story about a duel in which he had fired his shot at the financier and killed him in a fair fight, if a duel under the entirely unorthodox conditions described by him could be called fair. The story of that duel had been to Vereker's mind completely at variance with the nature of the wound which Sutton Armadale had received. He had been perfectly certain that the financier had been shot by some one standing to the right of him and probably at fairly close quarters. On Captain Fanshaugh's description of the duel, he had at once seen this discrepancy and had immediately concluded that Degerdon had lied to Fanshaugh. Swiftly reviewing the matter, it had appeared to him that Degerdon had probably shot Sutton Armadale after the latter had handed him his automatic pistol for the combat, but had subsequently cleverly adapted his story for Fanshaugh's consumption.

Fanshaugh was his friend and knew that the fight was to take place. Degerdon, astute as he was, had failed, however, to perceive that the angle at which the bullet had penetrated Armadale's body would prove conclusively that his story was pure fabrication to a man trained in observation and with a knowledge of gunshot wounds. And then had come this bombshell of a confession by Peach that he had fired the fatal shot! With that confession all the fabric of his carefully constructed theory had been swept away like leaves in a whirlwind. It was disappointing; but, after all, disappointments were of the texture of life on this imperfect planet.

In a restless mood he glanced at his watch. It was eight o'clock. The night was young, and sleep in his present frame of mind a remote possibility. Picking up his hat and stick, he left the inn and walked up to Vesey Manor with the intention of inquiring after Basil Ralli. On his arrival, he was at once conducted to the patient's room. To his surprise, he found Ralli sitting up in bed propped up comfortably with pillows and placidly reading a book.

"Hello, Vereker, I'm damned glad you've called. I expected you and gave instructions that you were to be admitted at once. It's frightfully dull sitting here all by myself and being cosseted like an invalid when I'm perfectly all right except for a bit of torn tissue. Tomorrow I shall be all right; Trixie has promised to come and nurse me. Amazing business this of Peach's; what do you think about it all?"

"To tell the truth, I'm feeling a bit fed up with it all at the moment and want to forget it. I've been walloped all along the line. Perhaps it's good for my self-conceit, but like all medicine it's rather unpleasant to swallow. What's this preposterous yarn about Angela's necklace?"

Ralli smiled rather wanly and replied:

"It's somewhat fragile, so we must handle it delicately. Still, all's well that ends well. Miss Cazas found it, as you probably know, behind a chest of drawers in Angela's room when looking for her lost diary. The maid who had searched the room on the day after the burglary was perhaps one of the most amazed and annoyed people in the world that the pearls should have been so simply retrieved. She came to me afterwards to give notice that she was leaving, and told me emphatically that she'd moved that chest of drawers out purposely to search behind it on the morning of the loss of the pearls. I pacified her by telling her I believed her word before any foreigner's born, and asked her for my sake to say nothing further about the matter."

"I wonder what caused the foreigner to make such an unexpected and magnanimous restitution," remarked Vereker ironically.

"That's a simple story. The night before she came to bid me good-bye, I wrote to her telling her that we had discovered a codicil to Sutton's will, made only last Wednesday, and witnessed by Dunkerley and Frederick. In that codicil my uncle had bequeathed to her in case of his death all the jewellery which Angela had returned to him. I think Mademoiselle, after careful consideration, thought that a certain restitution might be tactful, to say the least of it!"

"Very neat, very neat!" exclaimed Vereker, laughing heartily. "She beat me by her long nose on the post, but in extenuation of my failure I must say she had all the luck of the draw. There's a touch of sardonic humour in the fact that she risked so much to pinch her own pearls, and it makes me feel heaps happier!"

"And, as for Sutton's murder, I suppose recent revelations have put the lid on all your sleuthing, Vereker?" said Ralli.

"It was a disappointing finish to a fine race from my point of view," replied Vereker, and related the whole story of the case as it was known to him to an attentive and amazed listener.

"The inspector's a decent sort, and I'm jolly glad for his sake," said Ralli, and the conversation turned on Ralph Degerdon.

"He came up to see me this afternoon shortly after the accident," continued Ralli. "I'm sorry for Degerdon. He's still a bit upset and has made up his mind 'to sile awye' to Australia. I told him I thought it wasn't a bad plan to put a few thousand miles between himself and the charmer who was indirectly the cause of his latest trouble. I also promised to 'shove out the boat' from a financial point of view. But there's one thing I particularly want to ask you. Let's change the subject from murders to marriages. Trixie and I have fixed up the date in November. Will you be my best man?"

"Glad to, Ralli," replied Vereker.

"The wedding takes place a month before Angela and Stanley's, to which I can tell you you are to be asked."

"'Hell-for-leather's a lucky man!" exclaimed Vereker. "I wouldn't mind swapping places with him this very moment. Angela's a beautiful woman, and her English temperament's a secret ideal of mine. I could worship her. I'm born for disappointments!"

"You impressionable ass, Vereker! In any case, don't let's have any more duels. One's enough for a lifetime. There's a decanter and glasses on that table over there. You need a comforter in this discouraging hour, and my shoulder's a bit painful. Perhaps a little stimulant—"

THE END

Lightning Source UK Ltd.
Milton Keynes UK
UKOW06f0959131116
287501UK00020B/414/P